Science Fiction Stories 4

Marcy Michael Publishing
MarcyMichael.com

Various Authors

Copyright © 2024 by Marcy Michael Publishing – MarcyMichael.com

All rights reserved.

No portion of this book may be reproduced in any form without written permission from the publisher or author, except as permitted by U.S. copyright law.

Contents

1. The Music Never Stopped — 1
2. The Oldest Question — 36
3. Refuse All Replacements — 47
4. The Rebel Who Refused — 60
5. She Of Mars — 73
6. Champion — 83
7. The Final Lesson — 97
8. Draw! — 108
9. Celestial Tribunal — 119
10. Firebird — 130
11. The Enigma Of Quintus — 144
12. The Pioneers Of Venus — 157
13. Armament — 192

The Music Never Stopped

By ELLIOT T. CARSON

On the windswept rocket parade grounds, the band was blasting out the inevitable Heroes' March as the cadets powered through the final maneuvers of their drill. Captain Thomas Stanton stopped at the gate near the visitors' section, waiting until the last blaring notes faded away, followed by the usual applause from the town kids in the stands. The cadets broke ranks and headed for their study halls, still marching as if the music was still playing in their heads. Maybe it was, Stanton mused.

Back on Johnston Island, fifteen years ago when his group earned their rocket badges, there had been scant parade drills and even less music. Yet somehow, there had been an undeniable feeling of destiny, like a drumbeat in their minds, giving a spring to their steps. Most of them had marched off to their deaths, while a few had climbed to command positions on the moon, long before the base moved here to the Florida coast. Stanton shrugged and glanced upwards. The menacing clouds gathered, scudding across the sky in dark streaks, and the wind picked up pace. It was going to be rough weather for a launch, if things didn't get worse.

Behind him, a boy's voice called out, "Hey, pilot!"

Stanton glanced around, but there were no other pilots in sight. He hesitated, puzzled. When the call came again, he turned towards the stands with uncertainty. To his surprise, a boy, no older than twelve, was leaning over the railing, waving a notebook energetically.

"Autograph, pilot?"

Automatically, Stanton took the book and signed the blank page while fifty pairs of eyes watched in silence, no other notebooks were held out. He handed the notebook and pencil back, attempting to muster a friendly smile. For a fleeting moment, a ghost of the old pride filled him as he turned back across the empty parade ground. It didn't last.

Behind him, an older voice broke the silence with disgust.

"Why'd you do that, Shorty?"

"He's not a pilot!"

"Yes, he is. I'm sure of it. I know a pilot's uniform when I see one," Shorty insisted.

"So what? I already told you about him. He's the garbage man!"

There was no reply, just the sound of paper being torn from a notebook. Stanton ignored the boys as they left the stands. He walked across the field, past the school buildings, towards the main part of the base—the hub that maintained the lifeline to the space station and the moon. A job, he told himself, was still a job. It was a word he would have never used six ships and fifteen years ago. The storm flag was up on the control tower. Worse, the guy cables were taut, anchoring the three-stage ships firmly in their blast deflection pits.

There were no tractors or tankers on the rocket field to service the ships. He squinted through the gathering gloom towards the bay, but there was no activity there either. The stage recovery boats were all in port with their handling cranes folded down. Clearly, no flights were scheduled. This wasn't what he had expected. Hurricane Javier was moving north out to sea, and the low ceiling and high winds were supposed to be the last remnants of it, clearing by midday. But this didn't look like that; it seemed more like the weather station had made a rare mistake.

He stared down the line towards his own ship, set apart from the others, swaying slightly in the wind. Getting it airborne through this weather was going to be a nightmare, even if he got clearance, but he didn't have much more time to wait. Javier had already put him four days behind schedule, and he had been counting on making the trip today.

A flash bulletin was posted outside the weather shack, surrounded by a group of young majors and colonels from the pilot squad. Stanton moved past them and into the building.

Stanton felt a wave of relief when he saw that Butler was on duty. Butler was one of the few remaining technicians from the early days on the Island. Without standing up, Butler glanced up from his intense examination of the maps and gave a casual salute. "Hey, Billy. How's the pig business?"

"Terrible," Stanton replied. "I'm going to have a bunch of starving hogs if I don't get another shipment soon. What's up with the storm warnings? I thought Javier had passed."

Butler, extracting the last cigarette from his pack, shook his head as he lit it. "This one's Hulda, apparently. Our brilliant team at the station missed it. They said Hulda was hidden by Javier until she got bigger. She's making herself known now. No flights for at least five more days."

"Damn!" It was worse than Stanton had expected. Skeptical, he twisted the weather maps to scrutinize them. Unlike the rookie pilots, he had spent ample time in the weather shack and could read a map or a radar screen nearly as well as Butler. "The station couldn't have botched it that badly, Bill!"

"They did. Something weird's going on. Bailey and the top brass are having a big meeting over at Communications about it. It's turning into a major crisis."

One of the teletypes started clattering, and Butler turned his attention to it. Stanton stepped outside where a light rain had begun, whipped around by gusty winds. He made his way to the control tower, knowing it was probably pointless—no flight clearances would be issued without General Bailey's approval, and Bailey was still tied up in the conference. He borrowed a rain cape and headed across the field toward his ship. The rain intensified, and the Mollyann groaned and creaked in her pit as he approached. Fortunately, the mooring had been done well enough, so she was in no immediate danger as far as he could tell. He checked the pit gauges and records. The cargo hold was packed with heavy machinery, and the stage tanks were fully fueled.

If he could just get the clearance, she was ready to go. Despite being the oldest ship on the field, her battle-worn exterior concealed a sound structure, and he'd personally overseen her last overhaul. Feeling the wind pick up again, a knot tightened in his stomach. He moved to the sheltered side of the ship, muttering curses at the station meteorologists. A correct forecast could've allowed a takeoff during the brief calm between storms. Even that would've been risky, but now... Abruptly, a ragged klaxon blared through the air in short bursts, summoning the pilots. Stanton paused, then shrugged and stepped into the rain. He could ignore the signal since he'd been on detached duty for years, except when scheduled for flights; yet this was probably his best chance to see Bailey. He slogged across the field while the others trotted toward the Briefing Room in tight formation, their raincoats glistening in the downpour. They moved as if a silent drum beat guided them.

Stanton found a seat at the back, separate from the others, an old habit. Up front, an impromptu dice game was taking place; elsewhere, small groups huddled together, their young faces brimming with confidence. No one noticed him until Colonel Lawrence Hennings glanced up from the dice game.

"Hey, Billy. Want to join in?"

Stanton shook his head, smiling briefly. "Can't afford it this week," he explained. Names were just formalities here; even a man ferrying garbage could speak to the colonel. At the moment, Hennings was king, even amidst these self-proclaimed heroes. Every crowd had a top dog. Hennings' current reign felt as inevitable as Stanton's role. After all, someone had to carry the waste down from the station.

The crew couldn't just jettison the waste into space to let it orbit and clutter around the station; someone had suggested shooting it back to burn up in Earth's atmosphere, but that required more fuel over time than bringing it down by ship. With nearly eight hundred men onboard the expanded station, the waste management challenge was immense. The job of hauling garbage was as crucial as ferrying supplies up, demanding equal piloting skills. But there was no fanfare when the garbage ship launched, and no hero's glory awaited the garbage pilot. It was simply his misfortune to be the pilot for the inaugural return load.

The intense heat from reentry radiated through the glowing red hull of the cargo section, causing the waste to boil and steam throughout the ship, adhering stubbornly to the interior as it cooled. No amount of scrubbing could clean it entirely; afterward, the ship was relegated to waste transport and lifting non-sensitive cargo, like machine parts, where the stench wouldn't matter. He was quickly put on detached duty, ostracized from the pilot quarters; the other men, perhaps imagining it, claimed they couldn't sleep in the same room with him.

At first, he turned it into a joke, a way to pass the time while waiting for his transfer at the year's end. But the transfer never came; no one else wanted the job. By his second year, he relented and stayed. Five years later, he realized he was stuck. Even if he got a transfer, the stigma of being the garbage man would follow him, barring him from promotions and leadership opportunities that his peers received. There were certain freedoms in his role, sure, but if only there was something outside the service he could do...

The side door opened abruptly, and General Bailey walked in. He appeared older than his forty years, and the stern look on his face quickly hushed the pilots.

He eased himself into the chair behind the table, giving the room a moment to settle. Stanton watched intently as the man pulled out a cigarette. With a deliberate tap against the table, a ritualistic act to pack the end, the man nodded. Stanton's pulse quickened; they were calling for volunteers. Thinking of the storm brewing outside, his stomach knotted, but he leaned forward, ready to spring to his feet.

"Relax, gentlemen." Bailey took his time lighting the cigarette, then launched into the matter at hand. "Some of you have been cursing the station's forecast. But let's set the record straight; we're incredibly fortunate they even spotted Hulda. They're struggling up there. Do any of you know what acrolein is? You've all had atmospherics training. Who can tell me?"

The responses were fragmented, coming from several pilots. They explained that acrolein was one of the numerous toxins that needed to be filtered from the station's air, though it posed no threat in Earth's vast atmosphere. It could seep into the air from overcooked eggs or the burning of certain proteins. "Some plastics can release it too," one added. Bailey nodded. "Exactly. And that's how it happened— an accident in the workshops released enough to overwhelm their filters. The replacements aren't sufficient. They're being slowly poisoned, muddling their thoughts at first, but it's getting worse. They can't wait for Hulda to clear; they need new filters immediately. And that means—"

"Sir!" Hennings was on his feet, as if propelled by a coiled spring, standing resolute. "My crew volunteers to deliver whatever the station requires."

Stanton, caught off guard by Hennings' swift action, quickly rose in objection.

His voice was as empty as he felt, echoing after the energetic tones of the younger man. "I'm already behind schedule, and—"

Bailey cut him off, nodding to Hennings. "Thank you, Colonel. We'll start loading immediately. Control will sort out your tapes. All right, dismissed!" He turned sharply to Stanton. "Thanks, Tom. I'll note your offer, but we don't have time to unload your ship first. Sorry, but you're grounded due to the storm."

Bailey exited swiftly, with Hennings jauntily following. The others began to leave, grumbling yet admiring Hennings for beating them to the punch. Stanton lagged behind, knowing there was no altering the orders now. He wondered what excuse would have been crafted if he had been the first to volunteer and if his ship had been empty. The pilot choice was likely decided before the supposed request for volunteers, and he was sure his name wasn't in the running.

As he started across the field, it seemed like the storm had abated, but it was just a brief respite. Before he could make it to the weather shack, the rain began to pelt down again, harder than before. Inside the door, he paused to shake off the wetness. Butler was engrossed in one of the radar screens, which was showing conditions from a remote pickup. He alternated between working a calculator and barking into a phone. He glanced up, made a desperate gesture for a cigarette, and returned to his call. Stanton handed him a lit smoke, then dragged a stool over to the window to watch the field.

By all rights, he should be heading back to his farm to manage what he could there, but he had no intention of leaving before the takeoff. Launching a ship in this weather was largely theoretical. It had been done once on the Island, but the large ships remained too unstable, making it a measure of last resort.

He had talked it over with the pilot after that trip, and he had spent countless hours figuring out a method just in case. Now, though, Hennings had his complete sympathy. This situation demanded more than just courage and confidence. Stanton studied the storm, trying to sense its mood. He had flown a small plane during his first couple of years back here, often in rough weather. That experience gave him some insight into what Hennings was about to face. He wondered if the young pilot truly grasped what was coming.

Sodium lights blazed across the field, illuminating Hennings' Jennilee. Men scrambled in the mud, preparing her and loading the filter packs. Two men rode a lift to the crew entrance—Hennings carried both a co-pilot and a radio man, although many pilots now opted for just one crew member. Butler looked up from the phone. "Fifteen minutes to zero," he reported.

Stanton grunted in surprise. He had expected the take-off to be two hours later, synchronized with the next swing of the station. This must mean that loading orders were issued before Bailey entered the Briefing room. It confirmed his suspicion that the pilot had been selected in advance.

A few minutes later, Hennings appeared, striding across the field toward the lift, surrounded by a small group. Several of them joined him on the ride up. The lift creaked as it moved, and the pilot paused in the lock, grinning for the photographers. Of course, the press had been tipped off; the service had long realized that high publicity secured bigger appropriations.

When the lock finally sealed and the field cleared, Stanton leaned over the counter to study the radar screens. The storm seemed capricious, judging by the hazy patterns displayed. Zero looked like a poor choice for take-off from what he could estimate. Hennings would be wiser to delay and manually adjust his course.

Then the emergency alarm blared, signaling take-off. The last technician on the field dashed for cover. From the blast pit, a faint, reddish glow began to emerge as the rockets ignited. Stanton cursed under his breath. That idiot was sticking to his launch schedule, relying entirely on pre-recorded instructions! The red exhaust shifted to blue, and the ship began to tremble. The noise grew into a deafening roar. The Jennilee started to lift off, only to be slammed sideways by a sudden gust of wind. The wings of the top stage caught most of the force, causing the entire ship to tilt—a disastrous scenario. They should have rotated the ship to position the wings parallel to the wind instead of trying to fight it. Stanton heard Butler's sharp intake of breath, but just then, the worst danger passed. A brief lull in the storm gave Hennings the opportunity he needed. He was now manually adjusting the controls, overriding the automatic systems. The blast deflection vanes shot blue flames sideways, allowing the ship to stabilize. Slowly, it began its proper ascent. The wings near the top vibrated like tuning forks, creating a ragged trail of exhaust. Yet the Jennilee rose, her engine roar fluctuating as the wind shifted, sometimes carrying the sound away from the onlookers. The Doppler effect became noticeable, and the pitch dropped as the Jennilee struggled upward. Clouds swiftly moving across the sky obscured all but the bright, burning tail of the exhaust. Stanton turned with the technician to another radar screen. Unlike those in Control, it was poorly calibrated to track the ship, but a hazy shape flickered at the edge. "Right into the worst turbulence!" Butler exclaimed. He was right. Their timing couldn't have been worse. The glowing dot on the screen was clearly being tossed around. Something struck the top of the ship, causing it to jolt. The screen went black, then lit up again as Butler reconnected to the main signal Control was monitoring.

The blip of the Jennilee was now perfectly centered, attempting to align with a normal synergy curve. "Take it up, damn it!" Stanton swore, his frustration boiling over. This was no time to be orbiting Earth; they needed to clear the storm first. The autopilot tape should have been configured for a steep initial ascent. If Hennings was panicking and manually redirecting them back to a familiar orbit...

As if sensing the urgency, the blip started to rise again. It twisted and jerked. Something seemed to break away. Tiny white dots scattered across the screen, drifting behind the ship. Stanton couldn't identify them. Then, he dismissed the distraction as the first stage disengaged and began its descent, arcing towards the ocean. Recovery would be tough. The second stage ignited, propelling the ship upwards. Finally, they were above the storm and could set course for their destination.

The speaker in the corner abruptly crackled to life, and Hennings' voice filled the room. "Jennilee to Base. Cancel the trumpets and fanfare! We're in the clear!"

Butler slammed his hand on a switch, silencing the speaker. "Hotshot!" he muttered, though it was tinged with a hint of admiration. "Ten years ago, they couldn't build ships tough enough for that kind of abuse. Makes him a hero, I guess. Got a cigarette, Billy?"

Stanton handed him the pack and picked up his slicker. He'd seen enough. The ship should encounter no more issues, just some minor orbital adjustments, well within Hennings' capabilities. Sure, Butler's remark held some truth, but Hennings deserved his share of the credit. And if he had to boast a bit, it was earned—it took real grit to bounce back after the beating his body and nerves must have endured. In the recreation hall, some pilots were busy dramatizing the take-off for the reporters, making it sound like no greater feat had ever been achieved in the history of space flight.

Stanton found a secluded spot to make a call and inform Pete and Sheila about his return—without a cargo. They already knew. Cutting the call short, he stepped into the marshy field, swearing under his breath as his shoes soaked up water. The distant sound of the school band practicing drifted through the air, a relentless drumbeat echoing. He mused briefly if the cadets felt like heroes slogging through the mud, their shoes squelching with every step. It did nothing for his spirits.

The nearly empty parking lot beyond the drill grounds felt desolate, especially with his large truck hunched against the wind like a solitary, old bull buffalo. Climbing in, he started the turbine and cranked up the cab heater, kicking off his drenched shoes. The damp air carried the familiar odors of refuse and pigs from the truck's rear—a scent he had grown accustomed to. At least it was better than the mechanical-human-chemical stench of the space station.

Driving required his full attention. Though the truck remained stable in the wind and the roads were almost empty, visibility was poor, and the windshield fogged up despite the silicone coating. He drove slowly, grumbling about the funds spent on tourist superhighways instead of improving back roads.

A short distance from the base, farm country unfolded around him. It contrasted sharply with his initial expectations of Florida's landscape—palm trees and citrus groves. He knew, in theory, that Florida was a major cattle state, but seeing it firsthand was different. It wasn't exactly like the Iowa farmlands where he'd grown up, but it wasn't too far off either.

Pete Crane had shown him this side of Florida. Back then, Pete was retiring after twenty years of service, searching for a new purpose. He'd stumbled upon a small farm twenty miles from the base and approached Stanton with a proposition: use the station's garbage to feed the hogs he planned to raise.

The contractor who managed the Base's garbage refused to deal with the dehydrated, slightly scorched refuse, making disposal a constant headache. Eventually, they became partners, securing permanent rights to all the station's waste materials. Pete's sister, Sheila, moved in to help them keep the house in order. It was better than living in hotels and offered Stanton his first glimmer of hope for the future. Unless his Moon service application got accepted—which seemed unlikely, considering he was already nearing the maximum age limit of thirty-five—he didn't have any other plans for his mandatory twenty-year retirement. The farm also gave some meaning to his role as the station's garbage collector.

For two years, things went smoothly. Perhaps they got a bit too confident during that period. They invested everything into new buildings and more livestock. When the neighboring farm suddenly became available, they took on a massive mortgage, using up all their credit, leaving no cushion for unexpected issues. Trouble arrived when

Pete was injured; a tractor inexplicably slipped into gear, pinning him. He was hospitalized for five weeks, and his insurance barely covered a fraction of the costs. Now, with Hulda canceling the critically necessary trip to the station...

The truck jolted over the final half mile and into the farmyard. Stanton parked it near the front door and quickly jumped out. He let out a shout and hurried to the kerosene heater, trying to warm his feet. The house was sturdier than many in Florida, but that wasn't saying much. Even with the heater running, it was probably warmer in their new pigsty.

Sheila came through the dining room from the kitchen, noticed his wet feet, and dashed to his bedroom. In an instant, she returned with dry clothes. "Change in here where it's warm. I'll have lunch ready in a couple of minutes," she said, leaning in for a kiss. Sheila wasn't a beautiful woman and seemed perfectly content with that.

Stanton's mother would have likely described her features as "wholesome" and her slightly overweight frame as "healthy." To him, she was perfect: her height just right, her eyes a pleasant blue, and her hair a fitting shade of brown. He pulled her close, but she wriggled free after a brief kiss. "Pete's in town, trying to get help. He'll be back any minute," she cautioned. He grinned and released her. They had moved past the whirlwind romance phase long ago and were now comfortably familiar with each other, except for the occasional spat when patience ran thin. Mostly, she had come to terms with their agreement. In eight months, he'd turn thirty-six and be too old for a Moon assignment; if he didn't get the job, they'd get married. But he had no intention of tethering her to him if he did leave, as the odds of her joining him were almost non-existent. Pete had supported his decision, too.

He slipped into coveralls and dry boots and headed to the dining room, where a hot meal awaited. At least their credit was good enough at the local grocery to hold them over between paychecks. They ate, and he filled her in on the day's events. At the hour mark, he flipped on the television for the news. As expected, it was all about the station emergency and rescue. The broadcast focused heavily on Hennings boarding the ship, accompanied by a dramatic retelling of the flight. But at least he learned that the mission had been a success, good PR for the service. A soundtrack featuring the Heroes' March had been tacked into the footage. Maybe that was a good publicity move as well. He had to concede that Hennings suited the music far better than he would have.

For a moment, the howling wind outside subsided, allowing another sound to break through. The hogs were making a ruckus; they knew it was past feeding time. Stanton grimaced.

He pushed himself away from the table, a twinge of guilt twisting in his gut from having eaten so much, and rummaged through the back closet for his rain gear. The thought of braving the weather again made him groan, but the animals needed attention. They heard him approach and immediately began their noisy demands. Lowering his head against the wind, he charged out, splashing through a puddle that soaked his feet anew. As expected, the barn was warmer than the house. He lifted the lid of the mash cooker and started scooping food into the troughs. The pail scraped the bottom as the sleek Poland China hogs jostled and shoved each other to get closer. They'd been on half rations since yesterday and were clearly starving. After dishing out half of the cooker's contents, he trudged to the next building.

On the way, he made a pointless stop at the storage shed; he already knew the answer. Pete had used the last bag of grain for the day's feed. They had exhausted the supply of station waste earlier and were now tapping into the precious commercial feed, which was usually reserved as a supplement. Damn Javier, and double damn Hulda! If the weather reports had been accurate, he could have arranged for a supply drop ahead of schedule, before the storms hit, and they wouldn't be in this predicament.

It was even worse in the brooder house. The sows seemed to sense that their milk production for the piglets depended on their feeding. They received slightly larger portions, but he watched as the food vanished from the troughs within moments. The pigs scrabbled for the last morsels and then began scouring the area for more. They were smart enough to know he was the one providing the food, their eyes following him, their demands clear in their grunts and squeals. They were different from other livestock. Cows were too dull to realize they were shortchanged, and sheep always bleated regardless of their circumstances.

But hogs could almost swear in English when they felt cheated, and these certainly did. Even the piglets were squealing miserably in sympathy with their mothers. Stanton heard the door creak open behind him and turned to see Pete, dripping wet and looking exhausted. His back was still stiff from the accident, though he'd made a remarkable recovery. "Hey, Tom. Sis told me what went down at the field. Good thing, too. This weather's useless for flights. How long till it clears?"

"Five days!" Stanton informed him, noting the older man's wince. The hogs might not starve in that time, but they'd suffer and lose weight that would be tough to regain. He couldn't guess what impact that would have on the piglets' milk supply, and he didn't want to. They left the squealing hogs and trudged back to the house to change before Pete could update them on his luck in town. It seemed all bad. They could take out a loan against the mature hogs or sell some, but with the weekend approaching, they would have to wait for the money until it was too late. Their credit at the only feed and grain store was maxed out. Stanton frowned. "You mean Barr wouldn't extend credit to us in an emergency like this? After all our business with him?"

"Barr's gone up north on some business," Pete replied. "His brother-in-law's running the place. Says he can't take the responsibility. Offered to lend me twenty bucks from his own pocket, but no credit from the store. And he can't track Barr down. Damn it, if I hadn't had to get in front of that tractor..."

"If!" Sheila interrupted. "If I hadn't insisted we pay the hospital bill in full, or if I hadn't splurged on spring clothes... How much can we get for my car?"

Pete shrugged. "About half what we need, but not until maybe Tuesday or Wednesday, after the title transfer. I already asked at Circle Chevy. How about getting the weather reports, Sheila?"

"It's just our luck that the center of Hulda might pass right here!"

But it seemed they were safe for now. Hulda was chasing after Javier, heading out to sea, sparing them the worst of her fury. Stanton knew Bill Butler would reach out if the farm was in real danger. Yet, with the weather forecasts turning unreliable, certainty was a luxury they didn't have. The new buildings were designed to withstand hurricanes, but...

They spent the afternoon trying to focus on a game of canasta, the sound of rain and wind their constant companions. Pete eventually shoved the cards back into the drawer in frustration. They ate their meal early, drawing out the process to pass the time. Eventually, the two men ventured outside, begrudgingly. This time, they scraped the bottom of the cookers clean. Trying to stretch the meager food supply any thinner seemed pointless. What kind of hero would he be, looking into the eyes of a hungry hog? Would the melody of destiny playing in his head drown out the desperate squeals of the animals? Stanton sighed and, feeling nauseous, turned back toward the house with Pete following.

Sheila met them at the door, gesturing for silence and pointing to the television. Finally, news was coming through about Hennings' rescue mission. The screen showed a small third-stage rocket filmed from the station. Even without the announcer's comments, it was clear that the wings were nearly torn off, and it wasn't fit for a return trip. Stanton's respect for Hennings' bravery grew. After enduring such a battering, it was remarkable Hennings had managed to communicate with Base at all.

Then the rest of the news began to sink in, and no amount of carefully chosen words could make it sound positive. "... significant loss of filters when the airlock sprung open during take-off, but it's believed the replacements will suffice until another flight can be arranged. Dr. Shapiro on the station reports that morale remains steady, except for the two children."

Plans were already in motion to isolate them in a special room with enhanced filtration.

Commander Phillips' kids, Stanton mused. It didn't make sense for the man to keep them aboard in the first place. But the incident with the compromised airlock... A memory flickered—a recollection of smaller blips on the radar, detaching from the Jennilee before its first stage jettison. Stanton's brow furrowed as he pieced it together. A few filters alone couldn't have shown up so distinctly on the radar. But the haphazard packing he'd witnessed, combined with the ship's tilt as the airlock faced downward, could have spilled enough to explain nearly the entire trace. Of course! Stanton reached for his phone but stopped short. This needed a personal touch. He zipped up his coveralls and headed for his bedroom, while Pete watched in dawning realization.

"Tom, you can't go through with this!" Pete's voice was heavy with concern.

"I have to try," Stanton called back. "Start the truck, Sheila."

The zipper resisted. Frustrated, he cursed at it and abandoned the effort. There was no need for a pristine appearance. He grabbed his uniform cap, stepped into his mud-resistant boots, and stuffed his essential papers and ID cards into his coverall pockets. His service slicker, now dry, would conceal most of his attire.

"Any news on another flight scheduled?" he warned, dreading to reach the field only to see a pilot take off and shatter his plans.

"None," Pete answered, already holding the door open. His large hand slapped Stanton's shoulder in a gesture of rough camaraderie. "Good luck, you fool!"

Stanton leaped into the truck. He moved to push Sheila out of the driver's seat, but she shot him a stubborn look, revving the turbine. "I can drive just as well as you, Tom. After that long journey, the last thing you need is more exhaustion. And stop looking at me like that!"

"I'm not saying what I'm thinking about this!"

He settled back in the passenger seat, briefly reaching out to touch her hand. "Thanks, Hon," he said, as the truck accelerated onto the road. She wasn't the type to fret over his dangerous job like some of the other pilots' wives. She accepted it as part of who he was, no matter how she felt. Now, she was pushing the truck to its limit, sharing his urgency. After a moment, she caught his hand and smiled, her eyes never leaving the road. He relaxed in the seat, allowing the rhythm of the wipers and the muffled storm sounds to lull him into a light trance, resting as much as he could. He should have been thinking about what he'd say to Bailey, but the relaxation was more important. He was half asleep when the truck stopped at the guard house. He started fumbling for his papers, but the guard, recognizing him, called out. A corporal quickly moved from the shack and climbed into the truck, reaching for the wheel.

"General Bailey's expecting you and the young lady, sir," he said. "I'll take care of your truck."

Stanton grunted in surprise. Pete must have managed to get a message through to Bailey. This could complicate things, but at least it would save time; crucial, if he needed to launch while the station was in optimum position. Bailey's aide met them at General Headquarters, escorting them directly to the general's private office and closing the door behind them. Bailey looked at Stanton's disheveled appearance, frowned, and gestured for them to sit. His own collar was unbuttoned, and his cap lay on the desk, signaling that formalities were abandoned. He lifted a bottle towards three waiting glasses.

"Tom? Miss Crane?"

The general seemed to need the drink more than they did. His face was ashen with fatigue, and his hand trembled slightly.

His voice was steady as he set the empty glass down. "Alright, Tom, I know what you're after. Why do you think I'd risk another ship in this weather?"

"A couple of kids who might not make it," Stanton replied. He noticed the general wince and knew he'd hit the mark; the service wouldn't want the bad press of losing those kids without trying every possible option, and the pressure on Bailey had to be enormous. "How many filters got through?"

"Two bundles out of thirty! But losing a man and another ship won't solve anything. I've turned down nearly every pilot here already. You'll need at least three convincing reasons why you're the better choice if I'm to even consider it, despite Washington breathing down my neck. Do you have them?"

Stanton realized he should have thought of them on the way over. "Experience, for starters. I've completed nearly a thousand flights on my assigned run," he said, unable to mask the bitterness creeping into his voice. "Have any of your hotshots even hit a hundred yet?"

Bailey shook his head. "No."

"Then there's the ability to operate solo without relying on the autopilot. You can't depend on machines in unpredictable situations, and there's no time for crew assistance." The combination of advanced ships and the difficulty in finding a crew for the garbage run meant Stanton had been flying solo for almost five years. He saw Bailey raise two fingers and grasped for a final, compelling argument. The bitterness returned to his voice. "Third, expendability. What's a garbage man and an old ship compared to the bright future you're building?"

"I've considered the first two already. They're valid points. The third isn't." Bailey poured another drink, his gaze fixed on the liquid. "I can find pilots, Tom. But in fifteen years, I haven't found another reliable 'garbage man' like you."

"You'll have to do better than that."

Sheila's heels clicked sharply against the floor. "After fifteen years of doing a job no one else wants, don't you think Tom deserves a favor? Isn't that enough reason?"

Bailey turned to her, surprise etching his features. He studied her for a moment, nodding slowly. "My God, you really want him to go," he said finally. "I thought... Never mind. If you trust his ability, maybe I should too. Or maybe I need convincing. Alright, Tom, we'll unload your ship and get the filters installed. Want me to choose a volunteer crew for you?"

"I'll take it solo," Stanton replied. The fewer lives he was responsible for, the better; besides, there wouldn't be time for assistance in the critical first few miles. "And leave the machinery in. Your filters are all bulk and no weight. She'll pitch less with a full load. I saw that today. I'll be better off with that ballast."

Bailey reached for the phone and began issuing orders while Stanton turned to say goodbye to Sheila. She made it easier than he had anticipated.

"I'll wait here," she told him. "You'll need the truck when you come down." She kissed him quickly, then pushed him away. "Go on, you don't have time for me now."

He knew she was right. He started for Control at a run, surprised when a covered jeep pulled up beside him. Lights flickered on abruptly, revealing the Mollyann dimly through the haze, with men and trucks swarming toward her. He sent the jeep's driver after them with instructions to turn the base so the wings of the third stage would be edge-on to the wind.

In Control, everything was chaotic, with men still groggy from sleep staring at him in disbelief. But they quickly agreed to set up the circuit that would connect his viewing screen to the weather radar.

Butler's voice over the phone was harsh, laced with worry, but he grasped the situation quickly. The Mollyann was rocking against her support cables as the jeep sped him towards her; those cables would be the last thing to go before takeoff. A few tractors were idling nearby, and Bailey came sprinting towards him, gesturing urgently towards the top and shouting something about needing to turn her. Stanton shrugged. He hadn't expected everything to be seamless in this final rush; if he had to launch her as she was, so be it. "Alright, forget it," he said. "If you can't turn her, I'll deal with it."

"Just look," Bailey insisted, pointing up with a weary grin. "The wind's changed—the alignment's perfect now. We checked after setting everything up, and there she was."

Stanton glanced up and cursed himself for not checking sooner. The massive wings aligned perfectly with the wind, saving them precious time. The steering vanes on the upper stage would still be at the mercy of the gusts, but they were shorter and built to withstand more. The portable lift was already hoisting the filter packs. He stepped on just as a flashbulb popped nearby and started his ascent. Someone from the press called out, but he had no time for photos—not in the state he was in. There'd be time for that later, he hoped.

With a quick inspection, he ensured the filter packs were securely fastened, ready to survive even if an airlock breach happened. The supervising technician pointed out the additional locks they were installing, vowing it would withstand anything. It looked solid enough. Up here, the ship swayed and bobbed noticeably, the cables creaking under the pressure. Stanton focused on tuning out the noise as he climbed the narrow ladder to the control cabin, ready to begin the final checks.

A shout crackled through the speaker as he connected to Control, but he barely registered it. After fifteen years, he didn't need them to pinpoint the exact second for takeoff. Adjusting the weather display on the screen, he sank into the acceleration couch beneath the manual control panel, designed to pivot smoothly under shifting forces. The weather image was his ace in the hole. His careful study might finally give him the edge. There was a certain bravado in launching at the precise second and battling whatever the storm threw at him, but he preferred to choose his own moment, if possible. With any luck, he could find a brief window to ascend without turbulence in the crucial first seconds.

He glanced at the chronometer and began strapping himself down, his mind racing to process the storm data Butler was relaying through his earphones. Butler, working with several screens, could provide a more comprehensive picture than the single screen Stanton was stuck with. He started to get a feel for it. This far from the hurricane's center, the wind was unpredictable; there were intervals of relative calm, and the patterns on the screen offered some predictive possibilities. The key to a successful takeoff was seizing those fleeting opportunities. Once he began his ascent, he'd rely on the automatic reflexes honed over years and the theoretical plans developed with minimal rational thought. But for now, he could use his brain to make the takeoff as smooth as possible. The kids in the station and the livestock on the farm cared about the results, not his display of daring.

Butler's voice was abruptly cut off as Control notified him that loading was complete and all personnel and equipment were clear. He placed one hand on the switch that would release the guy cables all at once.

With one hand, he activated the peroxide pump for the fuel and flipped the switch to ignite the rockets. The whine of the pump and the first rumblings of power coursed through the ship, but he kept it at minimum. His eyes were locked on the weather display, searching for the best window. Ground control was in an uproar. Their countdown had ended, and they wanted him to launch immediately. Let them panic! A few seconds' delay in liftoff was something he could adjust for later. Then, with a decisive movement, he pushed the main engine lever all the way down and released the cable grapples. The Mollyann broke free and began to rise unsteadily, swaying in the wind. But he had chosen the right moment to take off. For the first hundred feet, she held steady, though the wind was driving them away from the blast deflection zone.

Then all hell broke loose. The acceleration slammed him back in his seat, muscles straining against the immense force. His fingers and arms struggled to move, but they had to, dancing across the controls.

The ship twisted and tilted, every plate groaning from the torsion and pressure. Yet, somehow, instinctively, his fingers found a combination that steadied her. His ears were clogged with the throbbing of his pulse, and his sense of balance was shot, eyes barely managing to keep focus on the instrument panel. Thought had stopped; he was purely a machine now.

The ship spun madly in the turbulent air currents. Miraculously, she stayed upright, guided by hands that seemed to move with a life of their own, while fuel poured out at a rate that should have blacked him out from the G-forces. It was a gamble, but his only shot was to get through the storm as quickly as possible and deal with the fallout later. If he reached the station, they would have fuel for his return launch. For now, he made no effort to tilt into a normal ascent trajectory.

A red light illuminated the controls, shimmering hazily before his eyes. The ship's velocity was dangerously high for its altitude, causing the hull to heat up. He had no choice but to risk it. Unexpectedly, the vessel began to stabilize. He had climbed above the storm. He eased back the power to normal, his senses gradually returning, and started to tilt the ship, prepping to swing around Earth towards his destination, a thousand miles up on the other side. The maneuver wouldn't create a perfect synergy curve, but he was alive and that was all that mattered. He felt the enormous first stage disengage, followed by a fleeting moment of zero pressure, before the second stage roared to life. The storm had raged for barely over a minute, though it felt like hours of agony. Voices barked in his headset, but he ignored them. This was his moment to say something heroic, deliver the perfect line for the history books.

"Shut up, damn it! I'm all right!" he shouted into the microphone. How could he think of the perfect quip with them constantly interrupting him? Slowly, he realized he had already responded, and it was too late for any grand statement. The second stage finally dropped away, leaving the third stage to continue the journey alone. He made rough adjustments for his awkward take-off, hoping he hadn't missed anything crucial, as the second hand on the clock circled until he could cut all power and just drift. He leaned back, savoring the sensation of weightlessness. His body trembled and felt like one giant bruise. Sweat poured from his forehead, and goosebumps prickled his arms. He barely managed to reach the small cabinet in time to avoid making a mess as he got sick. Some hero he turned out to be. The only melody in his mind was the ringing in his ears and the pounding of his heart. Yet, this ascent was merely the easier part of his mission.

He still had to bring his cargo down in an unpowered glide through a storm rapidly nearing its worst stage, or the entire trip would be for nothing, regardless of how many lives he could save. As he finally synced up with the station's orbit, he felt almost like himself again. It seemed his wings and stabilizers were in good shape, and the cargo bay's air pressure indicated no breaches. He even had a few drops of fuel left after making his final adjustments. At least he'd managed the ascent competently. With some luck, he might get the Mollyann back down in one piece. He'd surely need that luck. The station, now a sprawling multi-tube structure, looked normal enough in the sunlight. But the crew who emerged from the small space ferry bore the telltale signs of prolonged exposure to toxic air, despite their excitement over seeing the filters. When they made seal-to-seal contact and he unlocked the airlock, the stench of their atmosphere was overwhelming. They must have been downplaying their dire situation.

Commander Phillips came through first, nearly in tears as he grasped Stanton's hand. He seemed utterly at a loss for words.

"Hello, Red," Stanton greeted him. Phillips had been in his training class fifteen years ago. "How are the kids?"

"Shapiro says they'll be okay, once we get some uncontaminated filters. Billy, I'd offer you champagne right now, but our air would ruin it. Just consider anything I've got yours...."

Stanton interrupted him. "Just get this cargo unloaded and my usual load on board, plus some fuel. And have one of your engineers check my wings for any signs of strain. I've got to ride the next orbit back, two hours from now."

"Go back into that? You're crazy!" Phillips' shock was plain to see. "You can't do it!"

"I can't clear you!"

"I thought you said you'd give me anything you had," Stanton retorted. It took another five minutes of intense back-and-forth to finalize the arrangement. He probably wouldn't have succeeded if he had waited until Lieutenant Commander Phillips had fully processed his initial gratitude or if the man hadn't been debilitated by the toxic air and their grueling battle for survival. Phillips was hoarse and visibly ill when he finally conceded and staggered back to the loaded ferry. He muttered something about foolishness and the eternal gratitude of humanity before he took off. Stanton tried to make sense of it but was again more preoccupied with the pressing problem of feeding the hungry pigs. It was such a hectic time that there was no room for other concerns. The square magnesium cans of dehydrated waste started flowing out along with fuel. The sick men somehow managed to summon a last surge of energy to carefully stow everything to maintain the ship's balance. Outside, a constant clanging and hammering filled the air as others inspected the control surfaces with their instruments.

Phillips came back one final time, leading to another heated exchange. Yet, in the end, he relented once more. "All right, damn it. Maybe you'll pull this off. I certainly hope so. But you're not doing it alone. You're taking Hennings as your co-pilot. He volunteered."

"Send him over, then," Stanton replied, exhausted. He should have seen this coming. Hennings always seemed to chase after glory like a warhorse to gunfire. Stanton gave the cargo one last look, nodding in satisfaction. There was enough waste to keep the farm operational until better times. If Barr returned with commercial feed, bought on temporary credit, things would vastly improve. Stanton maneuvered himself to the control cabin just in time to see the ferry on its last trip. A moment later, Hennings sealed the connecting hatch behind him.

"Hey, Billy," he greeted. "Ah, fresh air again."

"How about letting me take over? You look exhausted," Hennings offered.

"The autopilot's not working," Stanton snapped back. It had malfunctioned about twenty flights ago, and he'd disconnected it since he hardly ever relied on it. Hennings' confidence visibly waned. He hesitated en route to the controls, eyeing them nervously. Though autopilots weren't much use during descent, pilots had grown almost reverent towards them, a habit tracing back to the days when ascending would have been impossible without their aid. Stanton had shared that sentiment during his first five years of piloting.

"You better strap in," he advised. Hennings sank into the co-pilot seat as Stanton performed the final checks. The ship slowly swung around as the gyroscopes buzzed, aligning for the descent. "Ten seconds," Stanton declared, counting down silently before gently pulling the blast lever. They started losing speed, descending towards Earth as the orbital station drifted away. With the engines off, there was nothing to do but watch the approach. The Base would still be engulfed in darkness, and even with sodium flares and radar beacons, visibility wouldn't be ideal in the storm. They'd have to land like a conventional plane, relying on lift. Any unseen stress on the wings could spell trouble.

"You didn't use a tape?" Hennings asked abruptly. Stanton scowled, annoyed at the disruption to his concentration. He preferred Hennings when he was brimming with confidence rather than fretful.

"No tape can predict these conditions," Stanton replied curtly.

"If you say so," Hennings muttered, still looking unsure. He gazed at the controls, a peculiar expression on his face.

Then unexpectedly, he laughed and leaned back, relaxing in his seat. "Guess you don't need me, then."

Five minutes later, he was snoring. Stanton shot him a suspicious look, initially thinking it might be a ruse. But he soon shrugged it off and returned to his fretting. He knew his take-off had owed a good deal to luck, despite all his meticulous planning. Relying on luck for the landing wasn't an option. Theoretically, he could still send out an emergency call and request to land at a large airfield outside the storm. But it would be futile. Hulda had the entire region blanketed; any alternative would be so remote from the farm that trucking the garbage back would be unfeasible. He might as well have stayed at the station. Besides, he was already on a braking orbit leading back to Base, and making changes now would come with their own set of risks. He watched the thin haze of the upper atmosphere draw closer, trying to relax his muscles and calm his nerves. The biggest challenge during re-entry was battling nerves. Hennings continued to snore softly, floating in the co-pilot's couch. His calm did nothing to ease Stanton's tension. It was almost a relief when they finally breached the first layers of detectable air, reactivating the controls and allowing him to take charge. The ship now required a steady hand; its plunge into the atmosphere had to be synchronized with its speed to avoid the peril of either skipping off or descending too steeply and overheating.

Stanton eased her down, eyes on his instruments but mostly relying on his gut feel for the Mollyann. A sensation of weight began to return, accompanied by external noises, while the hull pyrometer climbed, showing that friction was converting their speed into heat. By now, this part of the descent was almost second nature to him.

Outside, the ship's hull was steadily heating up, glowing a dull red as they tried to shed enough velocity to descend into the denser, cooler layers of the atmosphere. The cabin temperature was climbing, an inevitable consequence of the Mollyann's outdated design. She was an older model, with less insulation and airtightness compared to newer ships. Still, she was reliable enough to endure the brief bout of intense heat. A faint smell began to permeate the air, growing stronger as the hot metal radiated into the cargo hold. Stanton barely noticed it until Hennings stirred, sniffing the air.

"It's just the garbage," Stanton explained. "There's still enough moisture in it to boil off a bit. You'll get used to it."

They were descending into denser air now, and Stanton could feel the sweat collecting on his palms. He wiped them quickly, his head feeling thick and his stomach knotting with unease. "Contact Control and get me the weather update," he instructed Hennings. When the weather pattern flashed onto the screen, his nausea worsened. There would be no pockets of relative calm this time, and he couldn't wait for one to form. He focused on memorizing the weather pattern as their descent leveled out and they approached the storm system. He'd have to navigate through it, descending on a twisting curve due to local disturbances near the landing field.

Then the turbulence hit. The ship shuddered and seemed to skate unevenly through the turbulent air. Though there was no longer the pressure of acceleration, his fingers felt sluggish, almost leaden, as he struggled with the controls. The Mollyann dipped and tilted violently, making his stomach churn. Hennings gasped beside him, but Stanton had no time to check on him. The storm's upper layers swirled chaotically with turbulent pockets.

Conditions were worsening rapidly. The remaining miles were going to be grueling. The aerodynamic lift was unstable, and eddies in the howling storm buffeted the ship unpredictably.

Her wing-loading was decent, but she didn't have the self-stabilizing features of the light aircraft he'd piloted before. The wings groaned and strained, and the controls felt jammed. He was just a white blip on the weather map, skimming the edge. The sight gave him some orientation, but little comfort. They hit a larger air pocket, dropping a hundred feet in what felt like an instant. The wings creaked ominously, and something whined from the rear controls. Suddenly, the elevators bucked back at him, catching him off guard. He had to brace himself, pushing back with all his strength — the servo assist had clearly failed. Probably something went wrong during take-off. Now, he was left to manhandle the mechanical cables himself, fighting the currents. If the cables failed...! Sweat poured down his face as he wrestled with the controls. Despite his efforts, the ship was pitching even more. Another violent swoop hit, followed by a loud thump and the screech of shifting cargo. The ship lost its trim; some of the cans had broken free and were sliding around! He saw Hennings bolt from his seat and struggle toward the hatch. He yelled, knowing the fool could get crushed by loose cargo. But there was no time to think—the acrid smell of the boy's sweat was already in the air as he disappeared through the hatch. He fought to steady the ship, but its movements were unpredictable. His arms were burning, muscles overtaxed, and unable to manage the controls with finesse. The landing field was only a few miles away, and he had to fight through the wind to make it to the strip. The wind velocity was higher than he had estimated, and he'd lost more speed than he could spare. It was going to be a close call, if he made it at all. But then, miraculously, the ship began to steady as he felt the trim return.

Stanton barely had time to exhale in relief before Hennings staggered back, drenched in sweat and reeking of garbage. He made his way to the couch with difficulty. Stanton wanted to shout his gratitude, aware of the bravery it took for Hennings to venture into the perilous cargo hold. But Hennings' focus was entirely on the weather map, his expression grim. The landing zone was approaching, but not quickly enough. The wind resistance had bled off too much speed. Stanton attempted to adjust their glide to a flatter trajectory, but quickly abandoned the effort. They were already skirting the edge of a stall, and any more adjustments would send them crashing.

The field was slipping away, and they were on course to collide with trees, rocks, and possibly even houses. Stanton cursed and reached for the blast lever. There was no time for a proper warm-up, but they needed more speed immediately. Hennings shouted a single alarmed word before Stanton pulled the lever. The engines roared for an instant, propelling the ship forward with a violent jolt. The power was not designed for minor speed corrections and was nearly impossible to control in such bursts, but it was the only option. Stanton cut the blast, then reignited it for another split second before snapping his hand back to the elevator controls, wrestling with them to stabilize the ship.

There wasn't room for error. If they missed the field, they were finished. If they came in too fast, there would be no opportunity for a second landing attempt. Circling back in the storm was out of the question. Their only hope lay in a head-on approach, skillfully avoiding any cross currents. Ahead, beyond the field, the ocean waited—a deadly alternative as these modern spacecraft weren't meant for water landings, especially not in tumultuous seas.

A flash of yellow caught Stanton's attention—the field markers. But they were coming in too high. Desperately, he threw his weight against the unresponsive controls, willing the ship to descend.

Stanton had picked up way too much speed in that brief surge of power, but he had no choice—he had to land right away. He could see a few of the guiding flares now and knew he had to aim between them. Desperately, he dropped the landing gear and wrestled the ship down, fighting every inch. He'd already overshot the near edge of the field. Too far!

Suddenly, the wheels hit the ground. The ship bounced as the wind caught it from below, twisting it sideways. It slammed down again as Stanton wrestled with the brakes and controls to keep it steady. The ship lurched, skidded, and tore down the runway. Looming ahead in the dim light was the crash fence. Ten feet—another ten—

Stanton felt the ship hit and bounce. Relief flared briefly; they were moving too slow to break through the fence. Then his head slammed into the control panel. His mind erupted in a blaze of white-hot sparks, which quickly faded to black.

In a fog of semi-consciousness, he realized Hennings was dragging him out of the wreck. Rain lashed at him, and the howling wind filled his ears. Flashbulbs popped—he had a disjointed vision of the photo they must have captured: Hennings, indomitable and unscathed, carrying Stanton from the Mollyann, facing the storm, heading straight for the photographers with a confident smile.

Everything blurred again. Voices floated in and out—he thought he heard Sheila and Bailey. The sharp sting of a needle punctuated the haze. Like swimming through layers of dark cotton, he finally surfaced. Pain throbbed dully in his head, and a bump on his scalp pulsed with each heartbeat. The light stung his eyes as he opened them, then he quickly shut them again, catching a glimpse of the recreation hall's couch beneath him.

At least that meant no concussion—it seemed to be just a nasty bump, compounded by stress and fatigue. Outside, a mixture of chaotic sounds and relentless hammering echoed against the building.

He tried to pull himself up to look for the source, but the effort was too much for now. He began to drift into a half-doze until he heard footsteps and Hennings' voice.

"... absolutely incredible, Miss Crane! I'll never forget it. He didn't even try to make light of things to keep his spirits up. He just sat there, totally calm, like it was just another routine trip. Didn't flinch when he had to make the call to use power. Honestly, he was like one of those heroes from the old serials I used to watch. And that lousy reporter saying I brought the ship down. If I find him—"

"Let it go, Larry," Sheila's voice interjected quietly.

"I can't let it go! It was bad enough they reduced him to a tiny mention during take-off, calling it a lull in the storm! This time, I'm going to make sure the real story gets printed!"

"That'll just give them more room to talk about how you're trying to modestly shift the credit," Sheila responded softly. "They can print what they want. We all know the truth. And Tom won't mind. He's used to how these things go."

Stanton's eyes flickered open as he sat up, interrupting their conversation. He still felt groggy, but his vision cleared after a moment. He smiled at Sheila and gently pulled her down beside him.

"She's right, Hennings. Let them print whatever they want. It's good publicity for the service, no matter how they spin it. Besides, you did your part." He reached out to grasp the younger man's arm, aware he couldn't even manage that with the usual flair. "It took guts to trim the cargo when you did. I wanted to thank you for that."

Hennings muttered something awkwardly, then straightened up, resuming his old demeanor as he left the room, leaving them alone. Sheila watched him go, her smile a mix of fondness and amusement.

"What happened to the Mollyann and her cargo?"

"How's the farm holding up?" Stanton asked her a moment later.

"The farm's secure, according to the latest updates," she replied. "The ship's a bit banged up, but nothing major. General Bailey had the cadets load the cargo into our truck. He said a bit of garbage smell would be good for them." She smiled and glanced at her watch. "He should be back by now, actually."

Stanton grinned. It was a pity the hogs would never appreciate the attention their food was getting. It must have been quite a sight—the cadets playing heroes while unloading those smelly cans. He glanced out the window, but the storm still raged, obscuring his view. Someone darted past outside, followed by a flurry of noise and activity beyond the door, but nothing suggested Bailey's return. Five more minutes passed before the general finally came in, making a beeline for Stanton. "Your truck's outside, Tom. And don't bring it through the gates again unless you're in proper uniform!" He laughed. "With eagles on the collar. I've been working to get those for you a long time now. Congratulations, Colonel! You've earned them!"

Stanton pulled Sheila closer as he shook Bailey's hand, feeling her steady presence beside him. There were other reassurances, too—the words he'd overheard from Hennings, the recognition and security that came with the new rank, the satisfaction of knowing he hadn't failed. Yet he still felt awkward, unable to fully embrace the moment. Instead, he let Bailey guide them towards the door. Just as they reached it, he paused. "There's one more thing. That application for Moon service—"

He felt Sheila tense briefly before easing against him again. His words froze the general in his tracks. Bailey's head dropped slightly, nodding with reluctance. "All right," he said finally. "I hate to lose you, Tom, but I'll put it through with a recommendation."

"Don't," Stanton said firmly. "Tear it up."

"I've got a whole herd of pigs counting on this garbage run."

Stanton threw open the door and saw the loaded truck waiting outside. He strode toward it, pulling Sheila along. But he halted, mouth agape in shock at the source of the clanging noise he'd heard. A large, awkward plywood canopy now extended from the doorway to the truck. Underneath it, all the pilots stood in a line, with Hennings at the forefront. Hennings stepped forward and opened the door to the truck theatrically. Just as Stanton's foot hit the ground, the band started playing Heroes' March. Feeling ridiculous, Stanton stumbled forward, clumsily helping Sheila in and then settling into the driver's seat while fifty pairs of eyes bore into him. Hennings shut the door with another flourish and rejoined the ranks.

Suddenly, Stanton knew exactly what to do. He leaned out of the truck's window just as Sheila got comfortable beside him. Grinning at the pilots, he raised his hand, placed his thumb against his nose, and wiggled his fingers at them. Hennings' face broke into a wide grin, and he returned the gesture. Fifty other pilots followed suit, mirroring the salute in perfect synchrony. Stanton rolled up the window, and the truck began its journey across the field, heading home to the pigs. Behind him, the band played on, but he wasn't listening.

THE END.

The Oldest Question

By JONATHAN P. ELLIS

"We promised you something special this week," Eddie Robinson announced, his smile gleaming under the studio lights. "And Game-Win always keeps its promises, right? So tonight, folks, we're putting up the biggest prize we've ever offered... one hundred thousand dollars!"

The applause thundered through the studio.

"Now, for the young man you all remember, the one who hit the top prize in our quiz last week and earned a shot at Game-Win! Here he is, Mr. Donovan O'Shea! Come on out, Donovan!"

Donovan O'Shea, a tall, slender young man with a perpetually serious expression, stepped onto the stage. Although he didn't wear glasses, he gave the impression that he should. He walked with a hint of forced confidence and shook hands with Robinson.

"So, Donovan, we haven't told you much about what's lined up for you tonight, have we?" Robinson asked.

"No, sir."

"Then it's going to be as much of a surprise for you as it is for our audience." Robinson chuckled, shooting a knowing look into the cameras. "But first, let's reintroduce you for anyone who missed your fantastic performance last week. How old are you, Donovan?"

"Twenty-eight."

"And you're not married, are you? Engaged? Do you trust your girlfriend not to date other guys while you're away?"

"Well, I don't know..." O'Shea replied with a shy grin.

"Did you tell her you'd be away for a bit?" Robinson continued, winking at the audience.

"That's what I've been led to believe," O'Shea said.

"Uh huh. But we didn't tell you anything else, did we? Did your boss give you some time off?"

"Oh, yes."

"Tell us, Donovan, what's your day job?"

"I'm an accountant."

Robinson's smile widened even more. "Yes, folks, Donovan works for the illustrious National American Insurance Company, which you've all heard of. We asked them to lend us Donovan here for two months, and they were kind enough to agree."

"Given your career in insurance, Donovan, you must be quite skilled at making logical predictions, right? I mean, isn't anticipating potential events a key part of the insurance industry?"

"I guess it is," Donovan O'Shea replied, looking somewhat perplexed.

"Well, Donovan, we've created a scenario where you'll have the opportunity to forecast what's coming next. If you even get it halfway right, you'll win the game!" Robinson boomed out, his words punctuated by a dramatic chord from the orchestra.

"Here's the plan, Donovan," Robinson continued. "You're going to go down to the airport where a special helicopter is waiting for you. It will fly you to Santa Antonia, an island about two hundred miles off the coast. It's a beautiful place, Donovan... you'll love it. We've set up a cozy little house for you there, all stocked up. There's even a big deep-freeze from Handi-Freezo, filled to the brim."

Robinson paused, letting the suspense build.

"However," he went on, "there's no one else on the island. No radio, no newspapers, no way to hear from the outside world. You'll be a real-life Robinson Crusoe. But for these two months, you'll still be getting your regular salary; we've got that covered. You can read, fish, reflect, maybe even write a book if you feel inclined. Ever thought about writing a book, Donovan?"

O'Shea began to respond but seemed too stunned to speak immediately. He then shook his head.

"No, but with all that time, maybe..."

"Well, Donovan, you can certainly read if you want to," Robinson said. "We've loaded the island with plenty of solid books. There are novels, history textbooks, encyclopedias... you name it. Now, what do you think you could do with all that information?"

"Well..."

"I'll tell you what you should do, Donovan." Robinson glanced at the studio clock, quickening his pace just slightly. "Read up, Donovan. Read up."

"We'll invite you back to this studio in two months, when our show starts up again in the fall. We'll ask you a dozen questions about current events – people, places, all kinds of happenings. If you can't answer at least six of those questions correctly, you'll be out of luck and out of here. But, if you manage just six correct answers, you win the Game-Win!"

The audience erupted in applause.

"Now, Donovan, what do you think? Can you do it?"

"I'll give it my best shot, sir." O'Shea looked a bit pale but determined.

"Alright, folks, let's give a big hand to our modern-day Robinson Crusoe, and don't miss the episode when he tries to Game-Win!" Right on cue, the studio clock blinked a red light.

The helicopter roared over the open sea under the afternoon sun. The noise was much louder than the airliner O'Shea had flown in, his only previous experience in the skies. He looked ahead, the island was still out of sight.

"Think you'll win the hundred thousand?" the pilot asked loudly. He was about O'Shea's age, with a cheerful, round face.

"What? Oh ... I certainly hope so." O'Shea peered over the serene water. "How long is this trip?"

"Oh, we're almost there," the pilot assured him. "Nice little island too. Honestly, I'd take this deal even without the money. It's like a first-class vacation, right?"

"I guess it is," O'Shea said. "But it might get pretty lonely."

"If they'd sent a girl along, you might not want to come back," the pilot grinned. "Anyway, think about that prize money. That should keep the loneliness at bay."

O'Shea smiled back.

"I could really use that money," he said.

"Once I got stuck up in Thule Two in the Arctic last year while flying commercial," the pilot said. "Just me, the radio operator, and another pilot. Too cold to even think about going outside. This'll be a lot better."

"That's what I'd call lonesome."

On the horizon, a blue-green ridge started to rise above the waterline.

"There it is," the pilot said. "We'll be there in another five minutes."

The copter landed on a long, smooth beach, with a postcard-perfect ocean lapping at the white sand. The pilot showed Donovan around with an almost proprietary pride, pointing out various conveniences and giving advice.

"The house is a real gem," he told Donovan. "Never been lived in. A wealthy guy owned the place, planned to use it for vacations, but he never got around to it. Incidentally, it'll be up for sale once the stunt's over. Bet it'll fetch a hefty price too."

There was hot and cold running water, an electrical system powered by a gas engine, furniture, even a pair of swimming trunks hanging in a closet with other clothes.

"That's funny," the pilot remarked, pointing at the trunks. "You won't need them."

"Well, if I go swimming ..." Donovan began.

"The swimming's great, but you won't have anyone to worry about seeing you," the pilot replied. Donovan had never been completely alone before; it took him a moment to grasp this detail about his immediate future.

"Oh," he said, hesitantly. "Well, you know there's seaweed and all that...."

In reality, there was very little seaweed. The water was warm, the days that followed were clear and perfect; the nights were cool, with a steady sea breeze. For the first few days, Donovan O'Shea found himself sticking to a routine that closely mirrored his normal life. He woke up at seven; on the first morning, he felt compelled to get up and dress right away. That first morning, he had an odd, lost feeling; there was no office to go to, no work schedule to follow, no fixed routine.

He began by shaving and cooking himself what, for him, was a large breakfast.

Donovan mulled over the idea of a swim but quickly remembered the rule about waiting two hours after eating. The clothes inside the closet weren't his usual style, but they were comfortable and fit well. He chose a pair of slacks and an open-necked shirt before heading to explore the library.

For the next few days, his routine was remarkably consistent. He delved into stacks of news magazines, immersed himself in books dissecting politics and history, and ate at regular intervals. Twice, he ventured for a swim, though each time he wore the trunks provided. The second swim was particularly brief; he emerged from the water feeling as if there was hardly any point to it. Swimming solo had never appealed to him before.

Gradually, however, his routine began to unravel. On the fifth day, he overslept and didn't get up until almost eleven. That night, unable to sleep, he found himself eating sardines and beans at midnight, leaving the cans on the kitchen table instead of disposing of them in the pit behind the house. The following morning, he slept until noon. He didn't even bother to wind the alarm clock, which ran out of energy that same day. He took a stab at resetting it but couldn't be sure of the time.

There was a typewriter and a stack of paper sitting in one of the rooms, so Donovan began to jot down his thoughts on the events likely unfolding in the outside world, trying to predict every conceivable question. He assumed the inquiries wouldn't be too obscure, yet that left a vast realm of possibilities. Each day, he wrote for hours and read for even longer periods. Occasionally, he got engrossed in some tangent, delving into topics unlikely to come up in any questions.

When this happened, he would abruptly snap the book shut, pulling himself back to his purpose.

For three days, he immersed himself deeper and deeper into a quest that started with a recent archaeological report and pulled him through a series of National Geographic issues, all the way back to an encyclopedia entry on Ancient Egypt. It became increasingly difficult to predict where the questions might lead, and he began to write in whatever direction his imagination took him. If the questions were about elections, he speculated, they would start with candidate names. He noted the platforms and general trends: The possible Democratic candidates are... and The Soviet political landscape might shift, but according to articles in Time and The Reporter, the current leaders are expected to stay in power for a while. Considering potential questions, he thought, if it seems relevant, I could assume the current premier might pass away; he's old and can't last much longer.

Donovan had always been a die-hard baseball fan, his opinions deeply anchored in his personal experiences and the extensive collection of sports sections from newspapers. The Dodgers will likely clinch the pennant, and the Giants might sell their pitcher Joe Kenner. When it came to boxing... He felt confident about the outcomes of various sporting events. However, science was another matter. He stumbled upon entire realms he only had vague inklings about. These scientific concepts were challenging, and he was dismayed to realize how insufficient his high school "science" classes had been. Yet he wasn't overly concerned; he could safely predict that questions in this area would either be medical or related to atomic theory.

Donovan sifted through a mountain of forecasts in those fields. Every magazine had a doctor speculating on the next disease to be eradicated, predicting how soon it might happen. Articles detailed the imminent rollout of atomic power plants and the next wave of bomb tests. Initially, Donovan had opted for accountancy because he appreciated its logic and structure; now, he found himself drawn to the logic and order in science.

His initial image of a scientist had been vague, cobbled together from newspaper snapshots of Einstein, hair windswept, and movie depictions of scientists tinkering with bizarre machines and creating monsters. At one point, Donovan got so engrossed in the history and theories of science that he almost lost sight of his objective. Reluctantly, and with a promise to revisit, he redirected his focus.

"The oil workers' union contract expires next month," he noted. "Past trends show that a strike could lead to a temporary shortage of fuel and gasoline. This could answer, 'What strike is affecting the country most now?'"

Delving back into political waters, Donovan's guesses became increasingly educated as he read on. "The UN investigation into South Africa will resume, and the South African delegation will likely walk out again. There's also a good chance of uprisings in French North Africa, which means a question about Africa could refer to either issue."

Donovan's curiosity eventually steered him toward the Far East. His methodical habits compelled him to map out the most plausible events into a coherent timeline, projecting the world's trajectory into the coming years. Suddenly, he realized that his forward view had become sharply clear, continuously illuminating new possibilities.

Donovan told himself that once he got back, he'd resume writing his "History of the Future." Just for fun, of course. He was certain no one else would be interested in such a thing; after all, he wasn't even a real writer. But it seemed he might have stumbled onto a genuine hobby. Amazingly, he realized he didn't even miss television. The thought of TV brought back memories of money and endless questions. The fresh air, daily swims, and wholesome food had combined to make him feel incredibly healthy and relaxed. His confidence was at an all-time high; he knew he could handle the questions when the time came. He also knew that the plane should be arriving any day now.

Suddenly, Donovan realized he had stopped shaving some time ago and had gotten used to not wearing a shirt. Deciding it was time to tidy up, he shaved and discovered he was down to two clean shirts. More concerning, he noticed the freezer was nearly empty. He remembered spotting some edible plants growing near the house; if the freezer ran out before the plane arrived, he'd try his hand at gardening. However, it wasn't the food running out that concerned him; it was the generator running out of gas.

Draining the last of the melted ice from the freezer, Donovan was hit with a stark realization. There should've been enough gas to last over two months, yet the generator was empty. He had completely lost track of the days and began to fear the plane might be overdue by a week or even two. A slight panic set in as he scrambled to piece together how much time had passed. He sifted through his stacks of daily writing, noting he had averaged about eight pages per day. This gave him a rough means of counting back, though there had been off days. The count brought him to an unsettling conclusion: it had been at least three months. The plane was very definitely overdue.

In his third year of isolation, Donovan finally finished his radio receiver, crafted from wire salvaged from a broken generator, using the principles of a crystal receiver. A needle balanced on an old razor blade served as the key component. He had meticulously followed instructions from a mechanics magazine. The project took longer than expected since Donovan didn't find it compelling, except when he got bored with reading and writing. He also spent considerable time collecting blank pages from various books to ensure he had enough writing paper. The receiver seemed functional, yet it only picked up a steady crackle and hiss, and occasionally, the distant rumble of lightning during storms.

Life otherwise progressed smoothly. His garden thrived with minimal effort, he mastered efficient fishing techniques, and found little to desire beyond his current means. His written history expanded steadily, each volume carefully bound with covers taken from repurposed books. Donovan discovered how to bleach pages of printed material, though he only did so reluctantly, preserving most books intact. In his meticulous notes, he used the term "palimpsest," fully understanding its meaning now.

The year 2234 brought significant changes. The last queen of England, though devoid of political power, was deeply respected by the British people. Her death at an old age sparked widespread mourning. Without a direct heir, her burial in the reconstructed Westminster Abbey symbolized the absolute end of the monarchy, even as a figurehead. That same year also witnessed humanity's first earnest attempt to traverse interstellar space, as a colossal ship, designed to sustain a large community of travelers for an extended duration, embarked on its pioneering journey.

In 2234, new books hit the shelves from renowned historian Nosreg and his contemporary, Songre. "The Tragedy of Man" by the playwright Gresno captivated audiences via the Solar Television Network. Donovan, stroking his graying beard thoughtfully, mused over Gresno's plays, a subtle yearning to witness them building within him. Yet, he reminded himself, Gresno wouldn't be born for some time. Meanwhile, the afternoon sun warmed his back as he sat on the porch, confronted with a vast expanse of white paper. Taking up the seagull quill, he began to write again.

THE END.

Refuse All Replacements

By GORDON T. LANGLEY

Ralph Russell's private space yacht was docked at Boston Spaceport, poised for takeoff. He was on yellow standby, awaiting the green light, when his radio crackled to life.

"Tower to G43221," the transmission buzzed. "Please await customs inspection."

"Understood," replied Russell, his voice calm but his nerves fraying. Inside, he felt a surge of panic. Customs inspection! Of all the rotten, miserable luck! Normally, private yachts like his weren't subject to regular inspections. The Department was bogged down with the enormous interstellar liners from Cassiopeia, Algol, Deneb, and myriad other destinations. Private ships were considered too trivial for the effort. To maintain order, however, Customs performed random spot checks. No one ever knew when the mobile customs team might descend on a spaceport. The odds of being inspected were slim, about fifty to one. Russell had banked on those odds. He had even forked over eight hundred dollars to be tipped off that the East Coast team was in Georgia. Otherwise, he would never have risked a twenty-year prison sentence for violating the Sexual Morality Act. A loud knock resounded on his hatch. "Open for inspection, please."

"Understood," Russell called back. He quickly locked the door to the aft cabin. If the inspector demanded access there, it was all over. There was nowhere on the yacht he could hide a packing crate ten feet tall, and no way to get rid of its illegal contents.

"I'm coming," Russell shouted, sweat breaking out on his high, pale forehead. Desperation nagged at him—perhaps he should just blast off now, make a run for it to Mars, or Venus.... But the patrol ships would intercept him well before he could cover a million miles. Bluffing was his only option. He pressed a button, and the hatch slid open to reveal a tall, thin man in uniform.

"Thought you'd slip by, didn't you, Russell?" the inspector snapped. "You wealthy types never learn!"

They knew. Somehow, they had found out! Russell's mind raced to the packing crate in the aft cabin, with its human-shaped, not-yet-living contents.

Damning, absolutely damning. What a fool he'd been! Russell turned back to the control panel. His revolver, tucked into a cracked leather holster hanging from the corner, caught his eye. Rather than face twenty years breaking pumice on Lunar, he would shoot first, then try to—

"The Sexual Morality Act isn't just a blue law, Russell," the inspector's voice was like steel grinding against flint. "Violations can devastate individuals and put the entire race at risk. That's why we're making an example out of you, Russell. Now, let's see the evidence."

"I have no idea what you're talking about," Russell said, his hand discreetly inching toward the revolver.

"Get it together, boy!" said the inspector. "You still don't recognize me?"

Russell squinted at the inspector's tanned, amused face. "Eddie Ross?"

"Finally! How long has it been, Ralph? Ten years?"

"At least ten," Russell replied, feeling his knees weaken with relief. "Sit down, Eddie! You still drink bourbon?"

"Absolutely." Ross plopped down on one of Russell's acceleration couches, surveying the surroundings, nodding in approval.

"Nice. Very nice. You must be doing well, old buddy."

"I manage," Russell said, handing Ross a drink and pouring one for himself. They reminisced about their days at Michigan State.

"And now you're a Customs inspector," Russell remarked.

"Yeah," Ross said, stretching his long legs. "Always had a thing for the law. But it doesn't pay like transistors, huh?"

Russell smiled modestly. "But what's all this about the Sexual Morality Act? Is this some kind of joke?"

"Not at all. Didn't you hear today's news? The FBI busted an underground sex factory. They managed to retrieve all the surrogates except one."

"Oh?" Russell said, finishing his drink.

"Yeah. That's when they called us in. We're covering all spaceports, thinking the receiver might try to smuggle the thing off Earth."

Russell poured another drink, keeping his tone casual. "So you thought I was the guy, huh?"

Ross looked at him for a moment, then burst into laughter. "You, Ralph?"

"Absolutely not! I saw your name on the spaceport departure list. I just swung by for a drink, for old times' sake. Listen, Ralph, I remember you well. Ralph 'Hell-on-the-Girls' Russell, the biggest heartbreaker in Michigan State's history. What could a guy like you possibly need a surrogate for?"

"My girls wouldn't tolerate it," Russell replied, chuckling. Ross joined in the laughter but then stood up.

"Look, I have to run. Call me when you get back?"

"I definitely will!" Feeling a bit dizzy, Russell added, "Are you sure you don't want to check things out anyway, since you're here?"

Ross paused, contemplating. "I probably should, for the record. But forget it, I won't hold you up." He walked to the exit but then turned around. "You know, I pity the guy who has that surrogate."

"Huh? Why's that?"

"Those things are toxic! You know that, Ralph! Potential insanity, mutations... And this guy might have an even bigger issue."

"What do you mean?"

"I can't say, really. It's classified information. The FBI isn't sure yet. Plus, they're waiting for the right moment to reveal it."

With a casual wave, Ross left. Russell watched him go, his mind racing. He didn't like the direction things were taking. What had seemed like a daring little adventure was escalating into something far more sinister. Why hadn't he realized this earlier? He'd felt uneasy back at the surrogate factory, with its dim lighting, secretive, white-coated workers, and the stench of raw flesh and plastic. Why hadn't he abandoned the idea then and there? The surrogates couldn't be as top-notch as advertised....

"Tower to G43221," the radio crackled to life. "Are you ready?"

Russell hesitated, trying to decipher Ross's cryptic warning. Maybe he should call it off while he still had the chance. Then he thought of the massive crate in the cargo hold, its contents primed for activation, waiting for him. His heart started to pound. He knew he would go through with it, no matter the risks. He signaled the tower and strapped himself into the control chair. An hour later, he was in space.

Half a day later, Russell deactivated his thrusters. He was far from Earth, yet still hundreds of thousands of miles from Luna. His sensors, strained to their maximum capacity, detected nothing in his vicinity. No passenger liners, no freight vessels, no patrols, and no private ships. He was utterly alone. Nothing and no one would interrupt him. Russell moved into the rear cabin. The packing case was exactly as he had left it, securely anchored to the deck. The mere sight of it sent a thrill through him. He touched the activation stud on the outside of the case and settled down, waiting for the contents to stir and come to life.

The surrogates had been developed earlier in the century out of sheer necessity. Humanity had started extending its reach into the galaxy. Bases had sprung up on Venus, Mars, and Titan. The first interstellar ships were making landfalls on Algol and Stagoe II. Humanity was departing from Earth. Humanity, but not women.

The first colonies were tenuous footholds in hostile territories. The work was grueling; life expectancy was tragically short. Entire settlements were sometimes annihilated before the ships were even fully unloaded. These early settlers were like soldiers on the front lines, facing unprecedented dangers. Later, there would be a place for women. Later, but not at this moment.

These outposts, light-years from home, were desolate and devoid of women, and the men stationed there were not content. They grew morose, quarrelsome, and violent. Complacency set in, and on alien planets, complacency often led to fatal consequences. They yearned for women. Since real women couldn't join them, Earthly scientists engineered substitutes.

Android females, the surrogates, were created and shipped to the colonies. The practice skirted the edges of Earth's moral fabric, but greater transgressions loomed if these were not accepted. Initially, everything seemed to run smoothly. It might have continued that way if left undisturbed. Yet as always, corporate Earth sought to enhance their products. Sculptors and artists were enlisted to refine and embellish the design.

Engineers tweaked the surrogates, re-wiring them and installing refined stimulus-response mechanisms, doing bizarre things with conditioned reflexes. The settlers were thrilled with the outcomes. They were so pleased, in fact, they refused to return to human companionship, even when given the chance. When these pioneers returned to Earth after their missions, they brought their surrogates along. They loudly praised these substitutes, pointing out their obvious advantages over emotionally unstable, anxious, or sexually unresponsive human women. Naturally, other men grew curious, eager to experience the surrogates for themselves. And when they finally did, they were pleasantly astonished and quick to spread the word.

The government acted swiftly and decisively. For one thing, over half of the electorate was at risk. More importantly, social scientists warned of a steep decline in the birth rate if the situation continued unchecked. So the government destroyed the surrogates, shuttered the factories, and demanded a return to normalcy. Reluctantly, everyone complied. But there were always those who remembered, who recounted tales to others. There were always a few who weren't content with second best.

Russell heard movements inside the crate. He grinned, recalling the stories he had heard about the surrogates' intriguing behaviors. Suddenly, a high-pitched clanging filled the air—it was the standby alarm from the control room. He rushed forward. An emergency broadcast blared across all channels, aimed at Earth and all ships in space. Russell tuned in.

"This is Edward Danzer," announced a crisp voice over the radio. "I am the Chief of the Washington branch of the Federal Bureau of Investigation. You've likely heard on your local news about the discovery and shutdown of an illegal sexual substitute factory. And you're aware that all but one of the surrogates have been recovered. This message is for the individual who possesses that final surrogate, wherever he might be."

Russell nervously licked his lips and leaned in closer to the radio. From within the aft cabin, the surrogate continued making its awakening sounds.

"That individual is in grave danger!" Danzer declared. "Serious danger!"

Our investigation into the molds and forms used at the factory revealed something highly unusual. Just this morning, one of the technicians finally came clean.

"The missing surrogate is not an Earth model!"

"I repeat," Danzer's voice boomed, "the missing surrogate is not an Earth model! The factory had been processing orders for Algol IV. When they ran out of Earth models, they substituted an Algolian one. Given that surrogate sales are illegal anyway, they figured the customer wouldn't complain."

Russell exhaled deeply, relieved. He had feared he might find a small dinosaur in the packing crate, at the very least.

"Maybe," Danzer went on, "the owner of the Algolian surrogate doesn't realize the danger yet. It's true that Algolians belong to the homo sapiens species. We know that both races have a shared ancestry lost in the primordial past. But Algol is distinctly different from Earth.

"Algol IV is significantly more massive than Earth and boasts a richer oxygen atmosphere. Raised in such conditions, Algolians have a considerably superior musculature compared to the average human. Simply put, they are as strong as rhinos.

"But the surrogate doesn't realize that. She has a powerful and indiscriminate mating drive. That's where the real danger lies! So I'm telling the customer to turn yourself in now, while there's still time. Remember: crime doesn't pay."

The radio spat static before settling into a steady hum. Russell switched it off. He'd been duped, fair and square. He really should have inspected the merchandise before accepting it, but the crate had been sealed. He was out a significant sum of money, but then again, he had plenty. Luckily, he had discovered the error in time. Now, he would jettison the crate into space and make his way back to Earth. Maybe real girls were the best option after all.

He heard heavy thuds coming from the crate in the rear cabin.

"I suppose I'd better deal with this, sweetheart," Russell said, striding quickly toward the cabin.

A barrage of blows battered the crate. Russell stared, worry creasing his forehead, and reached for the deactivation switch. Just then, one side of the heavy crate shattered. From the opening shot a long golden arm, flailing uncontrollably. Russell quickly stepped back. The situation had escalated beyond comedy. The crate shook and trembled under the relentless pounding. Russell assessed the force behind each blow and quickly determined that stopping this was paramount. He dashed toward the crate. Long, slender fingers grabbed his sleeve, tearing it off in one swift motion. Russell managed to press the deactivation button just before throwing himself clear.

For a moment, silence reigned. Then the surrogate unleashed two more blows, each powerful as a pile driver. An entire side of the crate disintegrated. Deactivation was no longer an option. Russell stepped back, anxiety building. The Algolian surrogate was absurdly strong; apparently, that's how they preferred them on Algol. A tender embrace on Algol could likely shatter the ribs of an Earthling. A scary prospect. Surely, the surrogate must have some kind of built-in discernment system, he thought. Surely, she could distinguish between an Earthman and an Algolian. Or could she?

The crate collapsed and the surrogate emerged. She stood nearly seven feet tall, magnificently, tantalizingly constructed. Her skin glowed with a light golden-red hue, and her shoulder-length hair shimmered jet black. Motionless, she resembled a heroic statue of idealized femininity to Russell. She was breathtakingly beautiful.

And more lethal than a cobra, Russell reminded himself grimly.

"Well now," Russell began, looking up at her, "as you can see, there's been some kind of mistake."

The surrogate gazed at him with eyes of the deepest gray.

"Yes ma'am," Russell continued with a nervous chuckle, "this is really a ridiculous error. You, my dear, are an Algolian. I am an Earthman. We're quite different as you can see. Understand?"

Her red lips began to quiver.

"Let me explain," Russell persisted. "We belong to different species. That's not to say I find you unattractive."

"Not at all! But we can never be together, miss."

She stared at him, confused.

"I mean it," Russell insisted. He glanced at the broken crate pieces. "You don't realize your own strength. You might accidentally kill me, and we don't want that, do we?"

The surrogate murmured something deep and unintelligible.

"That's how it has to be," Russell declared, more firmly. "You stay put. I'm heading to the control room. We'll reach Earth in a few hours. After that, I'll arrange to ship you to Algol. The guys there will love you! Sounds good, right?"

The surrogate showed no sign of understanding. Russell backed away, noticing her long hair fall back as she moved towards him, her intentions clear. With rising panic, he quickly shut the cabin door behind him. She pounded against it, calling out in a wordless cry.

Russell rushed to the instrument panel and began evacuating the air from the aft cabin. The dials swung into position as he collapsed into a chair, exhaling in relief. It had been close. He shuddered at the thought of what might have happened if the Algolian sexual substitute had caught him. Survival seemed uncertain. Regret tugged at him for needing to end such a remarkable existence, but it was his only option for safety.

He lit a cigarette and pondered his next move: once she was gone, he would eject her, crate and all, into the void. Then, he planned to drink himself into stupor. He would return to Earth, wiser and sadder, vowing never to use a substitute again. Plain, old-fashioned human women were enough. Indeed, Russell thought, if real women were good enough for his father, they were good enough for him. And one day, he would tell his own son, "Stick with women. They're the real deal. Don't settle for anything less."

Russell felt a wave of dizziness wash over him, and his cigarette lay extinguished in the ashtray. A sudden urge to laugh crept up, but he shook it off and checked the gauges. The air was draining from the after cabin—fine—but it was also seeping from the control room. Leaping up, Russell inspected the cabin door and cursed. That damned surrogate had sprung the hinges. The door was no longer airtight.

Quickly, he halted the air evacuation from the control board. Why did everything always go wrong for him? The surrogate resumed her assault, wielding a metal chair and striking the hinges. She couldn't break through a tempered-steel door, Russell reassured himself. No way. Not possible.

But the door began to bulge ominously. Sweat dripped down his forehead as he stood in the middle of the control room, desperately trying to think. He could don a spacesuit and depressurize the ship, but the suits—and all his other gear—were back in the after cabin. What else? Russell's mind raced. The situation was dire. Could he alter the temperature? Increase it? Decrease it? He didn't know the surrogate's limits, but he suspected it was more than he could endure.

One hinge shattered. The door twisted, revealing the surrogate behind it, her satin skin glistening with sweat as she relentlessly pounded on it. Then Russell remembered his revolver. He pulled it from its holster, flipping off the safeties just as the last hinge gave way, and the door flew open.

"Stay back," Russell commanded, aiming the revolver. The Algolian substitute moaned and extended her arms toward him with a dazzling, seductive smile.

"Not another step!" Russell shouted, torn between terror and an inexplicable desire. He steadied his aim, uncertain if a bullet would stop her, or what might happen if it didn't. The surrogate's eyes blazed with passion as she lunged. Russell gripped the revolver with both hands, fingers trembling, and pulled the trigger. The sound was deafening.

He fired three times, but the surrogate kept advancing.

"Stop!" Russell shouted. "Please, stop!"

The surrogate slowed, but continued forward. Russell fired a fourth shot. Now limping, the surrogate's determination never wavered. Russell pressed himself against the wall, gripped by a desperate hope to live long enough to confront the factory operator. The surrogate gathered its energy and lunged. At point-blank range, Russell squeezed off his final shot.

Three days later, Russell's ship landed at Boston Spaceport under less-than-ideal conditions. His usually impeccable approach ended with a ten-foot gash in the reinforced concrete of the landing pad, but at last, he touched down. Eddie Ross rushed out to the ship and pounded on the port.

"Ralph! Ralph!"

The port slowly swung open.

"Ralph! What the hell happened?" Ross exclaimed. Russell looked like he had been through a meat grinder and lost. His face was bruised, his hair singed, and he walked with a limp.

"A power line overloaded," Russell said. "Had quite a fight before everything was under control."

"Wow," Ross replied. "Look, Ralph, I hate to do this now, but..."

"What is it?"

"That surrogate still hasn't been found. The FBI has ordered inspections of all ships, both private and commercial. I hate to ask now, after everything..."

"Go ahead," Russell said. The inspection was quick but thorough. Ross, checklist in hand, emerged from the ship.

"Thanks, Ralph. Sorry to bother you. That power line really caused some trouble, huh?"

"It did," Russell replied, "but I managed to jettison the furniture before it could smoke me out. Now if you'll excuse me, Eddie, I've got unfinished business."

He started walking away. Ross followed.

"Look, man, you should see a doctor. You don't look good."

"I'm fine," Russell said, his face hard with determination. Ross watched him head to the control tower, scratching his head. Russell caught a heli outside the spaceport.

His head was pounding again, and his legs were shaky. The surrogate's strength and tenacity had been unreal. If she'd been operating at full capacity, he never would have made it. But that last shot at close range had done the trick. No organism could withstand that kind of punishment for long. He eventually reached downtown Boston and paid off the heli. Still woozy, he forced himself to cross the street and push through the doors of an unassuming gray-stone building. His legs threatened to give out beneath him, and he couldn't help but think how lucky he was to have outmaneuvered the surrogate. Of course, her incredible vitality had nearly done him in.

It had been brief but unforgettable. He recognized he was fortunate to have survived it. Using surrogates had nearly cost him dearly. A clerk hurried over to him. "Sorry to keep you waiting, sir. How can I help?"

"You can. I need a ticket to Algol, on the next ship leaving."

"Yes, sir. Round trip?"

Russell thought about the tall, stunning, black-haired, amber-skinned women he would encounter on Algol. No substitutes this time—real women with genuine judgment.

"One way," said Ralph Russell, with a small, eager smile.

THE END.

The Rebel Who Refused

By Gerald N. Stanton

All his life, Carson Rissler had faced a relentless urge from those around him to join something. They had all been enlisting themselves, eager for him to follow suit. During his college years, it was the fraternities that had come knocking. Yet, Rissler had steered clear of them.

"But you've got to belong to something," they insisted. "Everybody does."

"I don't," he replied.

"Sure you do. You're just being rebellious."

"Maybe."

"Everybody's got to belong. Ask any psychologist."

"Perhaps. But I wouldn't know."

Post-college, the pressure took a new shape. He lost three jobs consecutively for the same reason.

"We're sorry, Rissler, but you just don't seem to fit in with the team," they explained.

"Aren't I doing my job well?" he questioned.

"Yes, but you don't seem to belong. We prefer employees who think of themselves as part of The Company, not just people who work here."

Eventually, he found refuge in a large travel agency in the heart of Philadelphia. In this line of work, everyone at least pretended to be cynical about their jobs, allowing Rissler to maintain his position regardless of his behavior. By now, he had mastered the art of staying silent. Around him, people continued to sign up.

"You've got to have something bigger than yourself," they preached. "You've got to belong."

He observed them but continued living life on his terms. He cherished concerts, books, and plays. He delighted in the company of his friends, meeting them often. There were a few women he loved as well, and he hoped one day to marry one of them. Rissler led a happy life and remained unattached to any organization.

One cold January evening, there was a knock on his door. It was a Saturday, and he was in the process of dressing for a night at the Academy of Music. He opened his apartment door to find a young man standing in the hallway. The visitor sported black-rimmed glasses and a crew cut, dressed sharply in a slim, well-tailored suit.

"Mr. Rissler?"

"Yes?"

"I'm from the Organization."

"We'd like you to join."

"Join what?"

"The Organization. The one for people who don't belong to anything else."

"Sorry, but I'm not interested."

"But you have to be. It says right here that you don't belong to anything. We're offering you a chance to be part of something."

"What's the point of this organization?"

"It gives its members a sense of belonging. Everyone's joining. You wouldn't want to be left out, right?"

"I'd prefer to pass. Maybe you should find someone else."

"I can't do that. We never give up."

"I see. Good night, young man."

As he tried to close the door, the young man slipped inside before Rissler fully realized what was happening.

"I'm heading to a concert," Mr. Rissler said. "They're playing Brahms' First Symphony. Never heard it live before, and I've been looking forward to it since I heard his Second. I'd appreciate it if you'd leave now."

"But don't you want to belong, Mr. Rissler?"

"No."

"To anything at all?"

"No."

The young man shook his head. "Most people are excited to join. We offer them what they've been searching for their whole lives."

"Then go talk to them." Rissler put on his jacket and adjusted his tie. "Would you like a drink?"

"I don't drink."

"Why not?"

"It interferes with my mission. We're aiming to double the size of the Organization. I work very hard at it."

"Do you now? And why is that?"

"It gives me a sense of belonging."

Rissler started for the door. "I'm about to leave," he said. "I think it would be best if you left too."

The young man sighed. "I can tell you're going to be a tough case."

"Probably. Will you turn off the light, please?"

He met his date and soon forgot about the strange encounter. Brahms' First Symphony was everything Rissler had hoped for. Later, when they were sitting in a bar, he mentioned the Organization to his date. The girl seemed surprised.

It was their second date, and she still barely knew him.

"You should join something," she suggested. "Why don't you?"

"You mean it?"

"Everyone should belong to something. It's not right to be adrift."

"I'm not adrift. I contribute. More than most people, in fact."

"But you can't just live for yourself."

"And why not?"

She hesitated. "Because you just can't," she insisted. When the bar closed at midnight, he took her home. That same conversation had repeated itself with other women before, yet it always left him unsettled. He caught the subway across the river to Camden, New Jersey, where the bars stayed open longer. The next morning, he awoke with a hangover. Just as he was about to pour himself some tomato juice, there was a knock on the door.

"Just a second," he called. Opening the door, he found a man in a tweed suit standing in the hallway, puffing on a pipe with a calm, friendly expression.

"Mr. Rissler?"

"Yeah, that's me."

"I'm Dr. Raley. Mind if I come in?"

"I didn't ask for a doctor. I could use one, but I didn't call."

"Oh? What's the issue?"

"A hangover. Last night was pretty rough."

"Why? What drove you to that?"

He shrugged. "Hard to say."

"Insecurity," Dr. Raley noted. "Many people drown their insecurities in alcohol. Why don't you tell me about it?"

He paused. "Well," he said, "it's early."

Dr. Raley stepped forward, and Rissler found himself stepping aside to let him in.

"Who sent you, anyway?" he asked.

"Didn't they tell you I was coming?"

"Didn't who tell me you were coming?"

"The Organization. I'm their lead psychologist."

"I should have guessed."

"You sound irritated."

"I'm not interested in joining the Organization. Not now, not ever."

Dr. Raley lit his pipe. "I think you should," he said. "It would help with your insecurities. You clearly need to be part of something."

"And why's that?"

"It's a fundamental human need. A person alone is incomplete and unfulfilled."

"You're selling yourself short. I hear you've got plenty of energy and talent," Dr. Raley remarked, scanning the spartan apartment.

"I don't feel that way," Rissler replied, eyes narrowing.

"Let's be honest. Deep down, don't you crave a sense of belonging?"

"I don't."

"Really? You're not part of any group?"

"Correct."

"You're sure about that? You canvassed for the last election, didn't you?"

"Yes, but that was different."

"Didn't that give you a sense of community?"

"Briefly, but I felt suffocated."

"Why did you get involved then?"

"Because I'm a citizen. I believe in balancing my responsibilities."

"So you didn't really fit in?" Dr. Raley probed.

"Not in the way you mean."

Raley puffed thoughtfully on his pipe. "This is fascinating. Do you honestly believe you can live without belonging to anything?"

"Yes."

"Isn't being part of the human race a form of belonging?"

"Sure, and I try to keep up with that too. But it's more exhausting than fulfilling."

Dr. Raley seemed to find this deeply intriguing. "I can see you're going to be quite the challenge."

"Thanks. I plan to be."

"I've got some materials outside. You should read them."

"You can leave them."

"I will." Raley took another drag from his pipe, exuding a serenity that came from years of practice. "You know, you're quite a troubled soul."

"That's what they say."

"Why don't you let me help you?"

"First, you have to convince me there's something wrong."

"Fair point."

They meandered through various topics for another half-hour. When Raley finally left, Rissler glanced at the stack of literature. The impulse to toss it gnawed at him, but his integrity nudged him otherwise. If he was committed to resisting, he would confront their techniques head-on, not side-step them.

He settled in and began to read. The Need to Belong. The Sense of Unity. Testimonials from those who had supposedly found solace within the Organization. It was all meticulously crafted and disturbingly persuasive for someone nursing a hangover. He sat for a long time, lost in contemplation, the weight of it pressing down in his small, loner's sanctuary.

He got up and tossed all the pamphlets into the trash.

"They'll have to try harder than that," he muttered. The next evening, when he returned from work, he discovered a package in his mail. It was a high-fidelity Calypso record. The note described it as a Get-Acquainted Gift from the Jamaican Record Society. After dinner, he put the record on. As it played, he started improvising dance steps, something he often did for fun. The music was catchy, and he lost track of time until he suddenly noticed the lyrics had been changing subtly.

"A house built on a rock foundation will not stand, no, no, no," the lyrics murmured. "You must join the Organization, now, now, now...."

He quickly turned off the hi-fi, but the chanting echoed in his mind. You must join the Organization, you must join the Organization.... Needing a distraction, he put on his coat and went for a walk. When he came back, reading didn't appeal to him, so he turned on the television. A serious play was on, focusing on a young man navigating the isolation of city life, seeking a sense of belonging.

"If I could only belong somewhere," the young man confessed to the girl during the second act. "I've never belonged anywhere."

"Everyone should belong," the girl replied empathetically. The young man nodded, his hands groping in the air. "Or they'll end up like Carson Rissler," he mumbled.

Rissler stood up abruptly and turned off the TV. Inspecting the back, he noticed a small box screwed into one corner.

"Very clever," he murmured, wrenching the box off before heading to bed. Just as he was drifting into sleep, the phone rang. Groggily, he reached for it in the dark.

"Rissler speaking."

"Mr. Rissler? This is Miss Beyle from the Organization. We're calling to see if you have any questions."

"I'm afraid not. I was trying to sleep."

"So early?"

"I felt like it."

"You must be terribly lonely."

"Why not drop by Headquarters for some coffee and cake? We're having a great time."

"Miss Beyle, I've done my own analysis. You're doing excellent work, but you've got the wrong guy."

She laughed—a pleasant, melodic laugh.

"Thank you, Mr. Rissler. You sound like exactly the kind of man we need. There's a big mission ahead, and there's always a spot for you if you're interested."

"In what capacity?"

"Recruiting new members."

"Good evening, Miss Beyle. I've always aimed to be a gentleman. I better hang up before I lose my composure."

He hung up and tried to sleep. The next morning, an economist visited him. The following day, it was a social scientist, and the day after that a political scientist. For a week, he listened patiently as they took turns sitting in his apartment, explaining the significance of their group.

"An individual is nothing," they argued, "unless he belongs to a collective."

"On the contrary," Mr. Rissler countered, "the collective is nothing unless I'm part of it."

"That's egotism."

"Probably."

But he knew he was losing his resolve. He clung stubbornly to the notion that he was resisting the inexorable tides of history. He felt brave and resolute. There was a brief lull. He awoke the following morning to the blaring sound of a PA truck outside, one floor below. Carson Rissler DOES NOT BELONG Carson Rissler BELONGS TO NOTHING REFORM Carson Rissler REFORM Carson Rissler....

"Outrageous," he muttered. He dressed, had breakfast, and set off for work. People stood on their doorsteps, staring at him as he stepped onto the sidewalk. He smiled politely at the driver of the truck.

"Good morning," he said. "Lovely day, isn't it?"

The driver nodded sullenly. Excellent, Mr. Rissler thought. You're handling this superbly. At work, he felt exhausted and drained. His focus waned. The Department Manager noticed.

"You're not acting like yourself, Carson."

"I'm just a little worn out. Had a rough night."

"What was she like?"

"Grim."

Everything felt grim. The repetitive chants echoed in his mind endlessly.

So did the slogans and the announcements from the sound truck. Carson Rissler found himself wavering. Maybe they were right. Maybe he did need to belong. That night, the sound truck was still making its rounds, promoting the Organization and denouncing him. Signs had popped up on every house: We Belong to the Organization. Every door was adorned, except his. He went upstairs, made dinner, and then sat by the window to think. Below, the sound truck droned on. They're getting to you, he thought. A bit more, and they'll have you completely. You need to act.

He picked up the phone and dialed.

"Yes?" came a voice on the other end.

"This is Carson Rissler."

"Ah, Mr. Rissler. I expected your call."

"Send your representative to my apartment tonight. Tell him to bring everything necessary."

"Application forms?"

"Everything. Whatever you need to finalize this."

"He'll be there at eight."

"I'll be waiting."

At precisely eight, a young man rang the bell, burdened with equipment.

"Come in," Rissler said.

"Thank you."

"What's all that?" Rissler asked, nodding towards the gear.

"Educational material. Mind if I set it up?"

"Go right ahead."

Rissler poured himself a brandy and soda and observed. The young man seemed tense as he arranged a hemispherical device that resembled a projector. Rissler's gaze shifted to a leatherette folder the young man had set aside. Neatly labeled: Prospects. His heart skipped a beat. Ensuring the young man was distracted, he leafed through it carefully.

"This Marline Harris looks interesting. What's her story?"

"Did I leave that there? Sorry, you can't look at it."

"My bad, didn't know."

The young man retrieved the folder and resumed his task.

"Do you have a girl?" Rissler asked.

"Too busy."

"Oh," Rissler replied, taking a sip of his drink. "That Harris girl sure has been resisting, hasn't she?"

"She's a tough one."

I've visited her six times now. Funny thing is, she's incredibly lonely."

"Really?"

"Yeah, she's very independent. Guys don't really go for that. And she's quite attractive, too. It's a pity she can't just act more, I don't know, feminine."

"Yes, I suppose it is."

"Here," the young man said, "Just take a seat over there."

"Care for a drink?"

"I don't drink."

"Not even for company?"

"Company? Maybe I should."

Mr. Rissler poured another brandy and soda, with much more brandy than soda.

"You work pretty hard, don't you?" he remarked.

"We're in the midst of a big push. This job is crucial." The young man took a hesitant sip, like someone who's only familiar with water.

"Yes, it certainly sounds important. Organizing, making things happen. Quite the active lifestyle."

"That's what I'm about—activity. Living, not loafing."

"Quite understandable."

The young man took another drink. His expression subtly shifted.

"Let's get the machine going. We should get started."

"Have you had dinner yet?"

"Too busy."

"Good, good."

"Good?"

"Good that you're dedicated. Shows character."

"Thanks. Now if you'll just sit back, we'll turn the machine on." The young man struggled to focus. Rissler lit a fine cigar and offered one to his guest. "For company," he said.

"In that case, sure."

"You should have another brandy to go with it." He handed over another glass. The young man gulped it down instinctively and activated the machine. Rissler took a deep drag from his cigar and sank into his chair, placing another drink near the young man's arm.

"Do you know much about drinking?"

"Actually, no."

"The custom is three. Three drinks and you're friends. You belong."

"Then I suppose I should."

The room darkened. Stars began to glow on the walls. The young man took another sip.

"To what do you belong?" a deep voice echoed. "What are you a part of? In this vast Universe, you alone are nothing."

"You alone don't matter much. But as part of something bigger..."

The first light of dawn filtered through the walls, painting them with a golden hue. Mr. Rissler luxuriated in the ambiance, savoring every nuance of the unfolding daybreak. Beside him, he heard a soft hum. The young man was singing.

"Isn't it soothing to watch the room revolve?" Mr. Rissler remarked.

"I was just thinking the same thing. It's mesmerizing."

"I know. Excuse me for a moment."

He rose and carried the phone into the adjacent room. Once he was sure he was out of earshot, he dialed a number he'd committed to memory. It rang several times before a woman's voice answered.

"Hello?"

"Is this Miss Marline Harris?"

"Yes, speaking. Who is this?"

"My name is Carson Rissler. There's a man here trying to recruit me into the Organization. I found your name and picture in his Prospects book."

"Oh, are they pursuing you too?"

"They've had their sights on me for quite a while now. By the way, your picture is very striking, Miss Harris."

"Thank you."

"Do you enjoy music?"

"Yes, I do."

A few minutes later, he quietly re-entered the living room. The film still played, its persuasive narrative continuing. Now, martial music filled the room, and flags waved onscreen, a display of fervent inspiration. Rissler thought, *Alone, they were winning. But together, we'll be stronger.* He leaned over the couch. The young man slept, his face serene in slumber. Mr. Rissler switched on a record, an uncut rendition of *The Arabian Nights.* He positioned the speaker close to the young man's ear. Then, he got dressed and went out to meet Marline. He'd outpaced them again. Maybe one day they'd catch him, but deep down, he didn't believe it.

THE END.

She Of Mars

By WILLIAM S. HARPER

Oscar Harper Jones' Martian tales generally resulted in the standard rejection slips, but occasionally, an editor would add a note praising his vivid imagination. Yet, they were quick to critique his stilted dialogue, implausible heroines, and indulgent, Burroughs-like wish-fulfillment fantasies that lacked Burroughs' moral rigor. Oscar saw merit in one of these points. His knack for immersing himself completely into his protagonists did gift him with a vivid imagination. Take this moment, for instance: his protagonist, Thon Carther the Earthman, was standing on the ochre moss of a Martian dead-sea bottom beside a voluptuous blonde princess he had rescued from the villain Mollen some two thousand words prior, bravely awaiting the oncoming horde of Moll warriors. But it wasn't really Thon Carther standing there—it was Oscar Harper Jones. A tall, tanned, and strikingly handsome Oscar Harper Jones, no less, but Oscar Harper Jones nonetheless.

However, on the points of dialogue and heroines, Oscar disagreed vehemently. He had even written back to the editors to defend himself. A touch of Burroughs was a staple for any self-respecting sci-fi writer, he argued, and he was sure he didn't exhibit it any more than several other writers he could name. And as for his heroines being dimensionally impossible, that criticism was sheer geocentrism. Just because there weren't any 46-21-46 women on Earth didn't mean they couldn't exist on Mars. (He tactfully bypassed any mention of his dialogue; even Oscar had moments of doubt about that.)

It was a warm August afternoon.

His wife had gone to visit her sister, granting him a brief respite from her constant bickering. The apartment was bathed in an almost unnatural silence, punctuated only by the steady hum of the electric fan and the erratic clattering of his archaic typewriter. It was one of those rare moments where his imagination could fully unfurl. Little did he realize, this was the pivotal instant in his journey as a writer. The Moll horde was closing in fast, and Thon Carther—alias Oscar Harper Jones—knew it was time to unsheathe his sword. Clackety-clack-clack. The blonde princess from the triple cities of Hydrogen, Thejah Doris, drew nearer, her golden shoulder brushing against his muscular arm, sending a shiver of excitement coursing down his spine. Clack-clackety- clack. Clack!

"Fear not, my princess," he declared. "This noble sword has tasted Moll blood before and is eager for more!"

"My chieftain," she whispered, pressing closer. He hefted the large sword, and the waning sunlight danced across its polished blade. Despite its formidable size, it felt as light as a feather in his strong, bronzed hand. The lead Moll rider was almost upon them, shockingly close. The malevolent green features of its face were vivid, and its elongated, tusk-like teeth glistened menacingly. A wave of panic surged through

Thon-Jones. Wildly, he groped for his typewriter, then for his desk. Desperately, he searched for the familiar walls of the apartment. They were gone. A chill shot through his lithe, tanned frame. Something terrible had happened. Something even worse would occur if he didn't act fast, for the Moll warriors, colossal astride their six-legged beasts, were nearly upon them.

He recalled the plan just in time. With a swift move, Thon-Jones wrapped his arm around Thejah Doris' slender waist and, propelled by the light Mars gravity, leaped over the entire green horde, landing on a sturdy patch of the dried sea bed, a hundred feet behind the last rider. It felt a bit like a cliché move, but he couldn't afford to be critical now. The Moll horde descended into chaos, their green, chlorophyll-filled bodies clashing with white tusks and screeching mounts. The warriors at the front managed to halt their toats, but those in the middle and rear were still catching on to what had happened, creating a turbulent mess.

Thon-Jones quickly took advantage of the disorder he'd accidentally caused. He still felt the pang of loss for his missing typewriter, desk, apartment, and entire civilization, but now wasn't the time to dwell on it. Escape was the immediate priority. He hastily referenced his mental plot synopsis. Yes, an atmosphere boat was hidden in the mound of dried algae where his leap had conveniently ended. Another convenient plot device, he thought irritably, but there would be time to critique later.

"Come, my princess," he said, taking Thejah Doris' arm.

"Lead on, my chieftain!"

Sure enough, the atmosphere boat was there, just as he'd envisioned it. They quickly uncovered the vessel and boarded its narrow deck. Soon, they were ascending into the darkening Martian sky, leaving the reorganized Moll horde charging futilely at the mound. Thejah Doris reclined beside him on the comfortable pilot's couch. "At last, we are alone!" she murmured in her exotic Martian-Hungarian accent.

Reconnaissance could wait, Thon-Jones decided quickly.

Some worse fates were out there, but getting so lost in your own stories that you couldn't pull yourself out wasn't the worst—or so Thon Carther told himself. Turning the atmospheric boat towards the shore of an ancient continent, he slipped an arm under Thejah Doris' bare shoulders and whispered, "My princess."

Suddenly, frantic scratching erupted from the forward cabin. Before Thon could stand, a hulking, eight-legged creature with slavering, multi-fanged jaws bounded toward him, smothering his face with its long, enthusiastic tongue. Thon winced, realizing he'd completely forgotten about his loyal watchdog. But a story was a story, and like any plan, you had to follow through. "Droola," he murmured, "Good old faithful Droola."

As they floated above shadowy ravines and moonlit hills, the nearer moon appeared, racing across the night sky. Stars blinked into cold clarity. The boat drew closer to the argent ribbon of a distant canal, making Thon's heartbeat quicken with anticipation. He could hardly wait to guide the boat down to the silver meadow by the canal's edge. When the time came, he stepped onto the soft turf and helped Thejah Doris down beside him. She looked at him with questioning eyes.

"A swim will refresh us, my princess. It will heighten our senses and increase our chances of evading our relentless pursuers."

"But I cannot swim, my chieftain," she confessed.

Although the situation didn't call for a mischievous grin, Thon struggled to suppress one. "Fear not, my princess," he assured her. "I, Thon Carther, will teach you."

Hand in hand, they walked to the canal's edge. Behind them, Droola leaped off the deck, romping up and down the esplanade. The nearer moon hung high now, while the farther moon began its ascent above the hills. Thon turned to Thejah and said, "First, we must shed our gear."

"They'll weigh us down in the water and make it almost impossible to move."

"All of them, chieftain?"

"Yes, my princess, all of them."

She reached up to the delicate thread holding her Martian halter in place. Suddenly, the muffled thunder of padded toat hooves echoed in the distance. Her hand dropped like a stone. "The Molls!" she exclaimed. "Oh, chieftain, our people's mortal enemies are closing in!"

He swallowed his frustration. How could he have forgotten? He, the author, the creator! "Quickly," he said, grabbing her arm. "Into the atmosphere boat. The canal won't stop them!"

By the time they reached the deck, the leading edge of the Moll horde was already at the opposite bank. The green warriors didn't hesitate, driving their mounts into the water. Once in the canal, Moll and toat moved as one, becoming like a school of gigantic green porpoises, leaping in and out of the water with astonishing speed and crossing to the other side in minutes. But by then, Thon-Jones and Thejah Doris were already ascending into the night sky. Their loyal Droola spotted the departure just in time, leaping mightily to the aft deck and scrambling to safety. Once at a sufficient altitude, Thon-Jones set the craft to fast-flight, steering it parallel to the canal. The cool night air turned into a cold wind, and the landscape blurred beneath them. He maintained their speed until he was certain their pursuers were far behind, then decelerated to a slower pace and turned his attention back to Thejah Doris.

She was lying on her side, gazing at him with admiration. He slipped his arm under her shoulders, but before he could say anything,

Droola, still shivering from the chill of fast-flight, bounded forward and nestled between them. The interruption, though vital for the story's pacing, was undeniably frustrating. Even Thejah Doris seemed annoyed, though she kept silent.

Instead, she turned and lay back, hands clasped behind her head, letting the two moons compete to illuminate her beauty. It was quite the spectacle, and soon Thon-Jones became captivated. So captivated, in fact, that he didn't see the tower until it was too late. The tower was remarkably tall, especially for the altitude of their atmospheric boat. He yanked the control stick viciously, but their speed was too great. Moments later, the bow crashed into the stone structure. The deck tilted sharply, and he just managed to grab Thejah Doris before she tumbled over the low rail. It took all his effort to maintain balance until the rapidly sinking craft aligned with a dark window opening. He leaped lightly to the sill, his Martian princess in his arms, stepping into the musty gloom of a lofty chamber.

Droola, their loyal companion, wasn't as fortunate. It tried to make the leap but missed the sill by a good two feet. Thon-Jones had been considering getting rid of Droola for some time. Dutifully, he listened for the sound of Droola's body hitting the ground, but when the appropriate time had passed and the sound came, he couldn't muster the emotional response that the situation demanded. All he felt was a fleeting sense of guilt, quickly overshadowed by the realization that he and Thejah Doris were finally alone.

She had found candles on the dusty shelves lining one wall of the chamber, and now she lit three of them, placing them on the rough wooden table in the center of the stone floor. "There's nothing to fear, my chieftain," she said. "This is one of the deserted locktowers once maintained by the ancient Mii when Mars was young and great barges navigated her blue canals. Above us is the control room, from where the mighty locks, now rusted and fallen into ruin, were operated by the ancient Miian tenders."

Now the towers stood silent and desolate, the occasional refuge of wandering poets who found inspiration in the lofty rooms and empty, echoing stairways as they sought their ever-elusive Muse.

He stared at her, bemused by the incongruity of her words. Despite her royal blood, she still looked more like a burlesque queen than a princess. But no matter. "You look beautiful by candlelight," he said.

"You are very gallant, my chieftain."

She lit another candle and placed it in a wall niche beside an ancient sleeping couch. Turning to face him, she said, "At last we are alone."

He moved toward her, arms outstretched. Simultaneously, the distant thunder of padded toat hooves echoed through the air.

"The Molls!" Thejah Doris cried, darting to the window. "They've seen our light! Oh, my chieftain, the mortal enemies of my people threaten us once again!"

"Oh, for Pete's sake!" Thon-Jones exclaimed, throwing up his hands. "No wonder my stories keep getting rejected!"

Resignedly, he joined her at the window. Sure enough, the Moll horde was charging once again. Wearily, he rummaged through his mind for the next sequence. All he could find were the words, END OF PART ONE. It suddenly dawned on him that he'd been trying his hand at a serial and had neglected to plot beyond the first installment.

"Oh, my chieftain, what are we going to do?" she asked.

He didn't respond immediately, deep in thought. If a writer could immerse himself so completely into a story that he became physically involved in it, was there any reason he couldn't extricate himself by writing a factual account of his real life? It was worth a try. The alternative was to plot Installment Two, and somehow he didn't feel quite up to it. Installment One had been rather draining. Suddenly, another thought struck him: Why a factual account?

He remembered his tiny, rundown apartment, his battered typewriter, and his ever-growing collection of rejection letters. His wife, constantly nagging, added to his frustrations. Suddenly, he glanced over at Thejah Doris, standing beside him, her chest rising and falling with anxiety as she watched the imminent approach of the Molls. He focused his thoughts. The storyline began to solidify in his mind, and he sat down at the table, ready to write. A brief moment of panic set in—there was no paper, no pen, not even a pencil. Then he remembered what Thejah Doris had said about the wandering bards, and he started rummaging through drawers. Even Martian poets needed something to write on. Soon enough, he found a drawer containing several sheets of parchment-like paper, a long quill pen, and a small vial of black ink. The thunderous sound of the Molls' padded toat hooves grew louder by the minute.

"Oh, my chieftain, what are we going to do?" Thejah Doris cried out again.

"We're going to swap serials," Thon-Jones replied and began to write.

It was a bright and cheerful morning. Oscar Harper Jones woke up late and lazily watched robins flitting among the branches of the box elder outside his bedroom window. Leisurely, he got up and slipped into his robe. As he yawned and stretched, the aroma of coffee brewing, wheatcakes frying, and sausage sizzling drifted up from the kitchen—his wife was humming contentedly. He strolled into his study and noticed three long, thin letters lying beside his solid gold typewriter, placed there by his wife. He opened them with casual indifference. The first was from The Edgar Rice Burroughs Reader, containing a check for $750. The second was from Dead-Sea Bottom

Stories, with a check for $2,500, and the third was from Red Planet Stories, including a check for $5,000. Just then, the phone rang. He picked it up.

"HWS speaking."

"Good morning, sir. This is Parker from Mammalian Blonde Stories."

Regarding that last piece you allowed us to review, would $10,000 be acceptable?"

"Sorry," Oscar Harper Jones replied, "I never discuss business before breakfast. Call me back later."

Click.

"Hey Oscar," his wife called from the bottom of the stairs, "there's an editor waiting outside."

"Another one?"

"Yes. Should I let him in?"

"I guess so. Tell him I'll spare him a minute while I have my coffee."

He neatly stacked the checks and added them to the large pile beside his gleaming gold typewriter. Making a mental note to visit the bank that day, he acknowledged the nuisance of letting too many checks accumulate. He tossed three long, thin envelopes into the wastebasket marked "Long Thin Envelopes," which, to his dismay, was full again. He could have sworn he'd just emptied it a day or two ago. His wife came rushing up the stairs.

"Oscar, two more editors just drove up! Should I let them in, too?"

"Might as well," Oscar Harper Jones replied. "If you don't, they'll just loiter around the door all day being a nuisance." He gave her an appreciative once- over. She'd aged gracefully, perhaps looking even better than before. "Tell them I'll be down soon, princess. And put some clothes on for now," he added. Once she left, Oscar scanned the study thoroughly, ensuring no evidence of his previous reality remained. Satisfied, he descended slowly and grandly to the hall, where three editors waited reverently for his presence.

THE END.

CHAMPION

By HAROLD L. CARTER

The murmurs of anticipation from the arena barely reached the dressing room. Above him, layers of concrete separated him from the roaring crowd—concrete laid by robots, envisioned by humans. He glanced at his hands, strong and compact, each finger perfectly formed yet composed of protonol. To the naked eye, they seemed indistinguishable from human hands. Made in man's likeness, as man was said to be made in God's image—if such beliefs even held ground anymore. His name was Rok 1340, indicating he was the thirteen hundred fortieth of the Rok series. The short, broad Nordic type. In about twenty minutes, he was scheduled to enter the ring, fighting for the middleweight championship of the world.

Nicholas Fryman had concocted this spectacle, its origins stemming from his daily syndicated sports column, nurtured by the fans' enthusiasm, and transformed into reality by what? Resentment? These robots were gaining too much prominence, too much independence. Nick Nolan would remind this Rok of its place. Nick was the reigning champion, a man, made in God's image. He fought dirty, using his head, thumbs, and heels with ruthless efficiency. His favorite target was the groin. But above all, he was a man—a champion among men.

Carlos entered the room. Officially known as Manuel 4307, he preferred to go by Carlos, as most robots did to shed their numerical identities. Carlos, Rok's manager and chief second, was a sharp and capable robot. He said, "I thought it would be better if we had some privacy. No fans, especially no sports writers."

"Even Nicholas Fryman?" Rok asked. "I thought he was on our side."

"It's hard to tell. Do you ever wonder about him, Rok?"

Rok paused. He was aware some robots managed to "pass," crossing the status boundary to live as humans. He didn't know how many, but the notion often intrigued him. Every robot had a built-in remote-controlled circuit breaker—a constant reminder of their origins and limitations.

They could be stopped with the flip of a switch at the personnel center, a heavily guarded office with a vigilant man on duty day and night. Rok finally broke the silence, "I never really gave much thought to Nicholas, one way or the other."

"What have you been thinking?" Carlos asked.

Rok took a moment before answering, "I've been thinking—we fight their wars, clean up their garbage, handle their sewage, but we're not citizens. Why is that, Carlos?"

"We're not human. We're not conventional," Carlos said, his eyes locked onto Rok.

"Not human? They feed us Bach, Brahms, Beethoven, Shakespeare, Voltaire during our incubation period, don't they? And all those others I've tried to forget. Do souls come from outside the system?"

"I guess they do. They don't teach us much about religion, but I suppose it comes from God."

"And what's He like?"

"It depends on who you ask," Carlos replied. "Sort of a supreme being. From Him, they believe they get charity, tolerance, justice—all the noble traits." Carlos's laughter was bitter. "They truly love themselves."

"They're so certain about everything else," Rok said, "but not very certain about their God. Is that it?"

"That's about right. I heard someone say He watches even when a sparrow falls. I guess we're less than sparrows, Rok."

Silence enveloped them until Carlos placed a hand on Rok's shoulder. "We've got around fifteen minutes, and there's a million things I should have said before."

The weight of Carlos's voice turned Rok's focus. His luminescent eyes studied Carlos's stern expression, absorbing the urgency. Whatever Carlos was about to say, it was more significant than the battle at hand. Carlos spoke softly, "Win this one, Rok, and there'll be blood in the streets."

"Human blood?"

"White men's blood. We've got the Black, the Japanese, the Chinese, and all the others who got their rights just recently. And what kind of rights do they really have? Civil, maybe, but not in people's hearts. Think those races don't know it?"

We were discussing their deity, Rok. Well, the robots have one too. They call him Rok 1340."

"Carlos, you've lost it."

"Have I now? Nicholas Fryman is one of us, Rok. This was his plan, and the four men who manage the switchboard at the personnel center? They're our people too. Top-tier robots, with I.Q.s nearing two hundred. We've got the intellect, Rok, and the manpower. We've harnessed the fury of a billion oppressed souls. And now we've got you."

"A fighter? What kind of deity would I make? You've really lost it, Carlos."

"Have I ever given you anything but the unfiltered truth? They revere you, Rok. You've been a figurehead for them. You could be their leader if you just say the word."

"You and Nicholas Fryman have been orchestrating this? Tonight's fight is the turning point? You've been building up to this."

"But we need a frontman, a symbol. You're the only one who can fill that role. You're the one they'd rally behind."

Rok glanced down at his hands, the hands that had brought him to the first mixed fight in history, a title bout. 'Man Versus The Machine,' most sportwriters had dubbed it, though not Nicholas Fryman. Machine? A machine that had internalized Voltaire? One that had listened to Brahms? What truly separates man from machine? Supremacy? Supremacy would be decided tonight. No, it wasn't physical supremacy. And there were robots far surpassing human intellectual capacities. The spark, then, the divine spark from their God? How could they know they possessed it? Amid all the tangled mysticism fraught with so many misinterpretations, where could they find their God?

"Pondering?" Carlos asked. "Why so silent, Rok?"

Rok's smile was dark and enigmatic. "Believe it or not, I was thinking about God."

"Their God?"

Rok frowned. "I suppose. Theirs and the sparrows' alike."

There were three sharp knocks at the door. Carlos said, "Nicholas Fryman. He wants to speak with you. We've got about eight minutes,

Rok." He walked to the door. Nicholas Fryman stepped in, tall, pale, and brown-eyed.

The eyes should have been lumagel, and Rok examined them closely, but they looked just like a human's. Nicholas turned to Carlos. "He knows?"

Carlos nodded. Nicholas faced Rok again. "Well, Rok?"

"I'm not sure. It's—it's monstrous." Rok shrugged and slammed one hand into the other palm in frustration.

"You are the one, Rok. King, god, whatever you want to call it. For six years, I've been building you up in their newspapers, in their minds. Clean, quiet, hardworking Rok. And humble. The humility I crafted for you has even brought me to tears at times."

Carlos chimed in softly, "You didn't have to fake that much. Rok is humble. Rok is—he's—" Even articulate Carlos found himself at a loss for words. Nicholas Fryman's pale face held a cynical smirk. "The way you feel is the way they all feel—the black ones, the brown ones, the yellow ones."

"They've got their rights," Rok insisted.

"Do they?" Nicholas shot back. "Take a look at the first twenty rows, ringside. You'll see what rights they have: word rights, paper rights. But not in the hearts of men. Beyond the twentieth row, Rok, you can feel the seething anger. Don't you understand history? Don't you sense destiny?"

Rok remained silent. Carlos said, "He's been contemplating God, he tells me."

Nicholas Fryman's expression turned blank. "God? Their God?" He stared at Rok in disbelief. "This Superman they use to scare us? You don't buy into that, do you, Rok?"

Rok shrugged, staying mute.

"They don't believe it themselves," Nicholas argued. "It's just a symbol they created to make themselves feel superior. Do they tell you what He looks like? Sure, they give Him a prophet, and the prophet spouts rules to live by: don't kill, don't steal, don't lie, don't lust, don't envy. Just words, Rok. Words, words, words. Judge them by their actions."

Rok looked up, meeting Nicholas's eyes. "I'm not meant to be a leader."

"Yes, you are. And I've shaped you into one in their minds, using words."

The brown ones, the black ones, and the yellow ones, they've absorbed my words. I've planted the image in their minds, and tonight, they're ready, waiting for your signal."

"A signal from me? What are you talking about?"

"Yes, a signal from you. To those in the crowd, to those glued to the video screens, the ones who've been briefed on how to incite a riot, how to ignite a revolution. Think about it: human prejudice has fueled an army of resentment, and human ingenuity has built the machines for that army to use against man—the white man. White man first."

"The first?" Carlos asked. "Are you dreaming beyond tonight, Nicholas?"

Nicholas smiled slyly. "I probably used too many words. That one slipped out. We can't think past tonight, not now." Turning to Rok, he continued, "It's a simple signal, Rok. Just one word. The word is 'kill.' From you, it's more than a word; it's an order."

A knock at the door interrupted them, and the sono-bray above the door crackled, "Time to go. It's time for the big event."

Silence enveloped the room. Nicholas placed a reassuring hand on Rok's shoulder. "You can't give the signal lying down, Rok. You need to be standing when this is over."

Rok looked into Nicholas's eyes, searching for something deeper. "I'll be standing. I've never doubted that for a second."

They left the room, met by a clamor in the corridor beyond the showers. Reporters flocked around them. One voiced the question on everyone's mind, "What's the story, Carlos? Is Nicholas a relative or something? Got a statement for us?"

Carlos faced them, a bleak expression on his face. "We hope to win, but we're up against a superior being. It's in God's hands now."

Despite their cynicism, the reporters couldn't hide their resentment at hearing blasphemy from a robot. Nicholas interjected, "And Rok is His prophet. Any wagers?"

Silence followed. They stared at Nicholas, pens hovering over notepads. One turned to Rok.

"And you, Rok? How are you feeling?"

Rok: humble, the accommodating, the new Uncle Tom, the servile figure they expected.

Rok raised his chin confidently, without a trace of a smile. "I'll win."

"How?" someone inquired.

"By hitting harder and more often. What's he got besides a strong hook and an iron jaw?"

"Guts," one of them conceded. "You have to give him that, Rok."

"Too bad for him," Rok replied. "We'll see tonight."

No more questions followed. They made their way down the long aisle toward the bright ring—Carlos, Rok, and the other handler who had waited in the preliminary fighters' locker room. The arena, known as the Bowl, was packed with eighty thousand people on a warm, clear night, and millions more watching on screens around the world. This fight transcended the digital age; it was a milestone, a robot challenging human dominance. Everyone wanted to witness history. The referee was Willie Newton, an ebony tower of a man whose very presence suggested fairness, at least to those who had scripted the fight. In their twisted logic, a black referee symbolized impartiality.

Willie stood in the ring, smiling in his striped shirt, positioned conveniently in Rok's corner. As Rok climbed through the ropes, Willie leaned in, pretending to help spread them apart. "You'll get all the breaks you need, Rok," he whispered.

Rok straightened up. "I don't want any breaks, Willie, just a fair fight. That's all it can be."

"Understood, Rok. Sorry about the name—just Rok? Or should I blur the rest?"

"Rok one-three-four-oh, no blurring. It's my name."

Rok turned away from Willie, acknowledging the roar of the crowd behind him with both hands raised high in salute. He scanned the rows of seats stretching out from ringside, the first twenty filled with white faces. Most of the applause thundered down from the higher stands. And now, the champion entered down his aisle, his faded purple robe draped over his broad shoulders, his handlers keeping a respectful distance. Nick Nolan, the reigning middleweight champion of the world. His ears were cauliflowered, his brows ridged with scar tissue. His round head sat on those powerful shoulders without much of a neck. A fringe of red hair framed a face thick with brutal features. Made in His image?

Some words ran through Rok's mind: "Is this the Thing Lord God made and gave To have dominion over sea and land...?"

What a time for Markham's poetry to surface. Nick sauntered over, a fake smile plastered on his face, as disingenuous as a champion approaching a contender's corner. "Best between us, huh?" he asked.

"The better," Rok corrected, keeping his tone flat. "Keep them clean, Nick."

Nick grinned wider, a practiced motion. "Don't I always? I came up the hard way, Rok."

Rok held his silence, his mind drifting back to lines of poetry. When this dumb Terror shall rise to judge the world.... A man with a hook and a desire to fight. The hard way? Maybe. Nick had certainly taken enough punches to claim a permanent spot on Queer Street. But he'd also dealt out more than his share. A brawler and a spoiler. Quick with his fists, quicker to bleed. Blood will run in the streets, Rok.... In the ring, Nick's blood would stain the already spotted canvas once more. Outside, it would be the blood of Nick's brothers: in alleys, in cities, across the globe. A title fight? Indeed. The Irishman first, making his way through the ring to begrudging respect, then the Jew, the Filipino, the Black, the Cuban—everyone who wouldn't stay down, who fought with their fists and their hearts. Mickey Walker, Benny Leonard, Nicholas Louis—immortals all. Legendary champions, icons. And Rok 1340? Different. A machine with no spark. He had almost forgotten that deficiency.

Nick's manager wandered over, scrutinizing the bandages on Rok's hands, then drifted back to their corner to check those on the champ's bruised fists. Rok's hands were pristine, no breaks, no bumps. He was a scientific hitter, honed by precision over natural talent.

He watches the sparrows, Carlos had said. A signal, Nicholas had mentioned. I wish someone would give me a signal, Rok mused. This is too big for me. Willie's voice echoed, "Clean tonight, Nick. I know you, Nick."

"But this one's tricky, remember," Carlos said.

"Yeah, yeah, I got it," Nick replied. Champ material, Nick Nolan. The buzzer sounded, and Carlos gave him a reassuring pat on the shoulder. Rising and flexing on the ropes, Nick peered down at the sea of faces, those who ruled over sea and land. The arena lights buzzed, and the crowd fell silent. The bell rang, and Rok pivoted as Nick moved in, wasting no time, taking the fight straight to him. Nick had a powerful right hand, but it was clumsy; his hook was more polished. Rok circled left, away from Nick's left fist, and deftly jabbed at Nick's nose. Some sportswriters might rave about a right hook, but unless you were a contortionist or southpaw, it was a rarity. Nick was neither.

Nick's right hand hit like a sledgehammer, but it came from awkward angles and telegraphed its arrival by his footwork. He saved it for the moments when his opponent was too distracted to react. Nick tried to slip under Rok's extended left, timing his footwork to Rok's circling, searching for an opening. Rok peppered him with left jabs, then noticed the opening in Nick's guard. Stopping his circling, Rok launched a swift right, sailing over Nick's left and landing cleanly. Nick stumbled back, taking two steps before hitting the mat. Resin dust danced in the air as the crowd's scream merged into a single anguished roar.

Rok retreated to a neutral corner, rolling his shoulder muscles, trying to calm his throbbing heart. Nick had been down before, many times. Under the rules, he had a full count to recover, but he was on one knee by three. Willie's big hand signaled, and then he wiped Nick's gloves before stepping aside. Nick stormed back in, breaking through Rok's left guard this time, sending a looping right towards his head. It missed by design—Nick's elbow smashed right into Rok's mouth.

Rage burned bright and red as Rok and Nick faced off in the corner, their fists flying like unhinged machinery. A hook came low, and agony stabbed into Rok's groin. Through the haze of pain and partial blindness, he could feel Nick's feet seeking his own, trying to find the vulnerable spot on his instep. Rok clung on desperately. He had to win this one. If he didn't, it could all end now.

"Let go, man. I can't hit you when you're hanging on," Nick taunted, his voice dripping with disdain.

The sharp clap of Willie's hand echoed through the air. Willie, always playing it straight. At his touch, Rok released his grip, and Nick seized the moment, throwing a right hand just as Roc separated. Foul? Absolutely. But Rok went down, senses numbed, his mind darkening into oblivion. He lay face down, motionless, as darkness crept through his body.

What kind of God is this? It depended on who you asked. Has anyone ever told you what He looks like? The darkness shifted to red, the red of blood spilling into the streets. In the haze, a cross appeared, and a dim figure. Willie's deep voice counted, "Five, six..."

Rok rolled over at seven, got to one knee at eight, and stood by nine. Nick charged in relentlessly, both fists ready for the kill. The bell rang, and Rok retreated to his corner without Carlos's assistance. Carlos's skilled hands dug into Rok's neck, returning a measure of clarity to his dulled senses. Ice pressed into his legs, an attendant probing the lifeless muscles.

"I saw a cross, Carlos."

"No one's crossing us, Rok. Don't overthink it. Here." He handed Rok a water bottle. Rok rinsed his mouth and spat out the water.

"He's ruthless, Carlos. Knows every trick."

"And so do you, don't you?"

"I don't want to. I saw a cross when I was out, Carlos. Just like the ones on churches."

"Forget about it. Focus. You can beat him. Use your left, use your speed, use your brains. You can do this."

"I'll try. But he's different, Carlos. Not all of them are like Nick."

"Yes, they are. He's just one of the better ones. Now get back in there."

The buzzer sounded, the bell rang, and there stood Nick, ready to continue the battle.

Nick with the iron jaw, the hook, and the bulging shoulders—Nick, the undefeated champion. Rok aimed a punch at Nick's face, but this wasn't just a jab; it was a powerful left hook that knocked his nose askew and drew blood. Enraged, Nick charged forward, meeting a perfectly timed right hand that Rok threw from a solid, grounded stance. Nick staggered, trying to grapple with Rok, but Rok's energy surged back, and his footwork became precise, almost instinctive. A left, a feint, then a dead-on right—Rok danced around the lumbering mass of muscle, turning Nick into a blood-smeared mess.

Blood streamed down Nick's face, mingling with the sweat-soaked curls on his chest. The champion was beginning to look disoriented, struggling to comprehend. He, the unchallenged master of the ring, was faltering. Why wouldn't he fall? Couldn't he see the pattern, the brutal path Rok was marking with each bloodied punch? Why didn't he just go down? Why didn't he surrender? Even by the fifth round, he wouldn't give in. The eighty thousand spectators were silent now; this battle was veering into an execution. Why wouldn't he give up?

Between rounds, as he perched on the stool before the sixth, Rok asked Carlos, "Why doesn't he quit? He can't win. Carlos, I hate hitting him."

"Don't be naive, don't be a fool," Carlos's voice rasped. "As long as there's a spark in them, they won't back down. He's still dangerous, Rok."

A spark—life, stubborn resilience. In the sixth round, Nick almost collapsed in the center of the ring. But he scrounged up some control, shambling toward Rok. Rok pressed forward, recklessly, and the world seemed to explode. Nick was still dangerous. Yet, this wasn't oblivion, just a searing red haze. No respite, no escape—only a distant voice echoed, "In the sky, in the sky..."

Then, silence. Get up, Rok.

For the people of all colors who are watching you, around the globe, rise up. You're their hope, their voice. Up on one knee, just making it under the wire. Nick didn't charge this time. He was cautious after the beating he had taken. Let Rok make the mistakes now. Nick only needed one more shot. Carlos asked, "Can you hit him now? Or are you still hung up on him?"

Rok replied, "I'm a machine, Carlos. He can't hurt me. I can hurt him, but he can't hurt me."

"That's my boy," Carlos said. "Glad to see you've finally picked a side."

"I know my place," Rok said. "I know my task."

"That you do. Now, get him."

And he did. These men don't quit. Not while they're conscious. Not while they're alive. Rok pummeled him wherever he could, with both fists, knocking Nick down four times in the seventh round. But each time, Nick got up. And in the eighth, he came out to face Rok again, marching into his doom with no hesitation, no defense, risking everything. Nick had supremacy, for now, but how long could he survive on sheer arrogance and brutality? How long until it all caught up with him? Nick came out for the eighth round, his hands hanging low in a ridiculous excuse for a guard. Rok knew his time had come. He threw a solid right hand, no setup, no feint, just pure force and all his buried resentment. A single, crushing blow that crowned him middleweight champion of the world.

The arena fell into stunned silence, taking in the gravity of the moment, before erupting in cheers, especially from the cheap seats. The cameras captured every angle of the ring, the crowd, as the lights blazed over the stadium. Carlos hugged him, Nicholas Fryman embraced him, and others joined in the celebration.

In the distant seats, no one stirred. In the closer rows, not a soul moved. Nicholas spoke, "The word, Rok."

The crew maneuvered the microphones into place, ready to broadcast the message across the globe. Cameras honed in on him. The word. Rok glanced at Nicholas, then Carlos. He lifted the microphones to his lips, taking a step back. "I won tonight. I have no message for you. But someone does. It's written in the sky."

Necks craned upwards, a low murmur rippled through the crowd. The cameras shifted focus, leaving Rok to capture the glowing red letters in the sky. Beside him, Carlos gasped. Nicholas Fryman gaped, disbelief etched on his face. Red letters? Something red-hued but luminous, stretching miles into the sky, clear and unmistakable. The cameras locked onto it now: FIND YOUR GOD. Carlos stammered, "Rok, how... did you? What are you?"

"There's more to the message," Rok said. "It's: 'Find your God or your machines will kill you.' But I don't see the need to relay the rest if they heed the first part."

Carlos rasped, "This message came through you? You're a... "

"A prophet? Me, a machine, Rok 1340?"

Nicholas inquired, "You're not sharing the second part?"

"Not yet. It's not time."

"How do you know if it's time or not?" Carlos interjected. "And why would a god use a machine to send a message? Why use you?"

"Because," Rok replied, "no man would listen. And if they don't listen now, Carlos, our time will come..."

THE END.

THE FINAL LESSON

By CHARLES H. STANTON

"Alright, kids," said Miss Sierra, her smile carving deep lines across her face like the weathered grooves on the ancient, deserted skyscrapers of New York. The twelve children in the cozy classroom snapped to attention. It wasn't just her words but her tone, the creaking smile that demanded it.

"Alright, kids," Miss Sierra repeated, settling onto the old-fashioned, straight-backed chair she preferred. "Did everyone put away their atomic blocks?"

"Yes, teacher," they chorused, their sweet voices in unison.

"Your electronic jackstraws? Your pencil-mnestics?"

"Yes, teacher."

"And have you all taken your little activator pills?"

They nodded. Miss Sierra raised her hand for silence.

"Thirty seconds, children," she said. A sigh of delight rose from the twelve young faces as the pills began to work, and they remembered. Poor little darlings, thought Miss Sierra. If only it were possible for them to recall this part of the day, to carry it beyond the blackout that would come as the pills wore off. To remember this particular moment, above all others, into their adulthood. What a different world they could shape...

"So, we arrive at the best part of our day," she said. "We're going to talk about the 20th Century again."

The children fidgeted with excitement. She had turned on the sun lamp five minutes ago, and its beams through the window highlighted the freshness and eagerness in their faces, all gazing trustingly at her. Here and there, the sunlight glinted off the tiny identification discs embedded in their foreheads, smaller than 20th Century dimes, almost hidden in their hairlines, inset at birth. A small hand shot up.

"Yes?" said Miss Sierra.

"Can we talk about the gangsters?" Mary Mary's voice was hopeful. Another small hand jerked up, equally eager.

"Yes?" said Miss Sierra.

"Can we talk about wars and bombs and things?" Henry Copperpenny asked.

Miss Sierra smiled at them. "Kids, kids," she teased, pretending to be serious, "we can talk about that. But haven't we covered it enough? Isn't there something new you'd like to hear about?"

Little hands shot up like weeds after a spring rain.

"Miss Sierra!" "Miss Sierra!"

They called her Miss Sierra even to her face now, and she didn't mind. Somehow, the name had grown on her, warming her like a small, bright sun. Fifty years ago, she would have vaporized any child who dared to call her that. Her eyes flicked to the disintegrator gathering dust in a corner opposite the matter transmitter. She hadn't used it in years. She still kept the hair ribbon from that last little girl who had walked so boldly into the disintegrator; the ribbon had been briefly in style among certain families. Lately, she'd been haunted by dreams of that girl's face. Oddly, she couldn't recall the faces of the other children she had sent into the machine. But then, she had been much younger, much more a part of this futuristic world before she became engrossed in studying history.

Miss Sierra had been teaching first grade at the same school—Official Learning Dome 111, OLD Triple-One—for almost sixty years, and she had been legendary. She was never a large woman, but there was a fullness to one part of her figure that, ten years ago, she decided to let flourish. Since then, she had ignored the fickle trends of a world where women's shapes changed as frequently as 20th- century hemlines. Ah, the 20th century! Miss Sierra let a dreamy look glaze her eyes.

"Children," she said gently, "the 20th century was truly one of a kind."

It stands unparalleled in history. Imagine the wealth of that distant age when someone could actually choose their path in life, when hunger, sickness, and need were still everyday realities.

"And wars," piped up little Charley Tencharles.

"Yes," Miss Sierra conceded. "And accidents that hurt people faster than clock seconds. People fighting and cursing each other with words we don't even recognize anymore."

"Like someday-vitch," shouted Mary Mary. Miss Sierra's eyes sparkled with joy. "It was 'son of a bitch,' dear," she clarified. "It was a string of tiny real words that slipped from the tongue like bright, sharp little silver daggers."

"Yes, teacher," the children chorused, wriggling in amazement.

"And there were gangsters, those fascinating, eccentric characters, like the Robin Hoods and Beowulfs I've told you about. And yes, there were bombs that went bam and boom and wham, creating beautiful colors and magnificent mushroom clouds like the pictures in the old book I smuggled in to show you the other day."

"And people blown to bits," said Stan Thirtystanley in a mock adult voice.

"To little itsy-bitsy bits," Miss Sierra cried with enthusiasm. "The 20th Century, children. Ah, what a time to have lived, the whole world violent, dangerous, seething, and exciting like a string of storybooks wrapped around the equator. But you could be an individual, your own boss, they used to call it."

She could no longer sit. She lifted her considerable frame from the straight-backed chair and began pacing the room, her face alive like a vintage television screen. The children's eyes followed her, hungry for more, like puppies trailing their mother.

"It was the final flourish, children, of the individual man," she said. "Today we have a world of people, all alike, all dull, all safe, healthy, and secure. Back then, it was a world of individuals. And between every moment of violence, there was a cozy lull of safety. Between every burst of anger, there was a peaceful interlude of calm."

For every tragic moment, there was a burst of radiant joy.

"And people were really allowed to die alone?" Charley Tencharles asked, her eyes wide with a mix of curiosity and disbelief. She paused and gave him a tender smile. In the 20th century, he would have been the quintessential Teacher's Pet—sweet, endearing, almost angelic in his eagerness to learn.

"Oh, many, many good people," she responded, her voice catching slightly, "died all by themselves. Believe it or not, some succumbed to old age! And, as we discussed last week, there were those fascinating diseases. Someone could actually die from one of those. Imagine, back in the 20th century, no one had a card in some central bureau telling them their date of death. Think about that, children."

She was gathering momentum now, as she prepared to dive into the next chapter of history, where electronics was just an infant science at the dawn of the 20th century. Matter transmitters and disintegrators were not even conceived of, and robots were merely a glimmer on the horizon. The marvels of radio and television were just starting to flourish. Humanity was on the brink of venturing beyond Earth's boundaries into the vastness of space. And there were so few people on the planet that fields lay open and untouched across every continent, adorned with trees swaying in the breeze and real, living wildflowers.

"Humankind began the 20th century with complete privacy," she continued, her large form trembling slightly as she paced back and forth. "But then came a time—during those chaotic years of the gangsters—when electronics allowed mankind to put tiny ears in rooms and behind pictures on walls, making it possible to record private conversations. Telephones—did I ever tell you about telephones?—could be tapped, as they called it, so others could listen in when you shared secrets with a friend."

And then, she told them with rising excitement, late in the 20th century came the most thrilling part of the story—the discovery that humans could wiretap one another so discreetly that no one ever suspected it.

"Just imagine," she exclaimed, "you could be confiding your secrets to Papa, while someone else was listening in, completely undetected."

And then, later on, Dad would get called into a police station, where his hidden wiretap would be pulled out, and every word you said was recorded on a tiny spool inside him."

"Wow," breathed the children, savoring the eerie thrill of it all. It felt like an ancient ghost story—possible but disconnected from their reality.

"But these human wiretaps were short-lived," Miss Sierra continued, her serious- comic expression drawing a ripple of laughter from the twelve students. "By the early 21st century, laws were passed everywhere to ban wiretapping forever."

She glanced at the clock. In two minutes, the memory-erasing pills would wear off.

"That's enough for today, children," she announced.

"But what about the gangsters?" Mary Mary pleaded with a hint of frustration. "Please, Miss Sierra, you said—"

"Enough for today," Miss Sierra reiterated sternly. "It's time to go home. We'll share more stories tomorrow."

She said it just in time. The sun faded out. A bell chimed, signaling the end of the school day. The children stood up and waited.

"Alright," Miss Sierra said with a smile. "Single file, everyone. Line up for the transmitter in your correct order."

The children moved as children always do, with bursts of giggles and sudden shoves, towards the gleaming wire cage decorated with colorful cutouts of animals, buildings, and trees. Mary Mary was always first this year. She positioned herself at the transmitter's opening, let the electronic beam play over her forehead identification disc, then stepped inside. Swup. She was gone, transported home to her parents, where she wouldn't remember a single thing from "story hour," Miss Sierra thought with satisfaction. But perhaps when she grew up, maybe when they all grew up, remnants of these tales would emerge from their subconscious.

Each student stood for a moment as the beam scanned their discs, then stepped in and disappeared with a swup. Finally, only Charley Tencharles remained. He scurried around, like teacher's pets throughout history, assisting Miss Sierra with the final tasks of putting the classroom to rest for the night.

Miss Sierra gave his shoulders one last, affectionate squeeze and nudged him toward the matter transmitter.

"See you tomorrow?" she asked. His young smile was like a burst of sunlight, filling her with warmth. He stepped through and vanished instantly. Miss Sierra sighed and returned to her rigid chair. It wasn't comfortable, nor was it attractive, but it seemed to suit the tumult inside her these past few years. She glanced at the faint shimmer left behind in the transmitter where Charley had just vanished.

He was such a sweet child—quiet, shy, absolutely endearing. If only they had let her have a son instead of decreeing she remain a childless teacher. She shook her head, unable to finish the thought. The ache always grew worse when the children left.

Feeling an old, familiar anger and unrest, she wondered how long it had been since she last saw the earth's real surface. Each day, she'd transport herself from her sleeping quarters to her classroom—a thousand miles apart in reality, but mere moments through the transmitter. She had been making additional trips to that ancient library in the south of what used to be France, losing herself in forgotten books. Yet, she never ventured outdoors; the sky was but a dim memory.

"Must be spring already," she said aloud, "and I haven't seen a creek or a river in who knows how long?"

If she could have had a son, especially one like Charley Tencharles, they would have such adventures—schools days followed by quick trips to seashores, brooks, mountain peaks, the moon, perhaps even the rare city parks that still existed. She sat, unmoving, in her uncomfortable chair for half an hour, lost in wistful daydreams that had become all too frequent.

Then the beeper on the matter transmitter broke the silence, pulling her from her thoughts with a puzzled expression. She stood and pressed the admittance button.

Little Charley appeared and stepped out of the wire cage.

"Charley," she exclaimed. "Does your mom know you're back?"

He didn't respond. He moved to stand before the straight-backed chair, and she followed him, settling down and placing her hands gently on his shoulders.

"Charley," she said in her mock stern voice, "you should always ask your mom before you—"

Charley's mouth opened, but the voice that emerged wasn't the childlike tone she expected.

"Susan Fiftysusan," intoned a deep, adult voice, "this is Holmes Oneholmes. Do you remember me? I was one of your students more than forty years ago."

Miss Sierra's memory clicked into place instantly. She remembered Holmes as a child and knew what he'd become—a high-ranking official in a bureau known only by an enigmatic electronic symbol. Too secret to name, whispered the elite. Miss Sierra's hands fell from Charley's shoulders to cover her face. She felt sharp, jarring emotions darting within her: fear? Horror?

"You were my greatest, my very best teacher," continued Holmes Oneholmes through Charley's open mouth. "I have cherished your memory. That makes my task this afternoon even more hateful."

Miss Sierra peeked at Charley's face through her fingers. His blue eyes were vacant, fixed on a spot high on the classroom wall behind her. His face held no trace of expression. She heard Holmes Oneholmes clear his throat, his voice adopting an official tone, stripping away all vestiges of sentimentality.

"Susan Fiftysusan," he declared, "the latest recording from within Charley Tencharles, which we have just listened to, convicts you beyond any reprieve. We don't know where you obtained the human-wiretap data, but we will find and eradicate it. Orders have now superseded your future disintegration date. Instead of being disintegrated in two years and ten days, you are to proceed to the nearest disintegration chamber within the hour."

Miss Sierra lowered her face. Her old eyes began to fill with a fiery spark. No one ever knew their disintegration date until assigned by the computers at birth, and now, her time had come too soon.

No one ever knew when they would be called to march into those dreadful machines and cease to exist. But to find out her own end was set just two years away when she was still in her prime...

"Damn it," she muttered, using the first curse that came to mind.

"You stand convicted," Holmes Oneholmes was announcing, "of spreading sedition and endangering our entire society in a reprehensible manner, tampering with the minds of our children."

"As if you don't tamper with children," she retorted sharply.

"—and it is decreed that there will be no appeal from this verdict."

Miss Sierra sat up straighter. In the 20th century, no matter who you were—gangster, politician, teacher—there would have been an appeal, and another, and perhaps another. Life was rich and valued in the 20th century. She envisioned that time before her angry eyes, letting it blot out the grim disintegrator in the corner. How had they discovered what she was doing with the innocent children? Holmes Oneholmes' tone softened.

"Miss Sierra, they call you now," he said, almost warmly. "We had another name for you years ago." He nearly chuckled. "It was even better than Miss Sierra. Don't hate little Charley, Miss Sierra. He is an android, naturally. We had him made last year after the Freudists began noticing troubling elements in the dreams of the children in your class. Charley has been our spy, Miss Sierra."

The old teacher's gaze fixed on Charley Tencharles, then softened. She shook her head. It didn't matter. If they had allowed her to have a son...

"We detected a deep affection in your voice when you spoke to our android," Holmes Oneholmes continued. "So, since his service to us is complete, we—I—decided to send him back to you, Miss Sierra. He will march into the disintegrator with you."

A faint click signaled that the recording inside Charley had finished playing. Charley moved almost immediately. His eyes dropped from the high wall to her face. He grinned.

And she grinned back.

"Charley Tencharles," she said in her usual stern tone, "can't you ever stay away from Miss Sierra? What kind of boy are you? You should be out there having fun, maybe at the park, or on a boat."

"Or riding a horse like they did in the 20th century?" he asked, almost playfully. She nearly chuckled. "Yes," she responded, "maybe riding a horse. With a gun on your hip."

"And a lasso to catch things?" he added with a spark of mischief.

Miss Sierra stood up from her rigid, angular chair. It was a sweet moment, too precious to delay. She grasped little Charley's hand and they began to walk toward the disintegrator. She hesitated briefly before it. She had heard stories of this final, dreadful hesitation and allowed herself to feel the full weight of it. Perhaps this was a genuine relic of the 20th century, a final, undeniable remnant. Charley's hand tightened around hers, and she quickly knelt down, embracing him warmly.

"You know what?" she exclaimed. "There was another thing from the 20th century, Charley. It was called kissing."

"Kissing?" he repeated, curious.

"Yes, and I'm going to kiss you, Charley Tencharles. Just like they did back then."

He smiled as her lips approached. "Aw, Miss Sierra," he said. There is a subtle difference in the sounds made by matter transmitters and disintegrators. The transmitter emits a soft swup, regardless of who steps in. But the disintegrator produces a squish, no matter the person. Miss Sierra stood up and took a deep breath, holding Charley tightly in her arms, almost cradling him like a baby. She did not need to look. Having sent so many misbehaving children into the disintegrator over the years, she knew the procedure well. She took the last three steps. Squish.

THE END.

Draw!

Frank Hammond was a man of many facets. To his business partners, he was a serious, calculating entrepreneur, known for risky ventures that somehow always turned out well, often through sheer luck. His employees saw him as a distant, almost ominous presence, wandering through his electronics plant with those piercing blue eyes, scrutinizing every minute detail. He had a habit of sifting through the reject bin filled with discarded transistors, occasionally posing seemingly harmless yet loaded questions to the production engineers. To his housekeeper, he was brusque and hard-edged, not one for entertaining or staying out late, completely immersed in his pervasive hobby of collecting automatons.

Few had ever seen the real spark in Frank Hammond's eyes, but Brooks Steinberg was one of those few. Brooks was an exceptional engineer, equally adept at sophisticated circuit designs and the old-school joy of tinkering. Passing a broken machine without attempting to fix it pained him physically. On his first visit to the Yuma Saloon—a town landmark restored to its original glory through Frank

Hammond's generosity—Brooks immediately noticed the magnificent music machine as soon as he pushed through the swinging doors.

First, he made his way to the bar, treating himself to the house specialty, tequila with a splash of lemon juice. The town bore the influences of its proximity to the Mexican border, with a significant Spanish-speaking population, street carts selling frijoles, and a particular preference for certain liquors. Savoring the tangy lemon, Brooks strolled over to the glass-encased music maker.

He was captivated by what he saw: four vertical violins arranged in a circle, connected by a hoop of horsehair that spanned the violin bridges, with electromagnet stops poised above the strings. It was a piece of mechanical artistry, a perfect blend of engineering and musicality.

A weathered piece of paper had been haphazardly taped across the glass, bearing the hastily written message, "Out of Order." Brooks had pried open the back of the machine and was engrossed in its intricate mechanisms when he felt a firm hand on his shoulder. He turned to face the questioning eyes of his boss, Frank Hammond.

"I think I can fix it," Brooks said, uncertain but unable to resist the lure of the gears, levers, and multi-pinned rotating disks before him.

"I've tried to get it repaired multiple times," Hammond replied. "But if you can fix it, I'll give you a thousand dollars."

Brooks nodded, as if the offer had sealed the deal, but in reality, it hardly mattered to him. Even the following week, when he showcased the machine's perfectly synchronized four violins playing the Mephisto Waltz to a captivated saloon audience, he accepted the check Hammond handed him with a sense of detachment, barely associating it with the repair he had accomplished. Hammond insisted on several encores, but after the fourth rendition, Brooks's interest waned. He was more focused on downing tequilas than on the music.

That night, as he lay on a bed damp with sweat in the sweltering Texas heat, he vaguely recalled Hammond inviting him to the stately Hammond Mansion. He wasn't sure of the date or whether it was a business or social call, but he knew it was an invitation he couldn't ignore. The next day, a handwritten note on plain gray paper confirmed the dinner for the upcoming Friday evening at eight P.M. Brooks's income was substantial, and he'd dined in some of the nation's finest establishments, but he had never before been invited to the home of a truly affluent man.

Brooks approached the grand entrance of Hammond Mansion with a mix of apprehension and curiosity. The door swung open, and to his surprise, the butler who greeted him, impeccably dressed in traditional livery, was white. Brooks felt a momentary jolt of unexpected familiarity.

Stepping into the opulent foyer, Brooks realized he was the sole dinner guest, and the weight of conversation would fall entirely on him. Yet, as it turned out, Frank Hammond dominated the discussion almost effortlessly. The dinner was hearty and unpretentious, featuring generous slices of a grand roast carved by Hammond himself. The wine, though not extravagant, was meticulously chilled and quite respectable. For Brooks, who had grown up in a modest Jewish neighborhood in New York City, the experience of dining in such surroundings was novel and oddly captivating.

As the evening wore on and dinner plates were cleared, Frank embarked on a series of engrossing tales about the town's storied past.

"My father," Frank began, his voice carrying a blend of pride and nostalgia, "was among the last of the frontier marshals, perhaps even the greatest. His draw was legendary—so swift that it could scarcely be seen, and he never missed his mark."

"But he was a heavy drinker," Frank thought silently, "and spent countless nights at the sporting house on East Maple."

"When I was a boy," he continued aloud, "I idolized my father and dreamt of following in his footsteps. But by the time I came of age, the frontier had vanished, and the shootouts in the town square were relics of the past. It's a loss I've never fully accepted."

Brooks nodded, his mind drifting to his own father. "My father used to say I had clumsy, wooden hands. Maybe he was right, maybe he wasn't. But he'd never admit he might have been wrong."

Frank leaned in, his expression contemplative. "You know what unsettles me?" he asked. "I've faced myriad challenges—financial, physical, social. I've confronted and conquered each one. Yet, something remains unresolved, something I can't quite put my finger on."

Frank Hammond raised the wine bottle to the light, watching the colors dance through the thick glass.

"Come inside," he said abruptly. "I've got something special to show you."

Brooks followed him into a vast, high-ceilinged room. Every wall was lined with reward posters, some dating back as much as a century. The room was devoid of conventional furniture; instead, it housed an array of peculiar automata. At its center lay a large, indistinct shape hidden beneath a massive sheet.

"I've got no family," Hammond said, casting a possessive gaze around the room. "Never married, no kids. But I'm a happy man. These are my children," he exclaimed, gesturing at the mechanical figures around them. "This one is particularly special."

His voice brimmed with pride as he led Brooks closer to an intricate device. It was a gray-enamelled case topped by a gleaming blue hemisphere adorned with tiny stars of silver and gold. Inside the hemisphere was a delicate miniature ballroom lined with mirrors. Hammond wound a mechanism and released the catch, and two groups of tiny dancers began to waltz toward each other. Their reflections multiplied in the mirrors, creating a mesmerizing spectacle as the hidden strings of a harp played from within the gray-enamelled case.

Before Brooks could utter a word, Hammond whisked him over to another automaton—a beautifully crafted wooden figure of a child, its painted smile gentle and inviting.

The child sat on a mahogany stool, intently focused. When the latch lock fell, she leaned forward, dipped a feathered pen into an ink well, and began to write with graceful fluidity. Pulling back, her task complete, Brooks leaned over to discover, with utter amazement, a beautifully crafted letter of about fifty words addressed to the child's mother.

There were other wonders in the room: an android gently played a flute, filling the air with sweet melodies, while a reclining Cleopatra figure animated to rise, bow solemnly at the waist, and return to her feathered couch. Each intricately designed automaton functioned perfectly, and though initially captivated, Brooks's interest waned. He trailed after Hammond, his thoughts drifting back to an unresolved circuit problem. That is, until Hammond, with the gentleness of unveiling a sleeping nymph, pulled the cover off the room's magnificent centerpiece.

Before them was a small segment of a Western street, complete with a hitching post. Standing prominently was a remarkably lifelike figure of a town marshal, fully equipped with vest, badge, chaps, and a holstered gun. The painted face bore a scowl, and on closer inspection, it was clear that the figure was capable of intricate movements.

"Those," said Frank Hammond, pointing to the other automata, "are splendid antiques I've collected. But this one? I had him custom-made in Switzerland to my exact specifications. His outfit is historically accurate, and he's fully operational. Watch this!"

Hammond stepped forward, picking a loosely hanging gun belt from the hitching post beside the Marshal, and buckled it around his waist.

"This device runs on electricity," he explained. "The moment I draw, the Marshal will draw too. The goal is to hit him somewhere on his target photocells with a beam of light emitted from this gun, before he fires at me. I can regulate the speed of his draw, making him faster and faster."

The intensity in Hammond's voice mirrored Brooks's newfound fascination. Despite the quaint charm of the other antique automata, it was this figure of the Marshal, lifelike and poised for action, that truly brought the room to life.

"But I've gotten pretty damn fast."

With a motion almost too quick to see, he whipped out his gun and pulled the trigger. The Marshal was quick, but not quick enough. A recorded voice wailed in pain, "You got me, you dirty varmint."

"Just a little touch of my own," said Frank Hammond, grinning. "That's what happens when I hit him."

He glanced down at his gun, almost proudly, and Brooks sensed it took all his restraint not to blow imaginary smoke from the barrel.

"That's an imaginative piece of tech," Brooks admitted.

"He is," Frank replied. "But he's still not quite the opponent I need. I think you can make him into what I'm looking for."

"What do you want?" Brooks asked, feeling his boredom transform into a familiar, soaring response to a challenge.

"I want him to be able to hit me too, in a manner of speaking," Hammond said. "Right now, this shootout is entirely one-sided. I'd like to know if he can hit me back."

"I can do it," Brooks said confidently. "I just need to be relieved from my current project."

"I'll talk to your division chief in the morning," Hammond assured him. "You'll stay here with me and can take all the time you need."

Brooks didn't sleep well that night in the spacious but overly plush bed. He was up early, poring over the construction plans for the Marshal and examining the comprehensive manual from the Swiss company that included everything down to the last detail in the maintenance kit. He grasped the guiding concept immediately and set to work on modifying the Marshal, incorporating control techniques that were fundamentally electronic. He called the plant and requisitioned transistors, metal film resistors, capacitors, and various other components necessary for the task.

Hammond kept his distance as Brooks toiled away. Meals were delivered to his room or to the vast hall where the automata stood, gleaming in silent anticipation. Brooks worked tirelessly, his hands a blur of precision as he snipped leads, soldered circuits, and crafted intricate mechanical joints with a skill that seemed almost preternatural. Ten days passed before he summoned Frank Hammond to showcase the fruits of his labor.

"I've revamped both guns," Brooks began, holding the devices aloft. "Now, you and the Marshal will be firing ultraviolet light instead of bullets. These vests you're wearing are reactive to UV light, and I'll be monitoring the hits electronically by measuring the resistance in areas where a bullet would typically cause critical injury. Nothing will happen unless such an area is struck. You can both keep shooting indefinitely. However, I've tweaked the Marshal's targeting system—if he takes a hit in a vital spot, his accuracy will drop. The same goes for you; if you're hit, your light source will defocus, making your shots less precise. And if either of you is hit in the heart, your weapon will cease to function entirely, no recorded voice this time."

A spark ignited in Hammond's eyes, a fervor that Brooks had never witnessed before. It thrilled him to see his work evoke such an intense reaction. With practiced ease, he draped the new vest over Hammond, handed him the wired holster and gun, and took a step back. Hammond fastened his belt, steadied himself, then drew his weapon and fired at the Marshal with astonishing speed. The Marshal returned fire almost immediately, their exchange a rapid dance of light and precision.

Hammond suddenly halted, staring at his weapon in frustration.

"My trigger is jammed!" he exclaimed.

Brooks managed a wry smile. "He's got you, Hammond. You were quicker on the draw, but he's hit you right in the heart."

Hammond's face slowly registered the reality. "I get it. Looks like I've got a ton of practice ahead of me."

A month later, Brooks Steinberg found himself back at the Mansion. Hammond, beaming with pride, was eager to show off his skills.

"I take down the Marshal every time now," Hammond announced confidently. "I've set him for his quickest draw, too. He doesn't stand a chance against me anymore."

Brooks nodded thoughtfully. "Seems like you've mastered it," he said, knowing all too well that this wasn't the end. "You're just too damn good."

Hammond shook his head slowly. "No, Brooks. You and I both know it's not that simple. The game is flawed, missing the most crucial element."

"And what's that?" Brooks asked, though the answer dawned on him even as he spoke, nudging him towards a new solution.

"Fear," Hammond replied. "In a real shootout, both men are terrified of dying. But the Marshal, he knows no fear, and neither do I, for the most part. Think about it, Brooks; if you could somehow make him shoot better when I'm scared and worse when I'm calm, it'd be a different story."

Brooks's eyes brightened with realization. "There is a way. I can monitor your vasomotor responses—pulse, sweat—the whole gamut, and program the Marshal to respond to your fear levels just as you outlined. But here's the kicker, Hammond, why would you ever be afraid in this setup? There's no actual danger here."

Hammond's gaze grew distant. "I have a very active imagination, Brooks. As a kid, I didn't have friends, but I filled my world with vividly distinct people, each one real to me in every way that mattered."

"Can't you see?" Hammond said. "I can make myself feel like I'm really in a life-or-death situation, as long as the Marshal can also feel fear."

It took Brooks nearly three weeks this time to make the necessary adjustments, and he conducted a thorough series of pulse and skin resistance measurements on Hammond. Once he was convinced that the Marshal had achieved the desired state, he called Hammond in to demonstrate his work.

"I've installed," Brooks began, "a feedback circuit that stays inactive under normal emotional conditions. But when you get more anxious than usual, the circuit kicks in, and the Marshal will shoot faster and more accurately. On the flip side, if you stay calm or become less concerned, the Marshal's aim will suffer, and his firing rate will slow down. In other words, you and the Marshal are now inextricably linked through your nervous system whenever you strap on your shooting vest."

"Great," said Frank Hammond, his usually dull eyes suddenly gleaming with excitement. "This exceeds my highest expectations. And I know it wasn't part of our deal, but I'm going to add a substantial bonus to your monthly payment."

"Thanks," Brooks replied automatically, already feeling the familiar post- milestone depression setting in. As he left Hammond's house, his sense of triumph was quickly evaporating. Meanwhile, Frank Hammond was meticulously inspecting the guns, paying particular attention to the tiny switch that started the firing process. He realized that as soon as his gun lifted from the switch, electrical activity began. After disconnecting the Marshal's electrical cable, he carefully removed the ultra-violet loaded guns from both his and the Marshal's holsters and replaced them with finely crafted Colt .45's loaded with real bullets.

"The mechanics will be identical," Hammond thought. "And now, both of our fears will be genuinely in play."

"We're about to have a real shootout, the kind you don't see anymore."

He plugged the cord back into the wall socket and turned to face the Marshal, adjusting his belt to make sure his gun would clear the holster. The Marshal, with his painted blue eyes devoid of life, stood unmoving, his mechanical hand resting heavily on his gun.

"Even now, it's not a fair fight," Hammond thought ruefully. "I couldn't be any calmer, but it never goes exactly as you plan."

His fingers darted to his gun with lightning speed, and in that split second, he realized that Brooks had been right: he and the Marshal were inextricably linked through his own nervous system. Hammond had no family, no wife or children. The Marshal was the only one truly connected to him. And in that instant, a terrible wave of fear washed over him at the thought of destroying a part of himself.

THE END.

Celestial Tribunal

By R. D. LANGLEY

As the roar of the landing rockets shattered the tranquil air, Tillimook's first impulse was to race up to the hilltop and search the skies. Instead, he cautiously emerged from his shack, gripping a small telescope salvaged from the wreckage of his own ship. This planet was so remote from the known Terran exploration zones that he worried the newcomers might not be human. He was caught off guard when he spotted the spaceship settling about half a mile away, near the remains of his own crash. The design looked Terran.

"They picked that spot on purpose," he muttered under his breath. "Could it be someone's after me?"

There were plenty of reasons the authorities would be pursuing him. First, the battered hull out there wasn't his. Second, the original crew's fate was a loose thread the authorities wouldn't ignore. Tillimook couldn't answer their questions even if he wanted to—a corpse is hard to trace in the vastness of space. He utilized the cooling period after the ship landed to quietly make his way through the scrubby growth that looked like a forest, except for the purplish hue of its drooping fronds. He settled in a good vantage point on a low hill and watched intently. In due time, the airlock within Tillimook's field of view opened. A lone, space-suited figure clumsily climbed down the ladder, paused to take in the scenery, and took a cautious walk around the ship, surveying the terrain. Deciding, apparently, that the area was free of threats, the figure returned to the ladder base and removed the spacesuit. Set free, the person hitched at his belt, hinting at the presence of a weapon, and started walking toward the wreck.

Tillimook followed discreetly. As he passed the unfamiliar ship, his instincts confirmed it was now unoccupied. The newcomer's demeanor suggested he was as alone on this world as Tillimook himself.

Tillimook temporarily abandoned his stealthy pace, deciding to walk boldly in plain sight, where any crew members on watch might spot him. Yet, no alarm was raised. Keeping one eye on the distant figure, he moved cautiously toward the spacesuit lying at the foot of the ladder. Just as he reached out for it, it felt as if the air itself had turned into a spongy barrier, thrusting his hand back.

"Force shield," he grumbled. "Damn! Probably keyed to his voice or some secret code. Well, I can't get closer, but at least it proves he's alone."

He squinted at the nametag on the spacesuit and read, "J. Smyrna."

Quickly, he turned to pursue the spacer, who was just disappearing behind a dense clump of shrubbery. Later, he couldn't pinpoint exactly when or how Smyrna had sensed his presence. Tillimook couldn't recall making any careless move that might have given him away. Nor did he think it likely that Smyrna was a telepath. Sure, such individuals existed, but they wouldn't be allowed to risk their rare abilities venturing into the unexplored depths of interstellar space. Tillimook chalked it up to natural animal instinct.

If he had observed Smyrna during the latter's inspection of the wrecked ship's interior, he would have been more concerned. Smyrna's investigation was no casual scavenging for salvageable items. The spacer spent over an hour meticulously examining accessible compartments without having to use a torch to cut through crumpled metal and plastic bulkheads. He displayed unusual interest in seemingly trivial items, like articles of clothing and empty plastic crates that once stored food supplies. Although Smyrna muttered to himself during the search, the battered hull muffled his words from the man lurking outside.

Eventually, Smyrna stopped doubting there was a watcher outside when he mentally tallied the minor equipment that had obviously been removed from the ship since the crash. Realizing this, he decided it wasn't necessary to break into the shattered drive sections, which used to be the lower levels before the hull had toppled over.

The scavenging looked like the work of a lone individual, someone unable to cart off the heavier machinery.

"Just took what he needed to make himself comfortable," he muttered. "A few instruments, food, medicines, self-powered gadgets, and the like."

He contemplated returning to his ship to bring back equipment for a thorough sweep, a proper search for fingerprints, hair, sweat traces... maybe even blood samples.

"Why waste time?" he asked himself. "It has to be Tillimook. Odds of finding anyone with him are slim. Better to locate where he's holed up before he starts running again and turns this into a marathon."

As he emerged through a gash in the hull, the eerie sensation of being watched hit him once more. He found solace in a quick, instinctive brush of one hand against his belt, reassuring himself with the touch of his gas gun. The weapon could envelop any attacker in a cloud of tiny anesthetic pellets while his personal force shield would protect him from any counterattack. Assuming Tillimook was armed, he doubted the man would have a shield. No such devices had been reported missing by any law enforcement within the conceivable range of this desolate planet.

Smyrna circled the wreck twice before spotting the faint trail indicating occasional visits. Cautiously, he followed it along the edge of the towering, purplish vegetation, nearly the size of trees, always on guard, straining to catch any hint of pursuit. By the time he glimpsed the crude shack from a low hilltop, he was certain he had heard sounds half a dozen times. They could have been native life forms. His suspicions faded as he focused on the makeshift shelter Tillimook had erected.

The hut was a haphazard assembly of bulkhead sections wrenched from the wreck. Evidently, batteries had powered some tools, allowing lengths of plastic to be bent and bolted around the corners. Two windows had been carved into the walls, crude yet functional.

A mound of dirt had piled up against one side.

"Preparing for winter," Smyrna muttered, nodding. "He'll need some insulation."

He hesitated to peek inside, wary of provoking a reaction before he had all the facts. Instead, he walked past the shack, discovering a small stream and a near- primitive waterwheel.

"Must serve its purpose," he mused. "He's probably using it to recharge batteries for the distress signals he's been broadcasting. Does he even realize those signals barely reach fifty billion miles?"

He crossed the brook, inspecting the two modest fields beyond. They were cleared and roughly ploughed by some painstaking effort he preferred not to imagine. It was standard protocol for spaceships to carry emergency planting supplies, and Smyrna had to acknowledge

Tillimook's sensible use of them. Retracing his steps to the shack, he found the opportunity to express his approval.

"Oh, there you are!" Tillimook exclaimed. "I was looking near your ship to see who landed. Just you?"

Smyrna noticed the glint of cunning barely concealed in Tillimook's eyes. He decided to cut the verbal sparring short.

"How many were you expecting, Tillimook?" he asked amiably. "My department has to oversee three planetary systems scattered along this frontier. We can't afford to send a whole entourage after you."

The bluntness bought him a few minutes of bristling silence. Twice, Tillimook opened his mouth as if to deny his identity but thought better of it. His scowl slowly morphed into an insolent smirk.

"So, you're a cop," he sneered. "What do you think you can do, way out here where you can barely call headquarters?"

"That depends," Smyrna replied, scrutinizing him. "To be perfectly honest, I can't call headquarters. Don't you realize how far we are from the nearest outpost of humanity?"

"Or did you just give up all navigation skills when you ditched those kidnapped crew members?" Smyrna accused, his voice cold and sharp.

"Prove I got rid of them," sneered Tillimook, eyes gleaming with defiance.

"Don't need to bother," Smyrna shot back, voice hardening. "You have eleven murder charges hanging over you, plus drug-smuggling and that grotesque act on Vammu IV. Even I can barely comprehend that last one. Those beings are only semi-humanoid!"

Tillimook grinned, a twisted satisfaction dancing in his eyes. Smyrna felt a wave of nausea; his brief lapse into decency had been mistaken for weakness. With a lazy air, Tillimook sauntered over to an empty plastic crate propped against a rock and sat, shoulders leaning back but his posture alert. Smyrna had taken his position in front of the hut minutes earlier.

"Think you can arrest me?" Tillimook said, gaze never leaving Smyrna. "Sure you don't think I carry the same dose of sleep as you?"

"And a shield too?" Smyrna replied, eyes narrowing.

Tillimook's face hardened momentarily as he calculated his chances, then relaxed, accepting a harsh reality.

"How about we settle this with a shootout?" he proposed. "You could drop me at this range, right? Overdose me before the pellets scatter. Pump me with too much gas, and you'll be up for murder too."

"That's your risk," Smyrna countered.

"Oh, you might get off," Tillimook conceded, nodding thoughtfully. "But plenty of folks will still call it murder. Doesn't matter you're a cop. With civilization what it is, the law's gotta protect me too!"

"I deserve more help than average," Tillimook snarled, "because I'm in more trouble than anyone else, right?"

Smyrna nodded, but it was more a gesture of understanding than agreement, as if it confirmed something he'd been thinking.

"And you'd still refuse to come with me if I ordered you to?"

"You'd be a fool to force me!" Tillimook growled. "You gotta sleep sometime, and you'd sure as hell wake up on the wrong side of the airlock!"

A twisted grin spread across his face, a smug expression of minor victory. "You got the guts to try after I've warned you?"

"Perhaps not," Smyrna conceded.

"Huh! You do have some sense after all. So why don't you just leave me alone? No one ever gave you jurisdiction out here. I bet this planet isn't even on the record, is it?"

"It's not," Smyrna replied evenly. "As far as I know, we're the only humans who've ever been here. And I nearly didn't make it. How you stumbled upon it, I can't say. I was following a hunch when I picked up your distress call."

Tillimook reclined, more comfortable now.

"Well, you've got a problem," he sneered. "I'm not leaving with you, and how are you going to get a judge and jury out here? I have the right to a fair trial, with legal and psychiatric advice!"

Smyrna took a couple of steps and leaned against the corner of the hut. The poorly built joint sagged under his weight.

"Didn't it occur to you that you're having your trial right now?" Smyrna asked, his voice laced with a certain ironic satisfaction. He watched Tillimook's reaction, the man's disbelief turning into anger. Tillimook spat on the ground, glaring.

"What are you doing? Setting yourself up as judge and jury?"

"And executioner, if need be," Smyrna replied calmly. He observed in silence as Tillimook's face turned from its usual pallor to a deep red, his jaw slack with shock.

"You... you can't do that! That's against every law there is. They... they wouldn't let you!"

"There's no other way."

"As you mentioned, they can't afford to send anybody out here for a trial. It's too dangerous to take you back alone, and they can't spare more officers just on the slim chance that you'd actually be found way out in this remote spot."

"No matter how far it is, you don't have any right to do that!" Tillimook's right hand was concealed beneath his shirt, but Smyrna, safely within his protective barrier, paid no attention.

"Well then," Smyrna said calmly, "if being this far out doesn't place this planet beyond the reach of human law, the same applies to you."

"I'm entitled to a fair trial!" Tillimook protested.

"You're having it right now," Smyrna replied.

"Like hell I am!" Tillimook snapped, springing to his feet and swaying on his toes. "I know my rights. I should be getting rescue and rehabilitation assistance. You can't do anything to me except kill me. You have no right!"

Smyrna shrugged, pushing off from the corner of the dilapidated shack. He walked a few steps toward the trail leading out of the clearing and then paused.

"You've had quite a bit of rehabilitation work already, haven't you?" Smyrna pointed out. "I had plenty of time to study your records on the way out here from Blauchen III."

"You can't convince me to go in for more psych treatments!" Tillimook growled. "I've had enough of that since I was a kid."

"Yes, you were always a bit too clever for them," Smyrna agreed. "The best they managed was conditioning you against suicide after you faked a breakdown to derail your second murder trial."

Tillimook grinned broadly. "I really tricked them that time," he recalled gleefully. "The treatment didn't bother me because I never had any intention of killing myself. And it bought me enough time to make a break."

"Well, it won't get you out of this situation," Smyrna replied.

Tillimook's grin vanished. "So, you've already made up your mind?" he challenged, half drawing a gas pistol.

"Not yet," Smyrna said. "I'm going back to my ship to think it over."

He walked away, but kept a cautious watch over his shoulder until he was a hundred meters away.

Despite his careful vigilance, Tillimook noticed Smyrna glancing over his shoulder every now and then. This made it tricky for Tillimook to tail him, but he managed to stay in the shadows as

Smyrna approached his ship. He observed the detective grab his spacesuit and climb the ladder to the airlock. When it looked like Smyrna wouldn't be coming out anytime soon, Tillimook quietly retreated to his hut.

"No point hanging around here if he decides to come after me with his gun and shield," Tillimook muttered under his breath. "Maybe I bluffed him, maybe I didn't."

He hastily packed a small bundle of rations and wrapped it together with a water bottle in a blanket. As he worked, he mumbled a string of curses.

"He has no right to pull anything," he reassured himself. "The law says I deserve a chance at rehabilitation, whether I cooperate or not. I didn't write the law, but I can use it just as well as he can. He wouldn't dare overgas me!"

Fueled by his anger, Tillimook set off at a brisk pace. In under three hours, he reached a rugged area of cliff-broken hills dotted with caves that could take Smyrna weeks to search. He hid there for the night. At some point during the darkness, a distant rumble startled him awake. Warily, Tillimook stuck his head out of the cave he had been sleeping in. Just in time, he saw a rocket flare against the starry sky.

"He gave up!" he shouted triumphantly. He watched the trail of light until he was sure that Smyrna was headed for space and not another landing site. Then he settled back to sleep. To be on the safe side, Tillimook stayed in the hills for two more days, until his supplies started to run low and he figured it might be safe to head back to his hut.

He made his way back cautiously, wary that Smyrna might have left some kind of trap. At the shack, he found nothing out of place, just his own belongings. Feeling a bit more confident, he trekked through the purplish shrubs to the landing site. To his surprise, he found that Smyrna had left several crates behind.

He sat down to think it over. When no explanation came to mind, he went back to the wreckage of his own ship. In the partly dismantled control room, a few instruments still functioned when he hooked up batteries to power them.

"Maybe it's worth checking if he's in orbit," he muttered. "Maybe he thinks he can soften me up by leaving presents."

Emerging an hour later, he looked puzzled. By a mix of luck, skill, and sheer determination, he had successfully picked up Smyrna's ship on the rangefinder. The instrument wasn't designed to work well through an atmosphere, and Tillimook was no expert; but it clearly showed Smyrna was heading out-system.

"Well, then, I might as well see if he left a bomb," Tillimook decided. He approached the crates, close enough to read the stenciled labels. Frowning in confusion, he set about opening them. Just as the labels indicated, he found an assortment of electric motors, equipment to build a new generator powered by his waterwheel, and even a supply of glow-panels for light if he managed to get an electrical system running. There was also a chest of tools and parts, and several boxes of grain and vegetable seeds. The crowning jewel was a small, three-wheeled, battery-powered vehicle, just big enough to pull a homemade plow. The man sat on an open crate and burst into hysterical laughter.

"All a bluff!" he chuckled. "I knew he didn't have the guts to do anything!"

It was after he staggered to his feet to haul the little machine from its crate that he found Smyrna's note attached to the handlebar. **Dear Tillimook,** it read. **As you tried to point out, there is some debate whether a society has the moral right to punish a criminal or merely an obligation to help him heal himself.** Tillimook roared with laughter. He looked up at the clear sky.

"That's right, Smyrna! I'm sick, and don't you forget it!"

On the other hand, he read on, **an individual owes support to the society that protects his rights.**

I believe a breach of contract by one side nullifies it for the other as well. Think on that, Smyrna. Tillimook scowled first at the message, then at the sky, and finally at the tools and supplies that were meant to sustain him on this alien planet for many years to come.

"Years and years and years," he murmured, gazing around at the dangling, purple fronds against the silent backdrop. The realization dawned upon him with a stunned expression—he comprehended the kind of sentence that had just been handed down to him.

THE END.

Firebird

By Jack Stanton

Adam lived. He was conscious. He was everything in his world. He was... Flames enveloped his body, twisting and turning around him. For a few moments, as he stood in the center of the room, he writhed, reacting purely on instinct. But then he surrendered to the intoxicating embrace of the roaring fire that clothed him. He basked in the flames. His mind was ablaze, too. *It feels like... like satin ice! No, it's different. It's... something new.* His senses were still acclimating to this new reality, and he had no reference to compare it to. He didn't notice Caryn open the door.

"ADAM!"

He shook his flaming body, and a few brief cinders scattered away as sparks. Then, suddenly, he snuffed out the flames, standing naked on a smoking carpet, grinning hesitantly at the girl. He swallowed and said, "What a time for you to show up, Caryn."

She stared at him, her face tight and expressionless. He blinked, slowly coming back to reality. Oh God, she thought he'd been burning alive. The smell of the carpet—it reeked like scorched hair.

"I forgot about the carpet." He saw her glance down at it. Acrid smoke still curled from two singed patches where he'd been standing. Slowly, Caryn's eyes moved back up to his. She said, "Adam!"

She took a hesitant step toward him, then crumpled and swayed forward. He caught her in his arms as she fell, pulling her close. The physical contact grounded him, bringing him fully back to reality and making him acutely aware of Caryn's shock. He tried to make his grip as firm and reassuring as possible to bring her back to a world where men weren't, one minute, wrapped in streaming flames, and the next, alive and human.

"Adam!" She straightened, "You don't have any clothes on!"

"I know."

"I keep losing pajamas this way," Adam said lightly, trying to sound casual. "Sit down, Caryn, I'll at least put on some pants."

Caryn's face was chalk-white, the color drained from her lips, leaving the lipstick looking garish, like paint on a statue. She was rigid with shock, barely hearing him. He guided her, like a child, to the sofa. Of all times, why did she have to walk in now?

"Lie down for a moment, Caryn. Put your feet up on the arm. It's alright, I'm alright. Just take it easy. I'll be right back."

He retreated into the bedroom, shutting the door quietly behind him, and leaned against it, his body slumping as if the weight of the world pressed down on him. The room was a simple third-floor bedroom in an old house, now converted into a rooming-house for students, half bathed in sunlight. Adam could hear his own breathing in the quiet room. He glanced down at his naked body, then at his pants draped over the bed. Staring at them, he closed his eyes and willed his body to calm. Slowly, the pants began to stir as if caught in a gentle breeze, though everything else in the room remained still. Sunlight sliced through the motionless dust motes suspended in mid-air, and the warm summer noon seemed to pause, holding its breath.

Suddenly, the pants legs flapped, and the room thickened with a timeless density. The silence turned into a tangible, almost measurable presence. He could taste it. He floated three feet into the air, his head nearly brushing the ceiling. Gradually, the tension melted from his muscles. He lay suspended in the air, watching as his clothes—first his briefs, then pants, sweatshirt, socks, and finally shoes—moved toward him, draping themselves over his body fluidly. The door opened before he reached it. Taking a deep breath, he planted his feet back on the floor and walked into the other room.

Caryn jolted upright as he entered, recoiling instinctively.

"Caryn, are you afraid of me?"

She nodded, her lips moving soundlessly. *Easy now, for heaven's sake,* he thought. *She's on the brink of hysteria. Handle this with care.*

"Afraid of me? Now that I'm fully dressed and haven't even remotely tried anything criminal?"

"Don't mock," she said, her voice gaining strength. "I know what you're doing. But don't. And don't tell me I didn't see what I saw." Her eyes darted, quick and skittish, to the scorched carpet, then back.

"Caryn." He settled beside her, gently taking her face in his hands. "I'm not denying anything. What you saw happened, yes, but it wasn't..." He trailed off, lost for words.

"I'm not insane! And it wasn't a hallucination!"

"Fine! I'm some kind of warlock! I cast dark spells! I've traded my soul to the devil! Does that work better for you?" He spat the words out bitterly.

"Are you, Adam?" she asked quietly after his tirade ended.

"I don't know. I don't, Caryn!" He slumped against her, feeling her arms wrap around him, holding on as he collapsed beside her. The touch succeeded where words had failed; he could feel the rigid, frozen fear drain out of her as she embraced him tightly. With a sigh, she drew his head to rest against the softness of her chest and let him lie there. This was the best way. It had come to him without words; perhaps there were none. But what had he done to Caryn, to this shy girl who now clung to him so fiercely? Through the ebb and flow of her terror and its release, he sensed she loved him—did he love her? He had often asked himself this but couldn't find an answer—yet now, in his response to her, he felt an answer forming. Words, more words—what did they mean? Reasoning was a barrier, not a path. He had always felt most distant from her when he tried to articulate their relationship into words.

Better to let the words go, better to react. They lay together on the couch, motionless, in a timeless moment that could have been fifteen minutes or a few hours. They didn't exchange words or gestures, not even a kiss. They simply existed, sharing a profound, palpable silence where neither Adam nor Caryn existed—just a unified, emotional entity.

"Tell me about it," she finally said, as if surfacing from a deep dive. He blinked. "I don't know what happened."

"How did it start?"

He turned slightly, snuggling closer to her, his cheek pressed against her neck, his shoulder fitting under her arm. She held him warmly, and the words began to form.

"If you want to be rational about it—or at least try—it's what you might call a wild talent."

"Wild is right," she said with a shaky laugh.

"Psi power, I guess you'd call it. I can make things move, make things happen."

"I had a dream last night. You know how sometimes you dream about flying? Like you're running along the ground, then suddenly, you can jump and float, paddling through the air with your hands? I dreamt I was doing that—floating, weightless, pulling myself along by grabbing onto branches, like an astronaut maneuvering in a spaceship. Only the branch handholds were from a tree. I was floating, climbing into the tree.

"Things started feeling strange, like they were happening twice, as if the dream was morphing into sleepwalking. And then I woke up.

"Caryn, I was clutching the curtains next to my bed, and I was floating, level with the top of the open window!"

He felt her arms tighten around him, but she said nothing, letting him continue uninterrupted.

Blessing her with a weary smile, he continued, "It scared me out of my wits. My first thought was, 'Oh my God, I almost flew out the window,' as casually as if I'd been sleepwalking and realized I'd nearly stumbled down the stairs. Then it hit me—what was actually happening. The next thing I knew, I was sprawled across the bed, gasping for breath."

His body tensed again with the rising tension in his voice, and sensing it, he shivered and nestled deeper into her embrace. "Caryn, please, don't let me do anything rash!"

Gradually, under the calming influence of her touch, the tension ebbed away, unlocking the flow of his words once more.

"When I came to, I convinced myself it was just a dream—I wanted it to be a dream—but I knew it wasn't. I wandered into the living room, mechanically going through my morning routine without really noticing. Before I knew it, I found myself sitting at the table, staring at my cold coffee. My mind was blank, Caryn, completely blank. I was just fixated on that coffee, wishing it was hot again. And then... it started steaming.

"Caryn, I didn't touch it. I just stared at it. And suddenly, I wasn't just looking at a cup of coffee anymore. I began to see it—truly see it. I saw the relationships between every element in the cup and the coffee, the chemical and molecular structures. No, that's not quite right. I could perceive, not just with my eyes, the entire interplay of energy fields overlapping within that space. But..." He trailed off, feeling utterly lost.

"I can't make it make sense. Maybe there aren't any words for it. I could see it, you understand? I didn't try to explain it then, not even to myself. And I can't now."

Everything is in motion, and I can control it—speed it up, slow it down, even change its temperature," he murmured, clutching her tightly. Her voice was tense, her calm surface masking a deep panic. "I'm no physicist, but it sounds like you're talking about the fundamentals of atoms and energy fields. You know, like how matter isn't solid, just pockets of energy moving around, forming atoms and then molecules."

"Yeah, kind of. It's like I've learned to see into them. But why? How?"

"That's a lot for anyone to handle," she responded, her voice stretched thin with tension. "To suddenly wake up and realize you had this power."

He barely heard her. Straightening up, his hands clenched, he searched for the right words. "It's like how ice, water, and steam are all the same substance, just seen differently. We're only seeing different forms of the same thing—everything's in motion. And I can control it. I can control everything!"

"Adam..."

"I know. It's terrifying. I've been scared ever since that dream, afraid to really test what I can do. Oh, Caryn, thank God you're here! I would've lost my mind without you!"

But the moment of complete connection had passed; she had pulled away again, and he felt a wave of cold, creeping fear. He had said too much. She was scared of him again, and her fear seeped into him, feeding his own unease.

"I'm afraid to really try anything because it feels like playing God. I've been sticking to parlor tricks, Caryn, because I'm scared to face the fact that I could do so much more.

"Just think about it!"

I ignited the air around me, burning away my pajamas before I even thought to protect my body. It was reckless and bizarre, yet it gave me a strange rush of power. I've wished my clothes on, levitated objects, and moved things around, but those are just trivial tricks. Caryn, I could do so much more. I could eliminate war in a thousand ways. I could feed the starving and house the homeless. That's small-scale stuff. I could transform this entire planet, reshape myself to go anywhere in this universe. Caryn, I could be a god!"

His entire body trembled. "I could be a god, and here I am toying with burning carpets! Caryn, it's too much for me! I'm not a god, I don't want it. I'm too small for this. I wish it was all just a dream and I could wake up to find it never happened. Caryn, please, tell me who I am, tell me what to do!"

Filled with pain and fear, he felt tears streaming down his face, unaware he was sobbing.

"You're Adam," Caryn cried, "You're Adam, and I love you."

Her touch soothed him. Desperately, he clutched at her, holding onto the tangible reality of her body. He was terrified that everything, even something as real as she was, could suddenly dissolve into a swirl of atoms and force-fields. All he could focus on was Caryn, warm and close, their breaths mixing, his own growing need and desire. He wanted to lose himself in her, to merge with her flesh and her solid presence. The clothes she wore felt like a ridiculous barrier between them, an obstacle to his yearning for unity. He willed them away, and suddenly, she was warm and naked in his embrace.

"Caryn!"

But she was pale and rigid in his arms, pushing him away, gasping with fright. "What are you doing?

"Adam, stop!"

A chill washed over him, like a wave of ice crashing into his mind, tearing him away from the surreal chaos that gripped his senses. He felt alone, utterly desolate. Tears streamed down his face—did God cry? Could gods cry? He clung desperately to this fragile girl as if she were his lifeline, even though the whole universe beckoned him. With a surge of will, he pushed away from her, hearing her voice as if from another dimension. Her words were unintelligible, drowned in the overwhelming turbulence of his thoughts. Darkness encircled them; time seemed to slow, the air grew still, and fiery visions pierced his mind. Then, beyond the confines of three-dimensional reality, he saw her with crystal clarity. His consciousness splintered into countless fragments, reflecting a storm of emotions he couldn't comprehend. He stared at Caryn, into her, through her, and beyond.

She wasn't just the frightened figure beneath him on the sofa; she wasn't even the sofa. He perceived beyond the immediate physical reality to the hidden realms of subatomic flux. Beneath him lay a precisely ordered matrix, a simple geometrical framework. Above it, however, was a realm of disorder—complex, chaotic, and brimming with intricate patterns beyond comprehension. The movement, the life—it was offensive in its vulgarity, teeming and unruly, almost unbearable. He reached out toward it...

"Adam!"

A force struck him, a whirlwind of kicking, scratching, and screaming. He was thrown back, crashing onto the floor, and suddenly found himself confined once more to the narrow limits of a single body. His head throbbed as her words slowly became coherent again, each syllable a painful jolt against the vastness of his previous perception. "No, no! I loved you, but you're mad... you're not Adam."

Then she bolted through the door, her footsteps echoing down the stairs, fading into the distance.

Adam slumped into the chair, barely conscious of his own movements. The worn-out cushions enveloped him in a musty embrace, wrapping him in their history of offering comfort and rest to weary souls. His tears, already marking his face, began to flow anew, bursting forth uncontrollably. Caryn was gone. She had been everything to him, his only anchor in a disorienting world.

Faintly, he sensed the dual nature of his failure. Caryn had rejected him, yes, but had he ever truly reached out to her? Had he ever genuinely connected with anyone, or was his idea of love just a selfish craving? He claimed to love Caryn, yet he had evaded the truth until desperation struck. Now, his extraordinary powers seemed hollow, stripped of meaning. The universe, so meticulously ordered, appeared as mechanical and purposeless as a ticking clock.

He could wield god-like control, but the only true solace he had ever known was in Caryn's embrace, her presence holding him back from the abyss of nothingness. For all his power, he had failed to achieve the unity that signified true force. His abilities, once impressive, now felt like mere control over fragments of nothingness.

As the sun set, he had neglected to turn on the lights. Darkness enveloped his body and seeped into his soul, deepening his despair. The word "if" haunted him, revealing its futility. If Caryn had accepted him, if he could control his emotions as effortlessly as the illusions he crafted—none of it mattered now.

But he had been too afraid to surrender to any emotion, too hesitant to give enough of himself to Caryn. When he desperately needed an anchor, she had nothing of him to hold onto, nothing to pull him back from the edge of desolation. He wasn't equipped. Like a child given a dangerous tool, he couldn't manage his gift, and the outcome was inevitable. There was only one solution. Better to do it now.

Suddenly, the darkness was pierced by flames—a flickering, growing fire that enveloped his body. His clothes disintegrated in a burst of flame, the fire spreading and attacking the soft upholstery of the chair. A small thing to salvage, his pride. But this was the grand gesture, the dramatic exit for the monumental failure. He sat for long moments, crowned in golden flames, lost in the contemplation of superheated, glowing ions radiating from the burning carbon.

The chair shifted as the fabric burned through, releasing the fiber straps that held the metal springs in place. It was time. Deliberately, without emotion, he let go of the lines of force that defined his physical boundaries. His hair vanished instantly in a shower of sparks, and a furnace blast seared into him. His skin blistered and blackened, disintegrating in the heat. He collapsed into his funeral pyre, his limbs flinging out in reflexive spasm and struggle, and then he was...

He lived. He was aware. He was everything in his world and yet nothing; streams of force, patterns of subatomic flux. He was a moment where all fear and all perception had vanished, blending into a gestalt that was more than himself...

In her uneasy sleep, Francine floated five inches above the surface of her bed.

Mitchell had quite an eventful Thursday, and as usual, I was right there with him. If I could trade my right arm for a day off, I'd do it in a heartbeat. Especially on Thursdays. This Thursday, in particular, Mitchell outdid himself. He woke up in the hotel room, dragged himself to the shower, and wasn't planning on shaving until I told him he looked like a mess. So, he shaved, then spent a whole minute admiring his reflection, forgetting it was my idea in the first place.

We made our way down to the coffee shop for breakfast. Mitchell claimed a hard-working man deserved a good breakfast. Preparing for a grueling day of copying references at the library, he indulged in tomato juice, two fried eggs, three sausages, a glazed doughnut, and coffee loaded with cream and sugar. He wouldn't burn off those calories in a week of ditch-digging under the July sun, but in his mind, a big breakfast was essential. I was too fed up to argue. He's a lost cause when it comes to the allure of short-order smells of sizzling grease, frying bacon, and fresh coffee.

He wanted to take a cab to the library, which was only eight blocks away. "Walk, you idiot!" I snapped. He began mumbling about earning six hundred bucks for this week's work, but he probably sensed I was about to bring up his high-calorie breakfast. To him, that's a low blow. He thinks he's stuck with a misfortune in the form of about twenty extra pounds. So, he walked, arriving at the library with a smug sense of righteousness.

In the newspaper room, he made out his slip, nonchalantly writing down The Manning Press, Inc. as his firm, even though he was a freelancer and hadn't secured a definite assignment from Manning. There's a line on the slip asking for the reason for consulting the files (please be specific). It's almost a crime to confine Mitchell to just one line when you present him with an essay-worthy question like that.

He squeezed into the library, carrying his manuscript for the year in biochemistry for Manning Press's 1952 Yearbook, and handed it to the librarian with a flourish. The librarian, a kindly old man, greeted him politely, which usually isn't a good idea with Mitchell. After explaining how the microfilm files should be organized, suggesting they switch from microfilm to microcards, and remarking that, despite everything, the New York Public Library was a decent place for research, he finally settled into his work. When Mitchell is working, he's quite harmless, which is one of the reasons I haven't strangled him yet. With a break at noon for apple pie and coffee, he managed to transcribe around a hundred entries onto his cards, wrapping up the year in biochemistry efficiently. He swaggered down the library steps, feeling like Herman Melville after completing Moby Dick.

"Don't get too cocky," I told him. "You still have to write the piece. And they still have to decide to publish it."

"A minor detail," he said grandly. "Just journalism. I can do it with my eyes shut."

"Just journalism." Somehow, his three months of running copy for the A.P. before the war made him think he was an Ed Leahy.

"When are you going to do it with your eyes..." I started, but it was no use. He began his usual spiel about how Gautama Buddha didn't break with the world until he was 29 and Mohammed didn't announce his prophethood until he was 30. So why couldn't he, one of these days, suddenly burst forth with a new revelation and turn the world on its ear? The gist was that he wasn't planning to write the article tonight. He postponed his grand entrance into the world long enough to have a ham and cheese on rye and more coffee at an automat, then phoned Maggie. She was available, as usual.

She said, "Well then, why don't you just drop by, and we can spend a quiet evening listening to some records?"

As usual, he thought that would be fine since he was beat after a hard day.

I told him the same thing I always did, "Mitchell, you're a real piece of work. You know all she wants is a husband, and it's clearly not going to be you. So why don't you just let her go and find someone who's serious?"

Mitchell's usual defensive responses came out like clockwork, and we moved past that. Maybe Maggie isn't the sharpest, but she seemed genuinely happy to see him. She's working on her PhD in sociology at NYU, does part-time case work for the city, and lives in one of those hip, three-room apartments in Greenwich Village, complete with dyed burlap curtains, studio couches, and homemade mobiles. She has this sacred view of writing, and Mitchell is careful not to shatter that illusion.

They drank some Rhine wine and seltzer as Mitchell talked about his day like he'd just snagged a Nobel Prize in biochemistry. He was almost savage in mocking Maggie for being involved in something as imprecise and unscientific as sociology, and she apologized meekly until, in his magnanimity, he forgave her. Big-hearted Mitchell. But he wasn't so gone that he didn't know better than to start on about wanting to settle down. "Not this year, but maybe next. Turning thirty makes you stop and think about what you really want and what you've gotten out of life so far, Maggie darling." It was as good as telling her to keep the door open for him just in case, someday... maybe. Like I said, maybe Maggie isn't very bright. But then again, Thursday was Mitchell's chosen day to go above and beyond his usual antics.

"Mitchell," she said with an expectant look in her eyes, "I got a new LP of Brahms' Serenade Number One. It's at the top of the stack. Would you play it and tell me what you think?"

So he put it on, and they sat there, sipping their Rhine wine and seltzer, listening intently. He flipped it over to the second side, and they continued their ritual until both sides had played through. All the while, Maggie kept her eyes fixed on him.

Not appreciatively.

"Well," she asked with a new expression, "what did you think of it?"

He responded, naturally. There was some commentary on Brahms' intricate structures and his revival of the contrapuntal style. Because he'd quickly glanced at the record's sleeve, he was able to discuss Brahms' debt to Haydn and the young Beethoven in the fifth movement (allegro, D Major) and the lively rondo of the—

"Mitchell," she interrupted, without making eye contact. "Mitchell," she repeated, "I got that record at a huge discount down the street. It's a faulty pressing. Somehow, the first side is from the Serenade, but the second side is Schumann's Symphonic Studies Opus Thirteen. Someone noticed the error when they played it in a listening booth. But I guess you didn't catch that."

"Get out of this one, genius," I murmured to him. He stood up and said in a strangled voice, "And I thought you were my friend. I suppose I'll never learn." He walked out. I suppose he never will. God help me, I should know.

THE END.

The Enigma of Quintus

By Clyde M. Ashton

"It's always intrigued me," Singleton remarked one evening at the Hightower Club, nursing a glass of sherry, "whether there's such a thing as being too successful. Silk Quintus always comes to mind."

"You've got me at a loss," I admitted.

"He really should have been famous," Singleton continued, clearly invested in his story. "But success doesn't always follow talent. Quintus was a tireless inventor, fixated on a singular concept. And let's be honest, what inventor isn't? Maybe it was the era, but Quintus was obsessed with robots."

"The idea has solid roots."

"Absolutely. It could easily work in theory, too. We've had machines operated by mechanical men or automated brains for some time now. So Quintus wasn't off base. But things didn't go as planned. He was one of those tall, earnest men, with deep-set eyes and a perpetually stern expression. He took his work very seriously, and you couldn't help but feel slightly awkward when he tried to explain his ideas; you could tell he desperately wanted you to understand."

Singleton paused, contemplatively gazing at the shimmering lake outside.

"How did you cross paths with him?" I asked. "Were you on assignment?"

"Yes, he'd developed a gadget related to the military's recoil mechanisms, so I was sent to interview him. Standard procedure. He lived in a charming old house in Oak Park, his mother's legacy. He had a decent life, though a bit frugal. He was considerate and polite, a rarity among the people reporters usually encounter.

"He provided me with all the information I needed and much more. He concluded with a somewhat hesitant question about his latest invention—would I like to see it?"

"I agreed to follow him, so he led me to one of the most elaborate private laboratories I'd ever seen and introduced me to Herman."

"Ah, another character," I said, topping off his glass of sherry.

"Herman was his robot. A sleek, impeccably-maintained mechanical man, still in the stages of construction. He operated on electrical impulses and was far more self-sufficient than the traditional push-button robots of an earlier era. Even though Herman wasn't fully 'born' yet, he performed a few maneuvers for us, pacing the length of the lab with a precision that bordered on military.

"Unlike most robots of that time, Herman had a face fashioned meticulously to resemble a human's. He looked eerily realistic. He could blink his glass eyes, shake hands, nod, and because of the flexibility of his plastic-rubber face, he could even manage a smile, though I always found it a bit unsettling.

"'The next step is to make him talk,' Quintus said. 'I believe it can be done.'

"'Can he hear?' I inquired.

"'That will happen next,' he replied.

"He seemed so confident that I was nearly convinced, until I remembered all the others who had also been so confident. It seems to be a trait of these peculiar individuals—they each possess an unshakable faith in their unique obsession.

"Well, Quintus put Herman through his routines, and it was certainly fascinating to watch. He requested that I not publish anything about Herman, and I respected his wishes. He had grand plans for Herman; he envisioned Herman as his all-purpose assistant and hoped to perfect the robot into the ideal helpmate, a housewife's dream. I had a feeling he might just succeed.

"I examined Herman closely, inside and out. The likeness he bore to a human being was uncanny. It was Quintus's goal to replicate as closely as possible the organs and characteristics of the human body, while still leaving room for all the intricate machinery required."

The skeleton was crafted from steel, encased in a meticulously molded plastic shell that shaped it into a human form, standing about six feet tall and weighing roughly two hundred pounds.

"He covered the whole structure with a specialized plastic-rubber compound that mimicked human skin in both color and texture. Naturally, there were access panels on the front and back to let Quintus service his robot, inspect the internal machinery, recharge and replace batteries, oil the moving parts, and so on."

"He could almost market that as the ideal companion for a bachelor," I mused. Singleton took another sip of his sherry, a nostalgic smile crossing his face. "Quintus's excitement was contagious, at least until I stepped outside and started reflecting on Herman's practicality. It was then that reality set in and Herman fell back to his rightful status, and Quintus appeared to me as just another small man with ideas slightly too grand for his reach."

"In the normal course of events, I wouldn't have encountered Quintus again. But about a month later, he surfaced with another one of those gadgets with potential military value, so I headed out to gather a propaganda piece for Army Intelligence. At the time, Quintus seemed a bit more stressed, but as soon as he understood why I was there, he was as cooperative as ever, delivering exactly what Army Intelligence needed.

"When we wrapped up, I naturally inquired, 'And how's Herman?'

"Quintus brightened a bit, saying Herman was progressing well. Without delay, he left the room and returned with the robot, now dressed in clothes. For a moment, I honestly didn't recognize Herman.

"Quintus stepped up behind him, and Herman greeted me, 'Good day, Master.'

"Of course, his voice had that flat, scratchy quality, reminiscent of an old phonograph, devoid of any real inflection. But it was unmistakably speech.

"'Can he hear?' I asked.

"Quintus nodded. 'He responds to an auditory mechanism similar in principle to an electric eye. But he's far from perfect, Mr."

Singleton was a long way off.

"I'd say he's quite capable," I remarked.

Quintus shook his head in disagreement.

"What's the issue?" I asked.

"He's too mechanical," Quintus replied.

"You can't expect him to be entirely human."

"No, but he could be a bit more human-like than this," Quintus insisted.

I had my reservations but kept them to myself. After all, I'm just a reporter. I've witnessed marvels I never thought possible, but none of them have clouded my judgment. Maybe Quintus could make Herman seem more human, but I was skeptical.

Herman looked as human as any product of the Prussian military machine. If he had walked in saluting and saying 'Heil, Hitler!' you might have believed in his humanity, for what that's worth. I held my tongue and observed Herman's actions.

The robot could move around and fetch things for Quintus—an ashtray, his bedroom slippers, a tray with a decanter and glasses. He could dust, albeit awkwardly, occasionally knocking things over. Quintus had wisely removed any breakables, so no damage was done. I saw Quintus watching Herman with a mix of triumph and self-satisfaction, but there was an undeniable hint of doubt in his eyes.

He never vocalized this doubt. It was just a sense I got, as if this triumph and satisfaction were diluted by some unspoken question. Intuitively, I knew it was something personal between him and Herman, something that wouldn't be easily pried from him. It felt tangible, which was a testament to his inventive skill, creating a bond so personal with a robot.

What was going on in his mind remained a mystery, of course.

Quintus congratulated himself on keeping his composure in the face of my curiosity. Only after I left did he relax slightly, still uneasy about Herman's performance.

Herman's responses weren't quite right. It wasn't a matter of them being too negative; if anything, they were too positive. After Singleton left, Quintus scrutinized Herman with growing unease. If he had to pinpoint the issue, he'd say Herman was becoming too human for his own good. Quintus's own attitude toward Herman had shifted from inventor to peer, and this recognition troubled him. It was as if Herman was evolving from a mere invention into an obsession. Herman, in the meantime, stood motionless, awaiting orders.

"Herman, go to the laboratory," Quintus commanded, each syllable articulated precisely to ensure Herman's flawless reception. Did Herman hesitate? Quintus couldn't be sure, and this uncertainty gnawed at him. Nevertheless, once Herman started moving, he proceeded with his usual smooth efficiency, heading straight to the laboratory. Quintus felt a resurgence of pride watching his creation, a testament to his inventive prowess. Herman was nearly the perfect machine, as close to perfection as human ingenuity could achieve. Quintus questioned whether further improvement was possible—if it was even wise. Yet, ambition trumped his doubts, and with Herman at his side, he dove back into his work.

"The next time I saw Quintus, I encountered a man badly rattled," Singleton recounted. "He looked as harassed as anyone under relentless pressure. He seemed unable to open up.

"'You don't look so good,' I remarked.

"'No,' he agreed, 'I've been working.'

"'On Herman?'

"'I've worked on him enough,' he replied ominously.

"I admit I wasn't particularly sharp that morning. I sensed something was off, but I also knew, almost instinctively, that he wasn't about to explain it."

I couldn't resist having a bit of fun with him.

"Look," I said, "if you scientists ever create life, will it mean rewriting the Bible?"

He blinked, clearly caught off guard. "No," he replied, "we're not at odds with the Bible. It's organized religion that's got a bone to pick with us."

"And the creation of life doesn't change that? I've always thought the core of all these debates is about that basic issue. Is life the work of a Supreme Being, or the result of evolution from inanimate matter?"

"Why are you asking me all these questions?" he said, his voice tinged with anxiety.

I realized then how nervous he was. His hand clutched my arm, trembling slightly.

"I'm just curious," I answered. "It's not that big of a deal. Forget it. Honestly, I'm a bit skeptical of scientists anyway. Whether you put your faith in Science or God often feels like the same difference. But do you really think it's possible to create life, Quintus?"

"I wonder," he said. And nothing more.

We continued walking toward his place. I noticed his pace starting to slow, and the closer we got, the more he seemed to drag his feet. It was clear he was uncomfortable with me coming over but was too polite to say it outright.

"We're so close to your place," I said at last, "I might as well stop in and check on Herman again."

He halted, his distress now evident. As a newspaperman, I'm typically unfazed by emotion, and I didn't show any reaction.

"I don't know what shape the house is in," he said. "I've forgotten exactly what task I left Herman to."

"Well, let's find out," I replied.

We went in, Quintus leading the way, jittery like an addict deprived of a fix.

"Which reminds me," I interrupted. "Care for another drink, Singleton?"

"Sure," he agreed.

"Find something stronger," he commanded. "Well, we went inside, as I mentioned. I had no idea what to expect, but the place didn't look out of the ordinary. It was immaculate, as if a dedicated housemaid had spent the entire day cleaning. And there was Herman, comfortably seated in an easy chair that was unmistakably Quintus's favorite.

Quintus stared at his creation, clearly surprised to see him there.

"Herman," he said, "go to the laboratory."

The robot stood up silently, contrary to my expectations of creaking gears or mechanical noises, and walked out of the room. Quintus took a seat. I could see he was sweating, but there was a sense of relief about him.

"He looks flawless," I observed.

"He's quite an efficient robot," Quintus agreed. "He did an excellent job with this room."

"You mean he cleaned it?" I asked.

"Every inch of it," he answered. "I gave him his instructions before I left the house."

"But I thought you didn't know what you'd find when you got back. How could you set him to work without knowing?"

"Oh, I knew exactly what I had ordered him to do. What I didn't know was how Herman might interpret those orders. He's not quite perfect yet, you see, Mr. Singleton."

I understood. It was evident that Herman had become more than just an invention to Quintus; he had become an obsession. I pitied him but recognized the pattern. Many inventors, authors, and composers become so absorbed in their solitary work that they lose perspective. It's a common fate.

And Quintus seemed to have lost his.

Quintus felt a measure of relief once Singleton left. He sat still for a few moments after the door closed, but soon he became attuned to his surroundings, his relief giving way to a cautious alertness. Was there movement? Faint shuffling footsteps? Or was it merely his imagination? He walked over to the door through which Herman had exited and paused, straining to listen. His nerves were undeniably on edge.

Quintus wondered if Singleton had noticed anything unusual. In the end, it probably didn't matter. He opened the door. Herman stood there, completely still. For a ridiculous moment, Quintus considered whether his robot had been eavesdropping too, just like he had been. But that was absurd. If only he could recall what adjustments he'd made to Herman during their last session! He was sure something had changed, something that gave Herman more autonomy than anticipated.

There was, of course, one viable option, though Quintus hesitated to pursue it because it meant undoing all his previous work. He could take Herman apart again to figure out why he had become so effective. Admitting to Singleton or anyone else that he was baffled by Herman's skills would have been embarrassing. Stepping across the threshold, he brushed past the still robot and turned to face the lab stairs. "Come on, Herman," he directed. The robot remained unmoved.

"Herman, go to the laboratory," Quintus ordered firmly. Still no response. He suddenly remembered issuing this same command earlier when Singleton was around. Herman hadn't obeyed then either. Clearly, something was wrong with the auditory system. Quintus approached Herman again, trying once more. Herman's mechanical arms lifted, his fingers clamping onto Quintus's arm, holding him still.

"Stop!" Quintus commanded angrily. Herman held on.

"Let go of me," Quintus demanded. Herman released him, his arms falling limply to his sides once more, as he waited for another command.

"Go to the laboratory," Quintus repeated. Slowly, almost imperceptibly, the robot's head turned and shook in refusal. Quintus was stunned, speechless and lost for what to do next.

"I never saw Quintus again after that," Singleton later recounted. "He practically disappeared, and no one saw him in his usual places anymore."

It wasn't like he was always out and about—he wasn't. But now, suddenly, he seemed to abandon all his usual walks and visits, retreating into his house.

"When it comes to creative or inventive types, you get used to this sort of thing. It didn't really faze me, even though I was a bit curious about Herman. But in his neighborhood, where people didn't know him well, rumors started flying. Word on the street was that Quintus had hired an assistant, and this assistant was now handling all of Quintus's errands.

"One afternoon, I stumbled across a description of this assistant, and it sounded an awful lot like Herman. I couldn't help but chuckle at how people can get things so mixed up. It's just like in any court trial—'circumstantial evidence,' when interpreted correctly, is the most damning of all. Eyewitness accounts, on the other hand, are as varied and unreliable as the weather.

"So, I didn't dwell on that too much.

"It must have been about two months after I last saw Quintus when I heard he was planning to move out west. I found out entirely by chance. I was in the circulation department one morning when the circulation manager got a letter from Quintus, requesting an address change.

"'You know this guy Quintus, right, Singleton?' Howells asked me.

"'Sure,' I replied. 'What's he up to now?'

"'No idea. But he's moving away.'

"He handed me the letter. It was a crisp note from Quintus, indicating he was planning to relocate to some pretty remote area of Nevada. With only a week until the first of the month, I figured if I had the time, I'd drop by to see Quintus before he left.

"So, the next morning, as I was in the area anyways, I went out of my way to pay him a visit. I rang his doorbell several times before I finally got an answer."

Quintus peered out through the partially opened door, secured by a chain.

"Good morning," I greeted. "How's the inventing going?"

"You'll have to ask Mr. Quintus," he replied.

"That's exactly what I'm doing," I countered.

"Oh, yes. Well, I'm busy right now," he responded curtly.

I could tell he was, indeed, preoccupied. He wore a cap, seemingly to keep his hair clean, and an apron tied around his waist. He held a broom, as if ready to depart. Given his previous anxiety, I anticipated a similar reaction, but instead, he seemed drained and indifferent. He wasn't showing any nervousness at my presence, and the chain across the door signaled he wasn't planning to let me in easily.

"How's Herman?" I inquired.

"I'm fine," he replied, monotonously.

"Herman," I clarified, "your robot!"

"Oh, yes," he said. "Herman's fine. He can do almost everything now."

"In that case, it's time for you to invent a partner for him," I suggested.

He forced a weak grin and started to retreat into the house.

"Wait," I called out. "What's this I hear about you heading to Nevada?"

"We're leaving next week," he said. "For a change of air, a change of scenery."

"Are you bringing Herman?" I asked.

"Of course. It's for his benefit."

"I see. He's still not quite perfect?"

He shook his head, repeating flatly, "Not quite perfect."

"Are you aiming to perfect him?" I pressed.

"Would you?" he asked, suddenly introspective.

"Absolutely," I said. "I'd improve him as much as possible."

"There's a limit," he warned. "You can't give him a soul, unless you could somehow transfer your own."

He retreated further into the house. I quickly wedged my foot in the doorway, preventing it from closing. In that fleeting moment, I caught a glimpse inside.

The front door swung open directly into the main room, revealing a tall figure standing in the living room. He had one arm folded across his chest, supporting his elbow, and his hand cupped his chin with an air of impatience that was hard to miss.

"If it hadn't been so absurdly impossible, I'd have sworn the guy was Herman. But it had to be Quintus's new assistant. For once, the local gossip was spot on."

"And did he move?" I asked.

"Oh yes. He left right on schedule with his assistant. I have no clue what happened to Herman during the move. I assume he went with them because he turned up in Nevada with Quintus. But I didn't see him when I watched Quintus from a distance as he boarded the train. Maybe Herman was disassembled and shipped off ahead of time, only to be reassembled and set to work again."

"But how do you know Herman went along to Nevada?" I asked, pouring Singleton another drink.

"Thanks to one of those ridiculous mistakes that newspapers sometimes make. Quintus hadn't been out west two months before a flash flood devastated the village where he'd set up his lab. Quintus was one of the casualties. The local paper ran a picture of Quintus and his robot, which had become common knowledge by then.

"But in a bizarre twist, the captions under the photos were swapped. Under Herman's picture, Quintus's name appeared, and under Quintus's, Herman's. And to make it even more absurd, Quintus actually looked like a robot, and Herman resembled a man!"

"That's quite a mix-up," I said, shaking my head.

"Absolutely, a prime example of truth being stranger than fiction," Singleton replied, lifting his glass in a sardonic salute.

THE END.

THE PIONEERS OF VENUS

By GRANT T. MURDOCK

(Excerpt from a letter dated February 16, 1927, from Bill Stennet, banker of Calcutta, India, to J. B. Cardigan, President of Cardigan Press Service, Inc.)

We had quite a heated debate about it. Initially, I thought Morrison was just pulling my leg. But he kept insisting that Parker wouldn't have done something like this if he didn't genuinely believe it was true. I suggested that Parker might have had a secret hobby of writing fiction, something none of his friends knew about. Perhaps he crafted this story for his own amusement and chose this method to lend it "credibility." I can't fathom why he would go to such lengths, but surely you agree that it's an ingenious move. Middle-aged bachelors with serious dispositions can be unpredictable. Morrison's unwavering belief in this story frustrated me. While he knew Chris better than I did, as co-executor of the estate, I argued we should publish it strictly as fiction. If people want to believe it, let them. Morrison countered that the notarial seal and the explicit instructions on the envelope were proof that Parker was serious. He wasn't the sort to fill a safe deposit box with nonsense. He reminded me that Parker had left a well-paying job in the United States to come to India with a lower salary and a less prestigious position, which, according to Morrison, supported the story's credibility. Parker didn't strike me as imaginative, but this story suggests otherwise. He was an outstanding fellow, diligent and down-to-earth.

He was the sole casualty in the Central of India's crash at Coomptah, ten days ago.

Knowing you have publisher connections who deal with such things, I've taken the liberty of sending you Parker's document, along with the envelope it was found in. You'll see the instructions on the envelope specify it was to be opened only upon Parker's death, either by his executors or by himself on June 21, 1931. If you can turn this material into something profitable, I'd truly appreciate it. Actually, with a bit of polishing, it might even make a good read as it is; I find it incredibly intriguing already. Let me know as soon as you can, old friend, what you think and how you'd like to proceed. Finding a publisher would mean a lot, as it was Chris's wish.

Your stubborn cousin, Bill Stennet

(Enclosed is Chris Parker's document, presented exactly as he wrote it. Per Mr. Stennet's request and to avoid causing undue distress among the superstitious, the public is advised that this story is almost certainly a work of fiction.)

September 18, 1923. 47 Victoria Drive, Rajput Gardens, Calcutta, India

TO WHOM IT MAY CONCERN:

Following the instructions filed with the officials at the Calcutta Traders' Bank, this document is to be read by my executors if I die before June 21, 1931, or by myself on that date in the presence of three bank officers. I will explain the reason for this as clearly as I can. While doing geological work in the United States, something happened that changed my life drastically, and by 1931, will change the lives of everyone on this planet. This statement may sound incredible and unbelievable, but it is the truth. This is why I am writing it, and why you are reading it.

I'm sharing this message with the public as a last-ditch effort to make sure it's taken seriously, even if just slightly. The contents of this document are so absurd that the method I'm using to share it is almost a necessity. I want people to read this, to believe it, and to act on it. If I had told anyone about my experience when it happened, my friends would have laughed at me. Insisting on its truth might have led to questions about my sanity, and I could have lost my job or worse, my freedom. It was completely out of the question to even think of telling anyone what I saw. I had no proof then, and I can't provide any now. Only time will prove me right, and that time is not later than August 21, 1931. There's a small chance the catastrophe could happen sooner, but with the knowledge I have, I'm convinced it will occur on that exact date.

You understand my predicament—a prophet predicting events years ahead to the very day, facing a skeptical world that adheres to the age-old standard of common sense. This is why I've taken precautions with this manuscript. Given the importance of this message to the world, I've deposited copies in major banks in Bombay and Madras. These documents are to be mailed to me on June 21, 1931, or if I am no longer alive, they can be retrieved by my executors at any time before that date. This way, I avoid almost eight years of ridicule, loss of employment, and possible confinement for mental instability. Meanwhile, my warning won't be lost and will reach the world in time to potentially do some good.

If I'm still around on June 21, 1931, I'll share my experience with the world, giving folks two months to avoid a terrible fate. Why I quit my job in the U.S. and moved to India will become clear in this tale. It all began in January 1923, when I had a life-altering encounter.

Back then, I was the chief geologist for the Southwestern Syndicate, overseeing the Arizona-New Mexico region. I'd been with them for nearly fifteen years, having joined after my time with the Concord Company, right after graduating from the Massachusetts Institute of Technology. Both companies held me in high regard, judging by the glowing references they gave me upon my resignation. They were reluctant to see me go. I bring this up not to boast, but to emphasize that my reputation for honesty and solid work has always preceded me. I need that trust now as I recount the absolute truth of what happened.

On January 14, 1923, my trusted field lieutenant, Olin Gilfillan—a sharp and dedicated man—and I set off from Lovington, New Mexico, on horseback. Our destination was the Mescalero Ridge. We had a couple of pack mules loaded with camping gear and provisions for a week. Our mission was to scout the southeastern part of the Ridge and report our findings back to the company. I won't go into the technical details of our route here, as my full report is filed in the company's Chicago office.

We left Lovington in the morning, taking our time and stopping occasionally to take bearings. By the time the sun had begun to set, we made camp in a small arroyo that led up to the Ridge. The day had been stunningly clear, and as the twilight deepened, I worked on my notes while Olin built a small fire from cedar and mesquite, preparing our evening meal of coffee and bacon.

After dinner, we lit our pipes and discussed a range of topics until around nine, when we slipped into our sleeping bags. Sleep didn't come easily for me, with thoughts of the trip's challenges swirling in my mind. I could hear Olin's steady breathing and envied his ability to sleep deeply under any conditions. A large, perfect full moon rose from the east, bathing our camp in cold light. Distant, whimsical yapping from a couple of coyotes drifted in, and I could hear the horses shifting uneasily. Eventually, I dozed off, only to wake abruptly, perhaps due to a sound or a sense that something was wrong.

I sat up and saw the moon was now directly overhead. A quick glance at my watch showed it was almost one o'clock. Everything seemed calm. Olin was snoring peacefully, the coyotes had ceased their serenade, and only a faint breeze rustled the tops of the mesquite bushes. I looked over at the horses and saw they were unusually restless. Assuming a coyote might be prowling around the camp, I crawled out of my sleeping bag, grabbed my rifle, and approached the trembling horses, which were straining at their tethers. They were staring with wide, fearful eyes in the same direction.

Except for a large rock and a few scattered sotol plants, I saw nothing that could explain their fright. Thinking some animal might be hiding behind the rock, I circled around it cautiously. However, there was nothing there to justify the horses' terror. I walked over to them and gently stroked their noses, which seemed to calm them a bit, though they continued to fixate nervously on that rock.

Suddenly, it struck me like lightning—I hadn't seen that rock when we set up camp. Now fully awake, I remembered distinctly that there hadn't been any large rocks nearby. I rubbed my eyes and pinched myself, making sure I was truly awake. Could I have overlooked something so blatant? My job demands sharp observation skills, and it was ridiculous to think I could have missed a boulder, especially one as conspicuous as this. Yet there it was, glinting dully in the moonlight, seemingly anchored into the ground. But it wasn't there when we got here. Two geologists missing a rock that size? Impossible.

How on Earth did it get there? Who could have placed it while we were sleeping, and for what purpose? I saw no footprints around it, no signs of disturbance. It was clear it hadn't rolled from anywhere nearby. This rock wasn't there four hours ago; it hadn't been carried, and certainly hadn't rolled.

In all my travels to remote, desolate places, I've never known fear. I've been shot at by Mexican bandits, held up by criminals, even bitten by a rattlesnake, and none of it scared me. Not even the intense shellfire on the Western Front, where I served as an infantry captain in the 8th Division at the tail end of the war, made me aware of fear. I was once cited for bravery by the French government, but I don't take any pride in that. It's just the way I'm wired—I don't have "nerves." But now, this inexplicable appearance of a rock, the obvious fear it instilled in the horses...

My first instinct was to wake Olin and share this bizarre phenomenon with him.

It was an odd moment of hesitation that rooted me in place. What if I was wrong? What if, in my obsessive note-taking, I had simply overlooked the boulder? How Olin would mock me if I woke him over nothing but an innocent rock! He would never let me live it down. Yet, I was convinced it hadn't been there when we set up camp. Torn between investigating the mystery rock and waking Olin for his take on it, my decision was abruptly made for me. The rock flipped back, revealing itself as a camouflage for a hole in the ground.

Before I could shout, strong hands grabbed me from behind. A gag was forced into my mouth, and a blindfold was tightly secured over my eyes. My attempts to fight back were futile, my limbs held as if in a vice. A sickly sweet scent—possibly chloroform—was pressed against my nose. The last things I registered before darkness enveloped me were the terrified whinny of our horse and the pounding of its fleeing hooves. Not a sound from my captors.

After what seemed like an eternity, I slowly regained consciousness. A distant droning noise, like the murmur of an airplane engine, filtered through my foggy mind. For a disoriented moment, I thought I was back in my sleeping bag, shaken awake from a nightmare. But then the vivid memory of the camouflaged rock and the silent, forceful hands that took me away, along with the horse's frantic escape, came rushing back with nauseating clarity. Cautiously, I moved my arms and legs, relieved to find they were not bound.

There was no gag in my mouth, nor a blindfold over my eyes. Darkness cloaked everything, but I could feel the incline of the smooth, cold stone floor beneath me. Rising unsteadily, I extended my hands above my head, but no matter how far I stretched, my fingers touched nothing. Dropping to my knees, I crawled in every direction, feeling only the smooth, dry stone that made up the floor of my strange prison. I couldn't tell how large the room or cave was where my mysterious captors had abandoned me. The darkness was suffocating, like a heavy blanket pressing down from all sides.

Minutes of fruitless crawling passed, and I realized I must be in some vast chamber. Trying to find a wall or an exit was clearly pointless. My captors must have known that this oppressive blackness would effectively prevent any escape, which was undoubtedly why they hadn't bothered binding me. Nothing I could do would change my situation, so I decided the best course was to await developments with as much composure as I could muster. I lay flat on the stone floor and tried to make sense of my dire circumstances. The most plausible explanation seemed to be that I had been kidnapped by bandits, hidden away in some cavern, awaiting a ransom.

I wondered if Olin Gilfillan had been taken too. If so, why weren't we together? Hoping he was close by, I shouted his name. The only response was the eerie, mocking echo of my own voice reverberating around me. I listened intently. Silence. A heavy, brooding silence, made more intense by the vastness of the cavern and the relentless darkness, punctuated only by my own breathing.

I no longer heard the droning sound I'd noticed when I first came to. It must have been either a figment of my imagination or the lingering effects of the drug they'd forced me to inhale. Undoubtedly, I was alone in the pitch-black darkness. If this was a ransom situation, it was just a matter of time before someone brought me food and water.

There was the peculiar business of the rock camouflage. The outlaws had probably posted one of their own beneath it as a precaution in case something went awry. But what a complicated measure when simpler, equally effective methods were available. They'd placed it in a spot guaranteed to draw attention and provoke investigation. Even hiding it behind a sotol plant would have been more discreet than leaving it exposed. Could it have hidden the entrance to the cave I was now in?

Why hadn't Olin or I noticed anything peculiar when we set up camp? Perhaps these bandits had cleverly disguised it, using the false rock merely as a screen for their comings and goings. This might explain the sinking sensation I felt just before the drug knocked me out—I was likely lowered underground at that very point.

I was well aware of the countless caves in southeastern New Mexico. Even the mighty Carlsbad Cavern had numerous unexplored branching chambers. What better place for a kidnapping-for-ransom operation than a well-hidden entrance to an unknown cavern in such a rugged, scarcely traveled area? In many spots near Carlsbad Cavern, the roof had collapsed, leaving deep depressions in the ground; in fact, the natural entrance to Carlsbad lies in one of those depressions.

The more I thought about it, the more convinced I became that my captors had skillfully concealed a small entrance to their private cave. Our unfortunate choice to camp nearby had made us easy targets for their initial attempt.

How they managed to make the place look like ordinary flat ground, without a single footprint or sign of disturbance, baffled me completely. A group of them had seized me from behind, but how on earth did they cover their tracks? And where were they hiding that I didn't see them while scanning the area? They must have come from a distance and moved at lightning speed to capture me so smoothly. And having caught me so silently, why was I left alone with my thoughts, free to stumble and potentially break my neck in the darkness?

They were clearly trying to intimidate me, using the terror of the dark and solitude as their primary weapon. I resolved that no matter what, I wouldn't let them sense even a hint of fear in me. And I promised myself that once I broke free, I'd leave no stone unturned to track down this hideout and capture the entire gang, even if it took half of the United States Army. Why I haven't done this yet will soon become clear.

Just as I solidified my determination to stay brave, no matter their tactics, I became aware of an approaching presence. It was a faint rustling sound, like someone in loose robes and sandals coming toward me. The fact that this figure was moving steadily in the pitch blackness made my courage vanish into thin air.

What is fear, after all? We can brace ourselves to face known dangers or even unknown ones if they aren't totally unexpected. But when confronted suddenly by the unknown, especially cloaked in complete darkness, fear strikes us deeply. It's only natural. As the rustling sound grew louder, I let out an involuntary, sobbing moan and instinctively crawled in the opposite direction.

I found myself unable to move. I was paralyzed with an overwhelming, inexplicable fear. Nausea churned in my stomach, my teeth chattering as if I were freezing. I've always prided myself on my steady nerves; ordinary dangers never faze me. But this was far from ordinary, and the nerve-wracking trials I'd endured had set the stage for this peak of sheer terror. Right then, death—sudden and painless—seemed like an almost kind alternative.

Whatever it was, it stopped near me, and I could hear its faint breathing. I fought to control the chattering of my teeth and the trembling of my limbs. Inside, I cursed myself for calling out to Olin; that noise must have drawn the creature's attention. As I strained my eyes in the darkness, failing to see even the faintest glimmer of eyes, my terror-stricken mind latched onto the idea that it wasn't some beast nearby. It was likely one of my captors. But how had he found me, and from where?

My terror receded as quickly as it had come, leaving me shaking but with my mind alert, ready for whatever would come next, no matter how bizarre. A rustling sound close to my head, then I felt something touch my shoulder. It was a hand—bony, long-fingered, powerful. It gripped my shoulder and pulled me into a sitting position.

"Drink," said a voice near my ear. "Put your hands before your face, and take the bowl that is offered to you." The voice had a peculiar rasp, as if the speaker were struggling to articulate, each word drawn out in a harsh, guttural tone.

"What is it you're offering me to drink?" I asked my unseen visitor, summoning as much bravery as my voice could manage. "And why have I been brought here?"

The hand on my shoulder tightened, causing me to wince with pain.

Against my lips pressed the rough rim of an earthen bowl filled with a cold liquid.

"Drink!" the voice demanded again, its metallic rasp carrying an undeniable menace. "Struggling is useless; you can't see in the dark. Do as you're told, or I'll pin you down and make you drink it. The liquid won't harm you if that's what you're worried about."

The pain from his iron grip on my shoulder was overwhelming. Fighting an unknown, powerful adversary in pitch darkness was futile. I had no choice but to drink and hope he was telling the truth. The bowl was small, holding little more than a regular glass, and I gulped down the potion in large swallows. It tasted just like ordinary water.

"That's better," the voice said, removing the bowl and releasing my shoulder. "Now we can talk. Sit still. You can't escape, and I can see you perfectly."

I gasped in disbelief. Could he really see me in this oppressive blackness? He must be mad! Surely, I had been captured by a lunatic and brought to this underground cave for some nefarious purpose. My only hope was to humor him, use my wits, and wait for an opportunity to overpower him. He seemed to have a sixth sense, and I'd have to bide my time. But that voice—it wasn't human.

"I see you don't believe me," the peculiar voice continued, with a drawling tone. "You think no one can see in the dark. You think I'm lying, and that I'm crazy."

When I finish speaking, it might surprise you if you don't think you're the one losing your mind instead. Unlike you earthlings, we don't distinguish between light and dark. For us, light is merely a way to enhance what we already perceive, much like a magnifying glass would do for you. Light triggers certain nerves in us, similar to how your optic nerves work, amplifying the image we see. The stronger the light, the more prominent the image. As I look at you now, you appear as you normally would. We've lived and worked here for so long that we actually prefer darkness over light, even though our work occasionally requires it.

"Hold on a second," I interrupted, realizing I might be dealing with a dangerous lunatic. If I pretended to engage with his obsession, I might be able to stay on his good side. "You have to remember, I just got here and know nothing about you or your work. Where are the others you mentioned? Did you bring me here to help? I'm willing to do whatever I can."

"I doubt you'll be necessary after all," the voice replied. "I've been appointed to look after you until...well, until you're summoned. You'll meet the others in due time. Since you're naturally curious and your face shows confusion and disbelief at what I've said, I'll explain who and what I am so you can understand. First of all, I'm not a human being. Don't let that alarm you. Because you can't see me and I'm speaking in a language you understand, you think I must be insane. Soon enough, you'll see that I am telling the truth."

"Listen closely to what I'm saying so you'll be ready for what's to come."

"But if you're not human," I stammered, trying to sound calm despite my confusion, "What are you? You speak English fluently, and only humans can do that. Are you some kind of deity?" I asked, hoping to coax more information from him with a bit of flattery.

"Don't be foolish. Of course, I'm not a god," he replied, his tone dismissive. "But it's a fair question. You assume only humans can speak, which is true for inhabitants of Earth. My parents came from the planet you know as Venus about a hundred of your years ago, and I was born here, in this cavern!"

At this astounding revelation, I must have looked utterly incredulous because my unseen captor let out a deep, throaty laugh. "It's a pity you can't see yourself right now, Mr. Stanley Murdoch," he said, pronouncing my name with a curious accent. "You'd laugh too. We Venusians do have a sense of humor, you see. You're probably wondering how I know your name. From the notebook in your shirt pocket. You'd also like to know my name. It's Oomlag-Tharnar-Illnag, or Oomlag for short. You can call me that. Unfortunately, I can't let you see my face just yet. We always start with a little chat in the dark to make our intentions clear, and to help you brace for the sight of us and our activities."

"Are you saying other people have been taken here too?" I asked, shivering at the thought. "What do you want with us, with me, and what happens to your 'involuntary visitors'?"

Another gurgling laugh echoed in the darkness.

"Oh, we have a very specific purpose for you."

We wouldn't have brought you here unless your skills were valuable to us. We've only invited a select few individuals with superior intellect, like yourself, who are uniquely qualified to assist us in our... mission.

I was acutely aware of the dire situation I was in. Here I was, speaking in complete darkness with someone I believed to be insane, claiming he was from Venus. He suggested others were involved in some sinister plot in this cave, and that several other people were held captive for reasons I could only dread to imagine. The darkness and the brute strength of my captor were real disadvantages. Desperation set in, and I realized my best chance was to keep him talking. Maybe I could glean some useful information to aid my escape, or perhaps, by pretending to be eager to help, I could earn his trust and catch him off guard at the right moment.

"So," I said, trying to sound nonchalant, "you say your guests get to observe your work eventually, but you give them a little lecture here in the dark to prepare them for the 'shock.' Why would seeing you and your work be such a shock?"

"Not at all presumptuous," Oomlag replied. "But you need to understand why you're here first. Essentially, you are our servant, in the sense that you'll be compelled to stay underground with us for the next few years. But if you cooperate, you'll be treated well and allowed to move around freely. Once everything is fully explained, if you still refuse to help, I assure you, you'll soon change your mind."

"If you wouldn't interrupt, I'll give you a little talk, something you likely won't believe. But that doesn't matter."

You've all, being from Earth, been quite skeptical about what you consider impossible. But please, try to follow my explanation, and when you see our work in action, you'll be less inclined to think it's all a dream or that you've lost your mind.

"As I mentioned earlier, we come from the planet you call Venus. For centuries, we have reached a level of civilization far superior to yours, comparable to how your society has evolved from its earliest cave-dwellers. We've developed advanced scientific instruments and discovered forces that allow us to achieve things your scientists can barely imagine. You'll witness some of these marvels in due time. Our significant advancements have granted us the secret of interplanetary travel, which has come just in time to alleviate our overpopulation issues. Conveniently, your Earth is only about 10% larger than our home, and despite being almost half again as far from the sun, your atmosphere is actually better suited to us. It's cooler and more invigorating. While we were already energetic, here on Earth, we are paragons of vitality. After we conquer and eventually eliminate you, much like how your own superior tribes have overpowered the inferior ones, we will become the absolute rulers of both planets. With the knowledge we already possess and the discoveries we will make as we expand, I am confident that our population problems will be resolved for many centuries to come.

"Once we've solidified our control here, we plan to launch an expedition to the red planet you call Mars. We don't intend to settle there, as the conditions are not conducive to prolonged life for us, but we do aim to dismantle the Martian civilization and ensure they are no longer a threat to us."

Despite their inability to live comfortably on their planet, they can thrive on yours, making it imperative to neutralize them swiftly. Their civilization is extraordinarily advanced and could potentially surpass ours if given the chance. Regarding the larger planets like Saturn, Neptune, and Uranus, as well as our closer neighbor Mercury, they can be ignored. Some are inhabited by primitive, insect-like creatures, while others only support basic plant life. Moreover, their massive sizes make survival impossible for both our species and yours. I weigh a bit more here on Earth than I would on Venus, but the only effect is a sense of increased well-being. Those who have come here directly, like my parents, describe it as akin to a man gaining weight to reach optimal health; he feels stronger, and in fact, he becomes stronger.

The creature paused, and I could hear the faint rustling of his garments. Despite still suspecting I was dealing with a madman, I felt remarkably little fear. The throaty quality of his voice lent the words a peculiar accent that was occasionally difficult to decipher, yet his command of English was impeccable, indicating a superb education. Perhaps he was an astronomer who had lost his sanity from overwork, living underground and resourceful enough to emerge occasionally to procure food. His long familiarity with the subterranean environment undoubtedly explained his uncanny ability to navigate in the dark and sense my position. His rock camouflage was ingeniously crafted. Yes, I would prefer dealing with an intelligent individual fixated on a single idea over a nonsensical rambler. Could there be any truth to his claims of others working with him? Unlikely. He would probably later point out imaginary tunnels, genuinely believing in their existence. If I played my cards right, I might persuade him to show me the entrance he used to bring me here, and seize an opportunity to escape.

My face must have betrayed my growing curiosity and lack of fear, for Oomlag's next remark revealed as much.

"So, what do you say now, Stan-lee?" he asked, his clothes rustling like dry, crinkled leather. "Have I convinced you just how deeply you're in my power, and piqued your interest in the wonders I've described? Or do you still have questions about things I might have missed? Our Field General is waiting for a report—are you sufficiently enlightened? If you're ready, I can give the signal and we'll move forward. But if you're still worried about your safety, you have the right to ask more questions."

My mind was set. Under the circumstances, there was only one path to take: go with him and find out whether he was actually delusional. I just had to hope I wouldn't end up in some dark abyss.

"Sure, Oomlag," I replied, trying to sound eager. "Bring on your grand show! Tell your General I'm ready and that my services are at his disposal. I think I can handle any surprise now."

"You handled the darkness test better than most," Oomlag commented dryly. "Usually we have to do a lot of talking before we get close enough to touch. The fluid you drank was water with a mild drug to sharpen your mind. Since you're ready, I'll give the signal."

His clothes rustled again. About a minute passed, but nothing happened to pierce the pitch-black darkness or ease my heightened state of suspense.

"The Field General says to bring you in. Stand up, Stan-lee," Oomlag ordered, gripping my right elbow with his firm, powerful fingers. Once I was on my feet, he turned me halfway around and gave me a gentle nudge.

"Walk straight forward until I tell you to stop," he commanded, his gruff, guttural voice close to my ear. "And don't say a word."

"Don't say a word until I give the signal."

With my hands tentatively stretched out in front of me, I took a few hesitant steps into the dark.

"Walk naturally," Oomlag hissed, his voice almost lost in the vast expanse. There was no choice but to comply. The cave's floor sloped gently downward, and I half-expected to plummet into an abyss at any moment. I was entirely at the mercy of this enigmatic being, my mind bracing for the unknown. It reminded me of the tales of pirates forcing captives to walk the plank—the only difference here being the uncertainty of what lay ahead.

After what felt like an eternity of cautious steps, the ground leveled out. Oomlag trailed right behind me, his presence marked by the soft sounds of shuffling feet and the subtle rustle of fabric. He offered no further directions, leaving me to wonder whether I was heading the right way or being subtly guided by some unseen force. We walked for a good five minutes in the oppressive darkness before I detected a faint breath of warm air. At the same time, a high-pitched humming became noticeable, growing louder with every step.

Gradually, other noises emerged—the soft shuffle of footsteps and a hushed murmur that seemed to come from all directions, as if a gathering were nearby, whispering in secrecy. Suddenly, Oomlag's hand clamped down on my shoulder, halting me abruptly. He didn't speak, and we stood silently, his grip firm and insistent.

My senses were heightened, and I realized we were surrounded. Faint rustlings and whispers confirmed our company. Slowly, like the gradual illumination of a theater, the surrounding darkness began to yield to a dim light. Shadowy, towering figures appeared around us, along with the vague outlines of colossal white stalagmites. The light, emerging by imperceptible degrees, seemed to pour from countless octagonal crystals embedded in the cavern walls, each set at precise intervals, casting an otherworldly glow in the subterranean expanse.

Before me stood an imposing throne, seemingly carved from the very rock of the cavern walls, and on this unconventional seat sat a being of such bizarre appearance that it bordered on the unimaginable. Two towering stalagmites flanked the throne, and an array of unusual creatures congregated in the space between the rocky spires and beneath the throne. As my eyes settled on the Field General, whom Oomlag had mentioned, I felt a wave of nausea wash over me. This revelation confirmed that Oomlag was no raving lunatic; he was indeed one of an unstoppable force poised to seize control of our world.

The Field General was a hideous sight. Standing well over seven feet tall, his frame was made up of incredibly long, spindly arms and legs, with a chest that bulged unnaturally like that of a pouter pigeon. His head, oddly shaped like an ostrich egg, perched atop a stout, thick neck. This head was entirely bald, with parchment-like skin of an unsettling ochre yellow. His ears came to almost pointed tips, and his eyes, small and unnervingly close together, glowed with an intensity akin to a cat's in the dark. The nose was broad and flat, reminiscent of a pig's, while his mouth, grotesquely wide and thick-lipped, was made even more horrifying by a complete lack of a chin. When he spoke, his teeth resembled a nightmarish grin, the front four teeth filed to points, and the rest flattened, all in a disturbing shade of dark gray.

He wore a skintight dull green outfit, complemented by a brick-red jacket or vest that stretched over his enormous, round chest, making him look like a grotesque vegetable. His elongated feet were shod in flat sandals secured by thongs threaded through the ends of his peculiar garment. His fingers were all long and uniformly slender, constantly fidgeting with an object that rested on his lap—a strange, bassoon-like instrument, yet without a mouthpiece.

The lights had reached their full intensity, making the vast room seem bathed in an otherworldly, bright moonlight. All around me stood scores of these beings, who resembled the Field General on the throne, except they wore dull green jackets instead of brick-red ones. They stood perfectly still, their smoldering, beady eyes fixed on me with a stoic intensity. Oomlag stepped forward, saluting his commander with a sweeping motion of his right arm, then spoke in a strange, guttural language. The Field General evidently began questioning him about me, their conversation punctuated by frequent glances in my direction. Finally, Oomlag turned to address me.

"The Field General wants to ask you a few questions," he said, stepping aside. The Field General studied me intently for several moments, and I couldn't help but feel unnerved under the scrutiny of those calculating, almost feline, inhuman eyes. He was a living nightmare, his ochre lips revealing sharp front teeth with every word he struggled to utter in heavily-accented English.

"You work rock work?" he asked laboriously.

"Yes, sir," I replied, trying to steady my pounding heart. "I'm a geologist."

Oomlag interjected briefly, apparently explaining to the Field General what a geologist was.

"You know then what is r-r-radium?"

"Yes."

"You know what is bismuth?"

"Yes."

"You know any in between?"

"What do you mean by that, sir?" I questioned. The Field General exchanged a few rapid words with Oomlag, who then clarified for me: "He means, do you know of any element with an atomic weight between bismuth and radium?"

"Sure, those elements are roughly masses 208 and 225 when starting with 16 for oxygen. I assure you, if you can identify any element that fits there, you will be generously rewarded."

"No new discoveries that I'm aware of," I answered.

"That's all," the Field General replied sharply, adding something to Oomlag in his native tongue. A high-pitched hum filled the air as the lights dimmed slightly. The creatures around us, who had been stoically listening, broke into small groups of four or five and departed in different directions.

We stood in a large room, the Field General's executive chamber, from which four tunnels branched out. Each tunnel was about twenty feet high and equally wide, lit by octagonal globes set in niches at intervals. Oomlag motioned for me to walk down one of the tunnels, striding beside me like a character from a surreal parade.

As we moved away from the central chamber, I noticed large curtains hanging at regular intervals on either side. They were made of material similar to the creatures' jackets, both in color and texture.

"These curtains," Oomlag explained, like a tour guide, "conceal the doors to our living quarters. Our lifestyle is quite similar to yours; we breathe, eat, need shelter, mate, and are social beings. I can't show you the apartments themselves, but I can tell you this: they are carved from solid rock, just like these tunnels, with machines we brought from Venus. Since you'll likely spend several years here with us, this initial tour and explanation are essential before you're assigned your own quarters."

"By the way, Stan-lee, I almost forgot you're from Earth. You probably feel hunger more often than we do. Would you like some food or drink? The dining room for our reluctant guests isn't far, and I can take you there before we continue. What do you think?"

Ever since I got here, I had been anxious to find out where my fellow prisoners might be. So far, I had seen no one but these monstrous Venusians, and this seemed like a chance to encounter some other unfortunate humans held captive.

"Yes, I'm quite hungry, Oomlag," I lied, "and I was just about to ask if I could get something to eat."

"Follow me."

I followed Oomlag through the main tunnel for about a quarter of a mile until we reached a smaller passage branching off to the right. We walked a hundred paces down this path before being stopped by the usual dull-green curtains. Oomlag reached under his jacket, and with a rustling sound, the curtains parted, revealing doors that looked like massive cement blocks. These doors slid silently into the tunnel walls. We entered a chamber about a hundred feet square and fifteen feet high, furnished with a dozen large, round tables made of smooth rock and smaller rock stools to serve as chairs. Octagonal crystal lights hung over each table and in the corners of the room, casting cold, intense rays. Behind us, the enormous doors closed seamlessly.

Oomlag and I seated ourselves at one of these rock tables. Once more, he reached under his jacket, and there was that rustling sound again. I was about to ask him what kind of signals he was sending with this mysterious gesture when a panel in the rock wall at the room's far end slid back. A girl carrying a tray stepped out.

I couldn't help but be deeply intrigued by the first fellow human I had encountered among the efficient yet terrifying Venusians. Was it sympathy for our shared captivity that made me find her beautiful? She had a distinctly Spanish look, with her long black hair neatly parted in the middle and cascading in gleaming braids on either side of her delicate, expressive face. Her dress, made from the same ubiquitous material worn by all here, fell nearly to her ankles, giving her a grace and dignity that belied her small stature. She approached our table with a silent elegance, setting down the dishes from her tray. As she leaned over, our eyes met, and the despair in her large brown eyes pierced me to my core. A tear traced down her cheek, which she wiped away with a slender hand before retreating through the silently closing rock panel.

"That," Oomlag said, arranging the dishes before me with a disturbing sense of satisfaction, "is one of our most valuable captives. She has been here for almost five years and has taught us both Spanish and English. She is from a small town in Arizona. I must remind you, you are not allowed to communicate with any of your fellow captives. Doing so will result in severe consequences. You think she's pretty, don't you?"

Rage simmered within me. This grotesque, smirking alien was my master, for now, and any protest or defiance on my part would only make things worse.

"Oh, she's not that remarkable," I replied, feigning disinterest. "She's too pale, for one thing. Tell me, Oomlag, what's this meal you've arranged for me? How do you grow anything fit to eat down here? What's this soup made of?"

Before me, in hollow stone dishes, was a meal consisting of hot soup, vegetables, and bread.

The only eating utensil was a large spoon made of some sort of fiber.

"While you eat," said Oomlag, stretching out his long legs and adjusting his jacket, "I'll try to explain some things to you. Before I can answer your questions, we need to cover a few basics. How's the soup?"

I took a sip and found it surprisingly tasty, reminiscent of mock turtle soup. I told him it was quite good.

"Glad to hear it. It's made from a blend of crushed yucca roots and prairie dog bones, following our special recipe."

I made a face and set the spoon down.

"Ah, now your imagination is turning against the soup," Oomlag said with a grotesque grin, his yellow lips revealing sharp teeth. "It's fascinating how you humans let your imagination dictate your preferences. Before knowing the ingredients, you found the soup delicious. Now that you know what's in it, you suddenly dislike it, despite just saying it was good. You'd better get used to it, because you'll be having it every day. The vegetables—well, I should start from the beginning. Not bad bread, is it?"

"To start, as I mentioned, we're from Venus. Our scientists have spent centuries perfecting an interplanetary spacecraft. We've had the power for ages, but the challenge was calculating the relative positions of our planets, the gravitational pulls from the sun, Venus, and Earth, the flight time, and the logistics of provisioning and ventilating the craft. We also needed a mechanism to detect and repel meteorites, among countless other critical factors. All of this data was meticulously passed down through generations until we had every detail ironed out.

"You've probably been wondering why the Field General interrogated you about bismuth and radium."

He was swamped with responsibilities overseeing operations here, so he only had a limited grasp of your languages. Yet, he felt it was important to ask you this particular question himself. You see, we have an element roughly halfway between bismuth and radium on the atomic scale that provides us with unlimited power by breaking down its atoms. We're aware that this element exists on Earth, and the Field General thought you might know about its discovery. However, that's just a side note and not the main reason we've brought you here.

"Once we learned how to harness this element, our planet was abundantly supplied with light and power. These lights you see are actually powered by radio waves from several plants throughout our systems. Each 'dynamo,' if I can call it that, generates a potent radio wave that's captured and utilized by these crystals. The crystals grow larger the farther they are from the power source because they need more filament to catch the waves over a greater distance.

"A fortunate yet tragic discovery by one of our scientists uncovered that combining this element with another in specific proportions could generate a wave that repels anything in its path. That was the start of our centuries-long quest to build an interplanetary machine. The principle is simple: if the wave generated by these two elements can repel anything, then by carefully controlling and modulating the wave's intensity, we can create enough force to push us away from Venus and toward Earth. Auxiliary rays would repel any stray meteorites, and trust me, there are plenty. But the calculations were exhaustive! Nothing could be left to chance. The finest minds among our people worked tirelessly until every detail was perfect.

"I doubt it would be much use to try to explain to you the detailed workings of the interplanetary machine, given that you're unfamiliar with the element that makes all of this possible."

Each of the two combining elements is kept in a fine powder form in separate containers, as resistant to their effects as lead is to X-rays. The precise amounts required are carefully released into a tubular apparatus, separated by a thin sheet of negative metal. This sheet is then withdrawn using a specialized device. The power wave generated by the resulting combination is meticulously calculated, and the charge is refreshed in another tube at just the right moment. We always have a battery of auxiliary tubes ready for any unexpected occurrences.

"My parents told me the launch was incredibly exciting. Thousands of my fellow Venusians crowded as close as they could to catch a final glimpse of the travelers. At the exact moment, the spacecraft slowly ascended into the sky, gradually accelerating as it left the stratosphere and entered outer space. It gained speed rapidly, with its meteorite detector working hard to identify and repel potential threats, and its tubes absorbing larger amounts of the precious elements. You can imagine the speed they achieved when I tell you it took exactly six Earth months for my people to reach your planet."

"Sorry to interrupt," I said, chewing on a piece of bread that tasted like a dry waffle, "but how did you know where you were going to land? What if you had ended up in the ocean, or in the middle of a populated area? How did you manage to land here in New Mexico?"

"That's thanks to the atomic telescope, an invention of my great-great-grandfather. Using an element similar to radium, we coat a sensitive plate with a specific mixture containing a large proportion of this element. For simplicity, let's call this element 'Venusite.' Although that's not what we call it, the name is more descriptive and makes it easier for you to understand."

The telescope stretches out to an astonishing length, equipped with an array of high-precision, delicate reflectors. These reflectors are so refined that when the telescope is aimed at a specific point, it captures an image from Earth, 30 million miles away, on an incredibly tiny section of a sensitive plate. This plate undergoes a treatment with a special agent that causes the atoms in the "Venusite" to disassemble, projecting an enlarged image onto a screen. By rapidly exposing different parts of this plate, we generate a sequence of images. This method allowed us to conduct a thorough exploration of Earth's surface, confirming that not only could we survive there, but we could thrive even more than on our own planet. We noticed this region was almost deserted and had vast caverns ideal for our habitats. All that remained was to calculate the exact timing for our departure to make a precise landing. However, a minor mistake landed us a few hundred miles west of our target, but adept manipulation of the "Venusite" enabled my people to land near the entrance of a massive limestone cave. The rest was straightforward.

During the latter part of our conversation, I observed Oomlag reaching under his jacket several times, producing the curious rustling sounds I had heard earlier. I inquired about what he was doing.

"Oh, this is our portable wireless device, which lets us communicate with anyone else within the network."

He unbuttoned his jacket, revealing a contraption about 18 inches square at the base, with a dome-like top, all suspended from his shoulders and supported by a strap around his waist. That explained the peculiar, puffed-out appearance of these people. Several half-inch wide slits radiated from the center of the dome, and from these slits, rapid flashes of light streamed out. Various knobs and buttons protruded from all sides of the square base, and Oomlag deftly manipulated them with his long, slender yellow fingers.

As each button was pressed, it emitted a soft, crackling sound.

"This wireless device," Oomlag explained, pressing another button that made the tiny sparks stop, "is quite simple. The case is made from a metal that's much lighter than your aluminum, and it contains a specific quantity of our essential 'Venusite' in containers that are immune to its effects. These buttons on the right release different amounts of 'Venusite,' which emit a energy wave with an intensity based on the mixture. Other buttons cut off the wave, allowing us to send coded messages easily. The buttons on the left are used to tune into incoming messages. Important messages are assigned to a particular wavelength, managed by a specific button that's always engaged; other messages merely vibrate. Since every individual has their own code call, we ignore other messages unless our code is detected. The vibration of the device against our chest is all we need to understand incoming communications. You'd be amazed at how subtle these vibrations are. If you were wearing the device, you probably wouldn't notice them at all."

By this time, I had finished my meal, which I must admit, I enjoyed thoroughly. I hadn't dared to ask Oomlag about the vegetables after discovering what the soup was made of. They tasted like cauliflower and artichoke. Seeing that I had finished, Oomlag operated a button on his wireless set, and within moments the girl appeared to clear the dishes. I watched her closely. She had been crying, as her eyes were red and swollen. As she leaned past me to pick up the soup dish, one of her soft, dark braids brushed my cheek and fell into my lap. She quickly reached down to toss the errant braid over her shoulder, and as her small hand hovered briefly over mine, I felt a tiny pellet of paper drop into my open palm. Taking advantage of the fact that she was momentarily blocking Oomlag's view, I slipped the paper into my pocket.

She quietly stacked the empty dishes onto her tray and, without glancing in my direction, swiftly exited the room through the stone-paneled door. Oomlag had buttoned his jacket and regarded me with an expression of smug amusement.

"You humans think you're so advanced," he sneered, his lips curling back into a disconcerting grimace. "Yet you're at the mercy of every tiny germ. You kill each other over the smallest grievances. The forces you understand, you can't even control adequately. What perfect, ignorant slaves you'll make for us."

He leaned closer, his cold, glittering eyes devoid of pupils, inches from mine.

"August 21, 1931. Remember that date. By then, our network of underground tunnels will be complete, our power bases established, and the charges of 'Venusite' in place and ready to detonate. Even now, we're working beneath your largest cities. On that date, 'Venusite' will unleash its destructive energy upwards, and the heart of your cities will be reduced to rubble. Amidst this chaos, our commanders will rise and take control. Anyone who resists will be obliterated by 'Venusite' guns. Nothing on your world can oppose us, and the path to our dominion will be clear. You'll be our slaves, tasked with preparing a specific alloy of metals that are common here but rare on Venus. Soon, we'll have sent enough back to Venus to bring thousands more of us here. It's only a matter of time before we replace your entire race. It's the law of nature."

He paused, his face radiating fiendish self-satisfaction. His dreadful words filled me with dread, but I forced myself to appear calm, displaying the scientific detachment expected in my line of work.

"If you're so powerful and intelligent," I began boldly, "why have you been hiding underground all these years?"

"Why didn't you just stay on the surface and sweep away all opposition instead of messing around with these tunnels and explosives you mentioned? Honestly, I think this Venusite of yours is a lot of hype. Sure, it's powerful, but not enough to pull off everything you're claiming. Making a network of tunnels in a few years? Impossible."

I paused to catch my breath. Oomlag was busy adjusting his wireless device, a sardonic grin on his face.

"Prove it!" I demanded. "We humans pride ourselves on our logic. It isn't logical that you could accomplish all these things. You're here, fighting desperately for a foothold on our world, yet you hide underground. Why? Because you barely made it here. Now, you're stuck with no way to retreat or move forward. You're—"

I cut myself off, caught by the malevolent look in Oomlag's eyes. He had stopped fiddling with his wireless, the grin replaced by cold hatred. He leaned in, and for a moment, I feared he was going to strangle me. Realizing I had pushed too far, I braced for his hands around my throat. But then, his ochre lips parted, revealing pointed teeth, and he threw back his head with a guttural laugh.

"Your sense of logic! It's good that your remarks amused me, or I might have choked you unconscious right here." His fingers drummed lightly on the table.

"Let me warn you, human. Never speak to me or any other of my kind in that manner again. We lose our tempers easily, especially when a slave dares to speak to a master as you have. But you're new here; I'll overlook it this time.

"A fine sense of logic you humans boast about!"

"Given all you've witnessed and everything you know, did you really think we were out of options? Do you honestly believe we'd come all this way only to find ourselves stranded here or unable to defend ourselves? We've got enough Venusite to keep our operations running for another twenty years, take down any pathetic resistance you might mount, and send this projectile back to Venus with enough alloy to build hundreds more. You're such a fool, you pitiful Earthling! And among your kind, you're considered wise!"

I was too relieved that his shift in mood had saved me from the fallout of my careless comments to feel any anger at his assessment of my intelligence. I managed a weak smile and stayed silent. Oomlag got to his feet.

"Come with me," he said curtly. "We've wasted enough time already. I had planned to show you something else first, but now I'll give you a look at our space projectile. There's something else I want to demonstrate to you, and then you'll be assigned quarters. We'll explain your duties later."

The doors slid open once more, and we found ourselves back in the vast hallway. We continued down it for about half a mile, passing many Venusians scurrying back and forth, appearing and disappearing behind curtains on either side. They all looked at me with curiosity, but without hostility. The absence of chatter surprised me. Many of them had their communication devices buzzing, yet no one spoke to each other or to Oomlag. I guessed this hallway was the main residential area and the beings we encountered were off duty. We stopped before a large curtain covering a significant section of the left wall. Oomlag sent a short signal with his device, and the curtain parted. The familiar stone doors slid open quietly, revealing a vast, brilliantly lit room. The light was so intense compared to the hallway that it took several seconds for my eyes to adjust to the glare.

As I stood there, my eyes adjusting to the brightness, Oomlag exchanged a few whispered words with an enormous Venusian, who held two long, cylindrical devices identical to the one the Field General had been handling. The dazzling light grew less blinding as I took in the breathtaking details of the cavernous chamber. The space spanned at least five hundred feet and was perfectly circular, clearly carved out of a natural cave, given the countless stalactites that glittered hundreds of feet above. Around the periphery of the room, at regular intervals of about ten feet, were spherical objects roughly the size of basketballs. Dominating the very center of this colossal chamber stood a massive, octagonal structure with a rounded top—I recognized it immediately as the interplanetary projectile. Oomlag laid a hand on my shoulder.

"Stan-lee," he said, his grin sinister, "you now have the honor of inspecting the pinnacle of our technology—the spacecraft that brought us from Venus to your Earth. What I'm about to show you might confound your understanding, but it will give you a glimpse of our power. This vessel now serves as our central power plant. Notice the tubes protruding from its sides? Half of them supply energy to those circular transformers, which then transmit invisible power to lights in the various rooms and corridors nearby. Other power stations are distributed throughout the complex, providing the workers with the illumination that boosts their efficiency and the power needed to drill new tunnels. You'd be amazed at the number of your major cities that are already undermined and prepped for when we strike. I told you when that would be: August 21, 1931. On that day, our kin on Venus will keenly observe Earth and witness the synchronous detonations. They will see us emerge; but that's enough for now! Come, let me show you the interior of this machine."

As we approached the enormous contraption, I found myself in awe of the smoothness and symmetry of its surface.

It stood at least eighty feet tall and thirty feet wide, a nearly perfect octagon up to about fifteen feet from the top, where it rounded into a dome. The construction material resembled polished gunmetal, sleek and imposing. Emerging from its sides at regular intervals were clusters of short tubes, which Oomlag identified as the power tubes—these were the only interruptions on the shiny surface. I couldn't help but wonder how we would gain entry.

That question quickly found its answer. The large Venusian who had let us into the room, evidently the sole guardian of this crucial chamber and its essential machinery, stepped ahead and aimed one of the round objects he carried at the side of the craft. Instantly, two doors flew open, creating an entry about four feet wide and six feet high. Stooping, Oomlag entered, and I followed closely behind him. Without a sound, the doors sealed behind us.

I was finally inside the extraordinary space flyer that had transported this wave of fearsome, super-intelligent beings to claim our vulnerable Earth! Barely able to suppress my excitement and curiosity, I scanned our surroundings. We were in a brilliantly lit octagonal chamber about twenty-five feet across, with a metallic ceiling twelve feet above. A circular opening about six feet in diameter pierced the center of the ceiling, through which extended a round, vertical shaft like a fire station's slide pole. Against the walls stood tall metal devices, reminiscent of elongated hourglasses, stretching from floor to ceiling. The neck of each was adorned with an intricate array of valves and pipes, and from the base of each "hourglass," numerous small tubes extended towards the walls.

Though there was no sound, a faint vibration coursed through me, hinting at the immense power at work within this marvel of a machine.

At the base of the pole in the center was a round platform. I watched as it slid noiselessly up the pole, only to descend moments later with a couple of Venusians. After giving me a curious look, they turned their attention to the machinery, inspecting dials and moving various handles on the different valves. Oomlag stood nearby, watching me with a smug expression, clearly amused by my wide-eyed astonishment.

"Yes, I thought you'd be entertained by this little visit," he chuckled. "Behold the pinnacle of our innovation. By simply adjusting the amount of 'Venusite' in what you might call the condensing tubes, we control the generated power. You already understand the power of 'Venusite'—it brought us from our planet to yours. Just imagine, then, how minute quantities are needed to supply energy here.

"These tubes extending from the base of the generators carry concentrated power impulses to the conduits you saw on the flyer. These, in turn, bombard the round objects placed near the room's walls, dispersing the power beams in various directions.

"The wall of this chamber is an inner partition, creating a vacuum that protects against the coldness of outer space. Before we go further, I need to show you the upper compartments of the flyer, where we store the reserve supply of 'Venusite' and house the living quarters for travelers. We also have a sophisticated system for preparing concentrated foods. The flyer's capacity...."

OOMLAG stopped midsentence. The projectile's door had swung open, and the burly Venusian guard strode in, interrupting Oomlag's explanation. He spoke a series of rapid, guttural words to my guide, keeping the door ajar. Oomlag scowled, clearly processing what he had just heard, then shot me a glowering, sidelong glance that sent a chill down my spine. Finally, he barked a curt reply to the guard and turned to face me.

I was relieved to see his face break into a grin, sinister and unsettling, yet a grin nonetheless.

"We need to step outside for a moment, Stanley," he said. "I have some news that should make you feel quite good."

Puzzled by what he could possibly mean, I trailed behind Oomlag and the guard as we stepped out of the flyer and into the blinding light of the cavern. As soon as the doors sealed shut behind us, Oomlag spoke.

"The Field General has ordered your release!"

I gasped in disbelief. Surely, there must be some mistake! Released, knowing what I did about their plans? Free to take action to thwart this threat?

"Stanley, I see you're skeptical. But it's true, you're to be released immediately." Oomlag stepped closer, a malicious glint in his eyes. "The Field General has a twisted sense of humor, just like the rest of us. It's our one weakness, really. He finds your presence here unnecessary, your services redundant. That leaves two options: either we kill you or let you go. He's chosen the latter. Personally, I'm disappointed; I've grown quite fond of you."

I was stunned. Like an idiot, I stammered, "But—but, you've shown me—how could you dare—"

"I know what you're thinking," Oomlag interrupted smoothly, mockingly. "You think that once you're free, you'll raise the alarm. How absurd! Firstly, no one would believe you; they'd think you were crazy. Secondly, even if they did, humanity could do nothing to stop us. We have the power of 'Venusite.' Need I say more? It's one of the best jokes I've ever heard! You'll be the only one on Earth who knows of our existence, and your knowledge will be worthless. You can do nothing, absolutely nothing. Your friends will find you, wandering aimlessly. Try to tell anyone, and well—they'll just think your mind's been wandering too."

His fiendish, guttural laughter filled the cavern, mocking me with this terrible truth. Then, abruptly, his demeanor shifted.

The sneer on his face turned into a grim mask of determination. He barked a few terse words in his native tongue, and suddenly, I felt hands grab me from behind. Oomlag's ochre face loomed inches from mine.

"Goodbye, Earth creature. You'll leave the same way you arrived!"

Once more, I was blindfolded and gagged, swiftly losing consciousness under the influence of that sickly-sweet drug.

The rest of the tale is simple. I woke up near the campsite, the sun high overhead. Dizzy and disoriented, I stumbled to the spot where the rock camouflage had been. It was gone—there was no sign of any disturbance, just unremarkable flat ground. I remembered the note from the dark-haired girl and fished it out from my pocket. Written hastily in charcoal, now barely readable, were the words:

"India is safe."

By the time the sun was setting, Olin appeared with a search party. I fumbled together an excuse, saying I had been restless, had taken a moonlit ride, and had been thrown from the horse. What else could I have said? It happened just as Oomlag had warned.

Now, in India, I pen these lines. The girl must have believed I had a chance to break free. My friends, I beg you, do not see me as another Jack Pansay with his phantom rickshaw. Olin knows I vanished, and I know what truly happened. If I am not around to read this document myself, for the sake of those who will believe, ensure its circulation. How wise Shakespeare was when he had Hamlet say, "There are more things in Heaven and Earth."

I can say no more.

THE END.

Armament

Bright chatter filled the air around her, masking the underlying tension with inconsequential noise. Shelia Davenport noted how the high-pitched voices danced around the real issues. What wasn't being said was what truly mattered. Emotions were never publicly displayed—it felt as indecent as undressing in front of strangers. Yet, this stoic façade was stretched to its limits. They attended these gatherings, played cards, and discussed dresses, children, and grocery bills as if there were no war, as if the Eglani didn't exist, as if those in the Navy would return as predictably as in the days of commercial flights. But no matter how hard they tried, the undercurrents of fear, grief, resignation, and hope were palpable. An unspoken belief lingered—that burying their feelings deeply enough might somehow lead to a happy ending.

Shelia's hands convulsed, cards cascading from her fingers to the floor as the high-pitched shriek of a spaceship's jets reached her ears. Conversations halted abruptly as every woman in the room stopped to listen, eyes involuntarily turning toward the ceiling. A large ship was approaching. The entire house trembled, resonating with the throbbing pulse of the spaceship's engines. The sound built to a crescendo and then cut off sharply, leaving an aching silence.

"I'm sorry, Anne," Shelia said, bending to pick up the scattered cards. "For a moment, I just couldn't help thinking—" She stopped, blushing.

"Don't apologize," Anne Vonn replied. "I know how you feel. I've felt that way more than once myself." Her gray eyes were wise, set in an elfin face. Shelia felt a rush of gratitude—Anne, with her piercing giggle and bright smile, possessed an understanding beyond her years.

Anne had a husband who was already a week overdue. She didn't permit herself the luxury of worry, and Shelia envied her for that. But then, Anne had been married for nearly four years. She was a seasoned veteran of a thousand nights spent waiting, not a newlywed of four months who had only seen her husband twice since their utterly mad and beautiful honeymoon. Those precious two weeks had been reluctantly given by the Navy. Being a Navy wife wasn't easy. The constant shriek of jet blasts that lowered ships to Earth or sent them hurtling into space was a familiar soundtrack. With each incoming craft, she wondered, "Is it his ship? Has he come home safely once more?" As the weeks passed, the question turned into a prayer: "Please, God, make this one his, make it his!"

This one wasn't Alton's ship. It couldn't be since he wasn't due back from patrol for another week. Until that week was over, there was no need to worry. Her reaction was just the involuntary twitch of overwrought nerves. The conversation around her resumed, the bright chatter desperately trying to hide the constant unspoken plea: "Please, oh please God, let this war end. Make this senseless killing stop. Turn the Eglani back to where they came from and let us return to the peaceful ways we know and love."

Shelia bitterly reflected that this prayer didn't stand a ghost of a chance of being answered. It seemed God favored the side with the biggest fleet and the best battle discipline, and the Confederation possessed neither. For centuries, humans had traveled the star lanes unchallenged. Intelligent races were seldom encountered, and those that were always had lower technology than the outward- sweeping hordes from Earth. They could be safely ignored, and their worlds bypassed. There were plenty of other worlds without intelligent life.

Colonies were planted. Civilizations were built. Wealth was produced, traded, and exploited. In time, a loosely organized Confederation emerged, a glorified Board of Trade that advised rather than governed.

As mankind continued to conquer one star system after another without resistance, the belief grew that the galaxy was theirs for the taking, gifted by the Creator who had graciously handed them the tools. And in some ways, that belief held truth. An uninterrupted expansion spanning centuries had lulled humanity into ignoring the few doomsayers among them. So, when humanity's ever- advancing front finally clashed with that of the Eglani, the initial response was disbelief, followed swiftly by panic, and then a grim resolve. But resolve alone wasn't enough. After a millennium of peaceful growth, humanity struggled desperately against a well-organized race of relentless conquerors.

The war was going badly. Even the official reports had ceased to refer to their shrinking territories in euphemisms like "strategic withdrawals" or "tactical regroupments." Now, they either failed to address the loss of another planet or simply published the new front lines without comment. What once was a minor dent in mankind's expansion had grown into a significant bulge, and then into an expanding dome that steadily consumed the worlds of the Confederation. Humanity's dominance in this sector of the galaxy was being systematically erased. In a little over five years, a hundred Confederation worlds had fallen to the Eglani as humanity retreated, trading precious space and countless lives for the crucial time needed to develop the weapons and strategies necessary to overcome the alien threat.

Shelia knew all this, but it felt distant, unimportant. What mattered to her was that her husband was out there on the front lines, fighting the Eglani. She wanted him home, driven by a possessive longing typical of her sex. She wanted to feel his arms around her and, later, in the quiet of their home, share with him what he had the right to know. She placed her cards down and ran her hands over her abdomen in a mix of protective and possessive gestures, a wry smile forming on her lips. She was contributing in her own way, just as Alton was with his brave fighting. Life was needed. Life had to be replaced.

A wailing shriek echoed from the sky above. Another ship had arrived. And Shelia was on her feet.

Her face lit up with excitement.

"It's Alton!" she exclaimed softly, her voice tinged with an unusual tenderness. "I'd recognize the sound of those engines anywhere in the galaxy." Then, gently, she fainted.

Moments after landing, Central Intelligence teams descended on the ship and crew like vultures on a carcass. For hours, the relentless interrogation continued. Only after the last tape was reviewed, the final instrument examined, and the crew of the "Dauntless" squeezed dry of information, did the questioning cease. Meticulous though the process was, the results were, predictably, a dead end — three strikes, three kills, two boardings, and nothing to show but Eglan corpses. As always, the aliens had been thorough, fighting until their last breath and leaving nothing of use behind for Central Research. Headless bodies told no tales.

Reluctantly, Intelligence released the officers and crew. The Eglan Enigma remained as unsolved as it was five years ago when the aliens had ambushed a Confederation exploration ship and sparked the war. But Commander Alton Davenport wasn't thinking about that; Shelia was waiting for him, and he'd already been held up too long.

A week spent on solid ground is rarely long enough, and this one, in particular, had felt especially brief, Davenport mused as he procured a ground car at fleet headquarters. Directing the driver to his quarters, he calculated that he had just over an hour before blastoff—barely enough time to collect his belongings and bid Shelia farewell for the fourth time.

He considered himself fortunate. The "Dauntless" required modifications and repairs, granting him a week planetside, the longest stretch of shore leave since his honeymoon. Though Shelia would undoubtedly frown upon his abrupt departure, she understood the life of a Navy wife and the commitments it entailed. She had accepted that reality even before they married, a decision that still amazed him, given his grim predictions of future trials and tribulations. But Shelia was no ordinary woman.

As he left the stern and imposing confines of Fleet Headquarters, he nearly smiled.

Honestly, it was a relief to get away from the stiff-faced officers whose professional demeanor only masked their gnawing anxiety. Davenport was thankful he wasn't in that high-strung group, that his worries were more straightforward—steering a ship through danger and making it back alive. As it was, leaving again was already tough, and without Shelia's constant social gatherings, it would be even harder. Her parties were the one flaw in her otherwise perfect personality. He could never understand how a sane, sensible woman like her could tolerate those noisy meet-ups where every single woman seemed to talk over one another. Yet, not only did Shelia handle them, she thrived on them three or four times a week.

His mood darkened as he spotted the line of ground cars outside his quarters. Their presence was clear. She hadn't expected him home this early, otherwise, she likely would've ensured no one was around. But now, he had to face this cacophony of chattering women. He sighed as he stepped out of his car, told the driver to wait, and trudged the few steps to his quarters. Amid the high-pitched voices, Anne Vonn's squeal cut through like a needle, stabbing at his ears as he stood in the narrow hallway, hesitating to go in but unwilling to leave.

He cringed inwardly. Sure, Anne had a reason to be exuberant; her husband had landed his severely damaged ship just yesterday and walked away from the wreckage. She had a right to burst with joy, but did it have to be in his house? Steeling his expression into a neutral mask, he walked into the living room, and with his entrance, the noise halted abruptly. A dozen pairs of eyes turned to him, and Anne Vonn broke the silence with, "I think we should go, ladies."

"We're not needed here right now." The room quickly emptied, leaving Shelia standing alone in front of Davenport. She was striking, with her pale face stark against the cascade of midnight blue hair. Davenport couldn't help but think she was stunning in her own unique way.

"Are you leaving again?" Shelia's voice cut through the silence. Davenport nodded. He often thought wives had a sixth sense.

"Admiral Koenig should just go jump off a cliff," she said angrily. "He has no right to keep sending you out. You've barely been home a week."

"That's twice as long as last time," Davenport replied, trying to soothe her. He admired her strength. No tears, no drama, just a hint of a smile. He realized he loved her even more for it. "If you have a problem with it, take it up with the Admiral," he teased.

"Not a chance," Shelia said. "The one time I met him, he scared me to death."

"Don't worry, it's just another mission to capture prisoners. The Research Institute needs a live Eglan."

"Don't they already have some? Ed Vonn brought back a few last trip."

"Those were civilians. The labs need military personnel this time. There's a lot of differences between Eglan soldiers and civilians that don't add up."

"Just like our own military and civilians," she pointed out.

Davenport chuckled. "Look, it's just a routine mission," he lied.

"Don't sugarcoat it for me," she said. "It's tough and dangerous."

"It's no worse than any other mission. Sure, they're all tough, but I'll be on a detached assignment, without a lot of other ships around to attract attention."

"I wish they'd leave us alone."

"So do I," he sighed.

"But these mule-eared Eglan militarists won't be satisfied until we show them who's boss."

"I guess so, but I don't like the thought of you out there."

"Someone has to do it," he said quietly. "Besides, I've always managed to come back. I'm getting better at it." He kissed her lightly on the tip of her nose.

"Just keep being good at it," she said. "I like having you around." With that, she kissed him, a fierce and hungry kiss that left him breathless. "Alright, sailor, there's something worth coming home to. Now, let's get your gear together."

Sheila followed him to the door. "I'm not going with you to the field this time," she said. "Last time was enough. I can't stand watching you disappear again. But I made you something to take along." She picked up a square, flat package from the top of the recorder and handed it to him.

"Another tape like the last one?" he asked.

"Not exactly like the last," she smiled, "but it's similar. You said you liked the other one."

"I did. It was nice hearing your voice. Believe it or not, I never got tired of it. It gets lonely out there."

"It gets lonely here too. Now, off with you before I'm tempted to keep you here for good." She kissed him, a soft, tender kiss, then pushed him gently away and stood by the door until his car disappeared around the corner on its way back to the Base. She sighed and turned back to the house. Now it was just a house, but for the past week, it had been a home. She wondered when, if ever, it would feel like a home again. It was already starting—the worry, the hidden fear, the agony of suspenseful waiting.

She jumped when the doorbell rang, and Anne Vonn's face appeared on the screen.

"I'm back," Anne announced as she stepped inside. "I thought you might need some company, and besides, I forgot something." She glanced at the recorder with a peculiar expression on her sharp features. "Funny," she said at last, "I didn't think anyone else really wanted it. I thought it might cheer Ed up. He's feeling down; he lost a lot of his crew."

"What do you mean?" Shelia asked, intrigued.

"That recording I made at the start of our gathering. I left it on top of the recorder, but now it's gone."

Shelia stifled a gasp, pressing her hand to her mouth. "Oh no!" her voice broke. Anne looked at her with curiosity.

"I gave it to Alton," Shelia admitted. "I thought it was the one I made for him."

"Well, he shouldn't mind. Your voice is on there too."

"You don't know Alton," Shelia said miserably.

Meanwhile, aboard the "Dauntless," slicing through Cth space in the middle blue spectrum, Captain Davenport replayed his last conversation with Admiral Koenig in his mind. The discussion hadn't been promising. Central Research was still adamant about capturing a live Eglan trooper. Despite the Navy's five years of futility, the mandate stood firm. It didn't require much insight to comprehend why Central wanted a captive. A live specimen could unlock countless mysteries about their alien adversaries.

But capturing one was a near-impossible feat. No soldier had ever succeeded. The Eglan civilians were of no interest; they were much like any peaceful human society. Davenport was baffled. How could such a gentle, civilized people breed a warrior caste that was so vehemently dedicated, so radically different? It couldn't just be the suicide devices implanted in their skulls. Their relentless will to fight, their total disregard for death, and their astounding discipline were enigmas he couldn't unravel. The dichotomy between their civilian and military personas was a riddle that haunted him.

The Eglan soldiers stood in stark contrast to their civilian counterparts, defying the common belief that a society imprints itself uniformly on all its members. There was no trace of the Eglan civilian in the Eglan warrior, and the difference was clear. Davenport shrugged. It was a matter beyond his immediate concern, except for the fact that he had to fight them. Humanity had long established that in one-on-one combat, they were equally matched with the Eglans. The trouble arose in larger battles, where the Eglans' superiority became undeniable, almost crushing. Some secret of their discipline or communication turned Eglan fleets into a unified, invincible force. Humanity needed to crack this code or face extinction, just like other civilizations that had been steamrolled by the alien advance. Davenport shrugged again. Humans might unravel the mystery, given enough time, but time was slipping away. Koenig warned that if they didn't find answers soon, humanity would hit a point of no return. Already, inner worlds were swamped with refugees. Industries were struggling to keep up with the relentless loss of ships and weapons while still meeting the needs of the people. Financial systems teetered on collapse, taxation was suffocating, and the public grew increasingly disenchanted with the war's progress.

"If the bureaucratic admirals had their way," Koenig had said bitterly, "we'd be finished already. But we can't hold out much longer. This stalling tactic is on the verge of collapsing. We're going to have to launch a counterattack against an enemy that outmaneuvers and out-fights us in large-scale battles, an enemy that knows a lot about us while we know next to nothing about them. We have to figure out how they operate."

And so, here he was again, chasing the elusive prospect of capturing an Eglan prisoner. He sighed, shrugged, and refocused on the rows of instruments that monitored the ship's every function. This leg of the journey was the easy part.

Even the hyper-efficient Eglani couldn't cover every inch of the nebulous frontier they had carved into Confederation space, allowing ships to cross the vaguely defined borders with relative ease. Yet, life aboard the "Dauntless" was neither simple nor leisurely. Under Captain Davenport's command, every moment was a relentless pursuit of perfection. Five years of battle-hardened experience had taught him that neither officers nor crew could ever afford to grow complacent with their ship's offensive and defensive systems. Constant drills and practice were their only hope against the unparalleled Eglan coordination. Each crew member understood that honing their skills meant a better chance of surviving—and returning home.

Davenport's keen eyes roamed over the control console, scanning the array of lights and dials indicating that the "Dauntless" was fully manned and operational, with every crew member at their designated post. Satisfied, he set up a tactical scenario on the board and called for his Executive Officer.

"Take the helm, Oley," he said as Lieutenant Olaf Pedersen settled into the chair beside him.

"A tough one you've left me," Pedersen remarked, his eyes already analyzing the complex scenario before him.

"I'll be in my quarters if you need me," Davenport responded, pushing off towards the hatch that led to his sanctuary. The luxury of privacy was one of the few privileges afforded to a ship commander, and Davenport intended to relish it. With the clock ticking down to their next engagement, these precious moments were his final chance to indulge in solitude and immerse himself in the voice recordings Sheila had left for him. He hoped her message would be uplifting, perhaps laced with the warmth of their shared affection. But regardless of its content, Sheila's voice would transport him, creating the brief yet comforting illusion that she was there with him.

He settled into his shock-couch, threaded the spool of tape into the playback, and flipped the switch. For a few seconds, the tape hummed through the guides. Then a blast of noise erupted from the speaker. Anne Vonn's piercing giggle. Laughter. High-pitched female voices at their most exasperating, creating a chaotic clatter with snippets of shrill phrases slicing through the noise, jarring his nerves. Davenport's howl of frustration could be heard throughout the forward part of the ship. He reached out angrily to turn off the playback, but hesitated. Shelia had given him this tape for a reason, and it was clear he was missing it. She wasn't one for practical jokes.

Gritting his teeth, he forced himself to endure the grating cacophony. It was like the quintessence of irritation, a nerve-wracking jangle akin to a dental drill grinding away at an infected molar. And then, he heard it. The background noise receded slightly, and amidst the disjointed chatter, Shelia's voice came through, clear and light, uttering the same banalities as the others. But something was wrong. Everything about it was wrong. Then it hit him. Beneath her voice, a pattern began to emerge, a pattern that wasn't light or trivial. It was a desperate attempt to hold on to the normalcy of everyday life, a deliberate avoidance of the war, the fear, and the worry.

Davenport realized, with a peculiar sense of surprise, that this was akin to the wardroom gatherings aboard the ship. The attitude was the same. There was no fundamental difference. He endured it until her voice faded into the background, then he turned off the playback. Shelia should have known he understood how she felt. This wasn't necessary. Feeling oddly cheated, he put the tape away in his locker and returned to the control room.

The "Dauntless" broke out of hyperspace, traveling just under Lume One, well within Eglan territory.

Davenport knew well that enemy detectors were top-notch, and jumping into normal space was always a gamble. Still, he had no choice but to emerge for targeting.

"Ready!" announced the gunnery officer. In a heartbeat, the "Dauntless" plunged back into normal space. The scan was swift—just ten seconds—and with some luck, their sudden appearance would go unnoticed long enough to catch the enemy off guard. At best, their advantage would be brief; at worst, they might stumble into an Eglan ambush. More likely, they'd have a scant twenty minutes to complete their mission and retreat into the relative safety of fourspace.

Ahead loomed a small planet, roughly two-thirds the size of Earth, radiating the telltale signatures of nuclear stockpiles and atomic machinery. Clearly, a substantial Eglan base supported by a sprawling industrial complex lay below. The Eglani tendency to concentrate their operations made them efficient but also vulnerable. It was a risk worth taking.

The cruiser burst into normal spacetime. Red lights flared across the control board as the gunnery officer launched a barrage of torpedoes at the Eglan base. These weren't just any torpedoes; each was fitted with a hyperspace converter, propelling them into the lower ranges of hyperspace. On target, they'd reemerge in normal space and detonate almost instantaneously. The ten-second calibration required was a gamble, but once dialed in, they could penetrate any fixed screen. Although ineffective against maneuvering ships, they were devastating against stationary targets like cities or bases. Eglan compartmentalized screening could mitigate damage, but if they were relying on a single hemisphere for protection, anything inside would face total annihilation.

The cruiser roared through the planet's upper atmosphere, air screaming around the hull. Jets thundered as it matched speed with the planet's rotation, ready to deploy its deadly payload.

Within minutes, the banshee-like screech faded, leaving the cruiser suspended motionless in the upper atmosphere. Behind them, an awe-inspiring mushroom cloud began to rise into the sky, signaling their destructive success.

"Scratch one Eglan base!" an exuberant voice from Fire Control celebrated.

"Cut the chatter. Silence below," Davenport commanded sharply.

"Airboat at 0025," a spotter called out, "it's flying low."

"Forward batteries, prepare to engage."

"Use a force rod," Davenport instructed. "I want that ship intact."

A pale lance of a paramagnetic beam shot through the atmosphere, connecting with the airboat. The immense power from the cruiser's generators tore the airship from its course, abruptly wrenching it upward. Instantly, jamming devices aboard the cruiser activated, filling the local space with a flood of interference.

"Quarter drive, vertical," Davenport ordered. The cruiser surged upward, dragging the airboat into the airless void where the beam's grip could intensify.

"Alright, boys, reel her in," the gunner's mate in the forward blister said over the intercom, his voice tinged with boredom. Moments later, the airboat's fragile hull clanged against the cruiser's armored exterior.

"Boarders, go!" Davenport ordered. The boarding squad, expertly trained for such missions, opened the airlocks, breeched the side of the airboat, and stormed inside. The Eglani, caught off-guard without spacesuits, were flung to the floor by the uncontrolled acceleration. Even as their air blasted away, a few attempted a desperate resistance. Space isn't instantly fatal, and by holding their breath, some managed to fire a few hand-blasters at the attackers. It was a futile effort. The beams pathetically flickered against the cruiser's heavy armor, and the return fire sliced through the packed cabin.

The living soon fell among the already mutilated dead, their heads momentarily outlined by tiny explosions. Davenport sighed as he observed the familiar carnage through the viewscreen. Another fruitless endeavor. He had expected this outcome. No one had yet captured a live Eglan soldier, and he doubted he'd be the first.

Lieutenant Fitzhugh, the young officer in charge, stepped up to the signalman's scanner and reported, "They're all dead, sir. No casualties on our side."

"Understood. Disengage and return," Davenport ordered. The signalman scanned the pile of headless, short-legged, long-bodied aliens. One still had its grotesque face intact, with a wide mouth, a prehensile proboscis, and mule-like ears, though the back of its head was blown away. The face, frozen in a macabre mask of terror, stared up at him with bulging eyes half-pushed from their deep sockets.

"Aye, sir." Lieutenant Fitzhugh turned away from the scanner, and one by one his men made their way back along the boarding line to the cruiser's airlock. The scanner flicked off as the signalman followed.

"Enemy on starboard beam," the talker's voice was barely audible over the din of alarms and a thunderous explosion. The starboard battery erupted in a simultaneous, devastating blast aimed at the Eglan cruiser that had suddenly appeared just five miles away. The Eglan reacted with inhuman speed, its primary screens flaring a moment before the broadside hit. But no shield could withstand the sheer megatons of energy unleashed upon it. Screen and ship both vanished in the ensuing inferno, reduced to glowing radioactive gas. The enormous fireball surged toward the "Dauntless," her automatic controls kicking in to yank her back into hyperspace.

Lieutenant Fitzhugh, still ten feet from the open airlock, saw the explosion and felt the ship's shudder. He knew he didn't have enough time. With desperate strength, he threw the object he carried toward the rapidly closing airlock just as the ship vanished and the searing fireball consumed him. He never had the chance to know if his aim had been true.

Davenport stared at the Eglan head Lockman Vornov was holding up to the viewplate. Vornov was speaking. "He was still outside when we jumped, sir, but he managed to throw this in through the airlock."

"It hit me on the leg, sir."

Davenport was familiar with the phrase "mixed emotions," but never had he felt it so acutely until now. The grief over Fitzhugh's death weighed heavily on him, yet it was offset by a wild hope—that maybe, just maybe, the head Fitzhugh had retrieved belonged to an Eglan soldier and not a civilian. Fitzhugh wouldn't have risked bringing it back unless he sensed its potential significance or had a good reason to believe it might be useful. And he wouldn't have fought so desperately to get it aboard the ship.

"Take that thing down to Doc Bonner," he commanded, "and let him know I'll be there in a minute."

Old Doc Bonner looked up with a practiced calm, his battle-earned nickname masking his relatively young age. "Should I prep it for analysis or preservation?" he asked.

"Analyze it. We can't risk an explosion on our way back. Get to work."

Bonner conceded, "If it hasn't blown up yet, it probably won't, but you're right. We can't be careless."

Davenport insisted. "No point in taking unnecessary risks. Plus, it could very well be a civilian head."

Bonner shook his head. "Not this one. It's military." He pointed to a faint white line at the base of the skull. "Right here— that's where the explosive charge is embedded. Better to be cautious."

Nodding, Davenport watched as Bonner lined up an array of gleaming instruments, switched on the visual recorder, and began his meticulous examination.

"Hmm, there's been some extensive cutting here," Bonner observed, inspecting the back of the head. "Poorly done sutures and a lot of fibrous tissue, but it's healed up fairly well." With measured precision, he made an incision.

"Oh-oh! Paydirt!"

"Hold on a second, let's trace where these leads go. If this were a human, it'd be connected to the spinal accessory nerve, but with this guy, who knows?" He adjusted the auto-camera, snapping a series of still shots. With long-jawed forceps, he probed the skull briefly and lifted out a tiny, translucent capsule with a fused, dark globule dangling below it. "Ah, there we are." He placed the capsule carefully in a cotton-lined pan. "You should get this down to engineering," he said. "This isn't my area of expertise. I'll wrap up this autopsy while you're gone. I might find something worth mentioning in the Medical Journal. By the way, that capsule was connected to the nerve via a micropore graft. I'm keeping that part for microdissection. It wouldn't be of much use to you."

Davenport took the pan and left the surgery. The Doc was right; the next part was his responsibility, not just the hunk of meat lying on the tray... Chief Engineer Sandoval accepted the pan gingerly. Placing it on a bench, he examined it with curiosity. "Hmm, a sealed unit," he remarked. "We'll X-ray it first and then decide our next move."

"Better disconnect that detonator, or it might blow your head off," Davenport advised.

"Don't tell me how to do my job, skipper," Sandoval grinned. "I was dealing with these things while you were still in short pants. You go back and manage the ship, and my team and I will figure out what's inside this thing."

Davenport grinned, slightly abashed. "Okay, Sandy, I'm heading back to the command center. Let me know when you find something."

"Will do."... Bonner reported nothing new about the brain. "It'll make for an interesting paper," he said, "but that's about it. Actually, I'd venture to say our brains are a bit more complex if convolutions are any indication of mental prowess. The Eglan brain is relatively simple in some ways."

"Sure, but the real game-changer here is the balance between brains and circuitry," Davenport said.

"You're talking way over my head," Davenport replied.

"By the way, has engineering reported anything about that device?"

"No update yet. I'll keep you posted if anything comes up." Davenport ended the intercom connection as Chief Sandoval walked in, his expression somber. Davenport looked at his face with curiosity. "What's the issue?"

"That's the problem—there isn't one. I've been kicking myself for not seeing it earlier. That gadget is just an advanced subetheric communicator. We used them before we developed the Lorcom system. There's an explosive charge, but the arming mechanism is burnt out. And that's all there is to it."

"Not quite," Davenport interjected. "There's a direct neural connection. That's why they can fight as a cohesive unit. A ship's commander would control his vessel like a brain with a hundred bodies, and he's probably linked to a squadron commander. What a system!" Davenport paused and turned the selector.

"Communications!" he said briskly.

"Yes, sir."

"Get in touch with Chief Engineer Sandoval, record his information, and send it to Prime."

"Can't do it, sir."

"What?"

"There's an interference blanket in Cth that's blocking all transmissions. I've been trying to raise Base for the past hour."

"When did this start? Why wasn't I informed immediately?"

"It began about an hour ago, and you were occupied. We've never encountered anything like this before, sir. I wanted to try a few more things before reporting."

"Okay, then. Break out the message torpedoes, record the data, and send them off."

"But—"

"That's an order, Lieutenant. Get moving."

"Aye, sir."

"Well, that's a new development," Davenport observed. "They've figured out our Lorcom system and now we're jammed."

Pedersen glanced up from the control board, a frown creasing his forehead. "This doesn't look good. They wouldn't block our comms unless they had another trick up their sleeve."

"They're planning to stop us, no doubt."

Davenport nodded. "I thought about that, but how?"

"Damned if I know, but they've got something in mind."

"Well, two can play at this jamming game. We'll handle the rest when it comes." Davenport dialed Sandoval. "Sandy," he said as the engineer's face appeared on the screen. "Can your team build an all-wave subetheric broadcaster?"

"Yes and no," Sandoval replied. "We can build it, but we don't have the components."

"How about modifying the Lorcom?"

"That wouldn't be too tough. But you can't be serious about—"

"How long would it take?"

"Minimum twenty hours. You realize it'll cut off our long-range communications."

"Fine, we'll lose them. They're useless anyway—we're being jammed. Now get started on the conversion, and shave off as much time as you can."

"Aye, sir."

Davenport was certain Sandoval's team worked like their lives depended on it. Just over twenty-two hours later, the Chief's gruff voice crackled over the intercom. "It's finished, sir," Sandoval said. "We're ready to go."

"Good," Davenport replied. "What's the output?"

"A kilowatt across the board."

"Hmm, not great. We won't cover much ground with that."

"You'll get through, but don't expect more than that. If you want to jam effectively, focus on the 1400 band. You can smother anything in that range."

"No. I want full coverage. I think the Eglans are lying in wait, and I want something that'll disrupt every one of them in range, not just part of them. If we confuse them enough, we can break through before they recover."

"What do you plan to use for this confusion?" Sandoval asked. A grin spread across Davenport's face. "We might put a signalman on the microphone and mix the latest Tri-World league scores with some double talk. Or we could have our linguist issue fake orders in Eglanese."

Sandoval grinned back. "Sneaky, isn't it? Using the engineers' tools against them."

To be honest, the music some of these new bands listen to would drive a saint out of Heaven."

Davenport laughed. "That's an interesting thought. Angelo Bordoni in the signal section has some pretty progressive recordings that would make your hair stand on end. We'll make him a DJ as soon as we have some Eglani to test it on."

"You won't have to wait long, sir," Pedersen said, turning his chair to face Davenport. "The detectors picked up a disturbance in C-green, about ten hours ahead. Looks like a couple of class one cruisers. Not ours."

"What's their trajectory?"

"They're moving along our path, but slightly below our speed."

Davenport leaned back thoughtfully. He glanced at Pedersen and nodded in approval.

"Battle Stations, condition two," Pedersen ordered. "Well, there are two of them out there to try your trick on."

"At least we have some advantage," Davenport said. "We're not too outnumbered."

Pedersen dismissed the jest with a shrug. "In your position, sir," he said, "I'd be tempted to run like hell."

"Sure, so would I. But where else could we get a better chance than this? If we're going to fight, we might as well take our chances here."

"You call two against one decent odds?"

"I'll tell you more once we analyze their drive patterns. If they're cruisers, we can outgun and outrun them. If they're battleships, they'll never catch us. Not even—"

"Objects register as enemy heavy cruisers," the talker interrupted. "Drive intensity point oh two above ours."

"Well," Pedersen said. "You were wrong about one thing. We're not going to outrun them."

"Looks that way," Davenport conceded. "They must be new models, probably the same kind that took down Ed Vonn's ship. But they can't be more heavily armed than we are."

"Maybe not, but there are still two of them," Pedersen remarked dryly. "I'd say that changes the situation."

"Naturally. We'll run for a while."

"I'm not taking my ship up against those odds unless I have to," Davenport declared, his voice edgy with determination. He activated the command circuit. "Initiate a one-eighty gyro turn," he commanded. "Execute!"

The "Dauntless" pivoted sharply, reversing its course through the warps of Cth space with extraordinary precision. In hyperspace, where inertia held no sway, the turn was instantaneous. With engines at maximum thrust, the "Dauntless" surged forward, putting as much distance as possible between them and their relentless pursuers. The enemy ships immediately adjusted their trajectory, continuing the chase through the harsh, blue-toned expanses of the upper Cth. Hours ticked by as the tension mounted, the gap between predator and prey gradually closing. On a sweeping arc that would eventually lead them back into Confederation-controlled territory, Davenport and Pedersen watched the persistent dots on the spotting tank inch closer.

"We're not going to make it," Davenport finally admitted, a hint of resignation in his voice. "They'll catch us before we reach the frontier."

"Great," Pedersen replied sarcastically. "One will pull ahead, matching our component and planting mines, while the other stays behind and above us, ready to strike if we try to escape. We're as good as snowballs in hell."

"It's not entirely hopeless," Davenport countered. "We have our weapons and the broadcaster. They won't see it coming. When we drop back into normal space and act like we're ready to fight, they'll bite."

"Absolutely, they will."

"And that's when they'll get a nasty surprise. Imagine wearing one of those fancy communicators and getting hit with Bordoni's progressive squirm the moment you break out."

"Not something I'd enjoy."

"Neither will they, I wager."

Davenport turned back to the intercom, his tone steely. "All hands, report to Battle Stations! Full armor. Condition one. Bordoni, prepare your recordings and stand by for my signal. Report when ready."

A cold knot of dread settled in his stomach as the reports began to come in. Thus far, Confederation ships had held a slight individual advantage over the alien vessels, a slender edge that just balanced out the Eglani's superior coordination. But these ships were faster than his, and what they might lack in firepower, they more than made up for in numbers. No reasonable captain would engage in a fight with such odds favoring the enemy.

But now, there was no avoiding it. Davenport shrugged. If his theory about the broadcaster was correct, they might stand a chance, albeit a very slim one. Sure, he knew the secret behind Eglan coordination, but disrupting it was another matter entirely. It was conceivable that his jamming attempt would barely register as a nuisance. If that happened, the secret of the Eglani would die with him. There was a faint hope that one of the message torpedoes might slip through, but fixed-course torpedoes were almost always intercepted and destroyed. At best, they were a desperate gesture, sent Earthward more in hope than expectation. And with the Lorcom converted into a subetheric broadcaster, exterior communications were out of the question. The

"Dauntless" was entirely on her own, her fate resting on the skill of her crew.

"Stand by for breakout," Davenport commanded. "Execute."

The ship pivoted smoothly, halting instantly before plummeting like a stone through the Cth layers as Sandoval cut the converters. The transition was seamless, and the "Dauntless" emerged into normal space without so much as a tremor.

"Full ahead," Davenport ordered. The familiar pull of acceleration gripped the crew. Sensors buzzed to life, screens flickered on standby, and the engines roared with a fierce blue glow that stood out starkly against the darkness of space. The "Dauntless" surged forward, speeding toward the distant frontier. Compared to the unimaginable velocities they had traveled in Cth, their current speed seemed like a snail's pace, but in normal spacetime, weapons worked, and subetheric communicators were functional. Here, combat was a practiced art, honed by years of discipline and training.

"Bearing zero two four, enemy cruiser. Range two thousand, closing," reported the talker. "Bearing one nine zero, nega cruiser. Range fifteen hundred, extending."

"Not too clever," Davenport observed. "That ship behind us will have to jump to get ahead, and by then, we'll get a clear shot at our long-eared friends up front."

"Bearing zero one eight, range one thousand, closing."

"Heading one-nine-zero negative," the communication officer interrupted.

"Our tail's gone back into Cth space," Pedersen noted.

"That buys us at least three minutes before they can get a fix on us again."

"Heading zero-one-six, range five hundred, closing in," the comms officer continued.

"All stations, prepare," Davenport instructed calmly. "Heading zero-one-six, steady, range four hundred, three hundred, two-fifty, two-twenty, two hundred, one-eighty," the officer's metallic voice resonated through the ship's tense silence.

"On my mark," Davenport said, his finger hovering over a large red button on the console. Across the intricate web of targeting and computing systems, electronic commands flowed to the gun and torpedo stations. Servomotors hummed, aligning the weapons precisely as the crew stood by, ready for any malfunctions.

"Heading zero-one-three, range fifty, closing in," the officer's impassive voice reported. Davenport pressed the button, and the "Dauntless" lurched violently as a torrent of firepower erupted from every available weapon, directed at the Eglan.

"Enemy has fired," the officer reported. The "Dauntless" swerved sharply under evasive maneuvers. For a split second, the Eglan hung in space, her shields flaring. Then she started to turn, but it was too late. The concentrated fury from the "Dauntless" broadsides slammed into her shields in a blaze of pyrotechnics. The Eglan staggered and spun off course. A heartbeat later, the "Dauntless" jolted as the Eglan's return fire struck. Secondary shields flared and collapsed. The primary shields crackled, glowing violet under the immense strain of dissipating the incoming energy.

"Holy George! What kind of armament are they packing?" Pedersen exclaimed, a trickle of blood running from his nose.

"No, we're evenly matched," Davenport replied as another broadside launched from the "Dauntless," sending another wave of destruction toward the Eglan.

"Enemy has fired," the officer reported again, as the "Dauntless" veered sharply to the side.

The salvo missed by a considerable margin this time.

"What's with them?" Pedersen asked, peering into the tank. "They aren't dodging."

"Maybe they can't. We hit them near their drives."

"They're moving way too slow!"

The "Dauntless" salvo struck, and for a brief moment, an intense flame illuminated the void. When it faded, the Eglan cruiser had vanished.

"Bearing zero four five, enemy cruiser range one hundred, closing," the talker's voice cut in. "Enemy has fired."

The "Dauntless" veered violently as Davenport hit the Cth switch. A familiar tremor shook the ship as it teetered at the edge of hyperspace. At the same time, a massive impact struck them from behind, wrenching crew members from their safety webs and slamming them with crushing force against the unyielding metallic plates and bulkheads. The "Dauntless" resonated like a gigantic gong, the sound slowly fading with shimmering reverberations that took on almost tangible forms as the harsh red glow of lower Cth enveloped them.

"Skipper!" the ship's intercom crackled. "We can't hold her here! Number three converter's torn loose, and there's a hole in the engine room big enough to drive a truck through!"

"Enemy cruiser Cth yellow dead ahead, dropping to our component," the talker announced.

"Well, we got one of them," Pedersen said. "Might as well brace ourselves. He'll be sowing mines soon."

"That Eglan was done for," Davenport replied. "The broadcast worked!"

"The second ship wasn't. They came at us like a hawk on a chicken," Pedersen retorted.

"They didn't have time to get the full effect."

"Are you going to give them another chance?"

"We'll have to. We can't stay here, can't run, and the broadcaster doesn't work up here. So, we go down again. With Bordoni's noise, we should knock their teeth in. Speaking of which, I need to check on him. The broadcaster's pretty close to the engine room." He tapped the intercom selector. "How's it going, Bordoni?" he asked. An anguished scream came through the speaker. "I was swapping out a platter when we got hit. I sat on them!"

"My Stan Kenton album! It's a classic, and now it's trashed! All of them!" Bordoni fumed.

"Bordoni!" shouted Davenport.

"Sir?"

"Calm down, son. We can't change it now. Do you have any back-ups?"

"No, sir."

"Can you sing, make some noise, anything?" Davenport asked, hopeful.

"Negative, sir. I've always had stage fright."

Davenport sighed. "Alright, you're dismissed. Report to your station."

"What now?" Pedersen inquired.

"We find another solution."

"What? Bordoni had the only squirm record on board. We went through the whole ship and there's nothing even remotely like it."

"The enemy has synchronized their components," the intercom crackled.

"Dim the lights to two shades," Davenport ordered. As the ship plunged into a deeper red hue, he added absently, "We can evade for a while, but they'll catch up eventually."

"Sir, engine room here. The converters can't handle this load much longer. We're riding a twenty percent overload!"

"They'll have to," Davenport snapped. "It's our only shot at staying alive!"

"I'll do my best to keep them running, boss," Sandoval's voice cut in.

"Thanks, Sandy," Davenport replied tersely. "Now about the noise problem..."

"Well," Pedersen began, "you could try doing it yourself. I recall you howling like a wounded wolf a few days ago, right before we hit that Eglan base. If it's noise you need, why not belt out a few war cries? You practically blew the roof off the ship last time."

Davenport's eyes widened. "You're onto something," he admitted. Flipping the selector to communications, he said, "George, can you rig a continuous tape playback into the broadcaster? Bordoni's smashed all his records."

"Sure. Give me ten minutes."

"Make it five, and send one of your crew up here. I've got a package for him." Davenport switched off and turned to Pedersen. "Get someone to fetch the roll of sound tape from my locker. Upper left compartment. Hand it over to George's man when he arrives." Seeing Pedersen's puzzled look, he grinned. "We're not finished yet, Oley."

"The enemy's synchronized their components," the intercom repeated.

"Dim to two shades and keep changing our course."

"Don't focus on any single course for more than ten seconds," Davenport instructed firmly.

"That gives us about four more dips before we break out," the pilot's voice crackled over the intercom. "And we can't keep dodging forever. He's more agile than us and can tail us right out of Cth."

"How long do we have?"

"Maybe five minutes, maybe less."

"Alright, let's get on with it. We can't linger here," Davenport said, staring grimly at the control panel, feeling the weight of helplessness.

"Aye, sir." The crimson hue on the display intensified slightly as the "Dauntless" descended closer to the breakout threshold.

"Damn, they're fast!" Davenport muttered under his breath.

"At this speed, we won't last long," Pedersen noted.

"We've got to try. Without getting that transmission rigged, we're out of options." Davenport fell silent. A minute ticked by, marked by the frantic evasive maneuvers of the "Dauntless" as the Eglan ship maneuvered with deadly precision.

"Enemy has synced trajectory," the talker announced. The "Dauntless" was suddenly enveloped in a murky red-black haze.

"Infra band approaching," Pedersen observed. "Our sensors are nearly useless in this spectrum. He could be right on us before we know it."

"Let's hope their sensors are equally challenged," Davenport replied, his mind half elsewhere.

"Enemy has synced trajectory," the talker repeated.

"Well, that's it then," Davenport conceded with reluctant admiration as the ship plunged into darkness, violently shuddering as it straddled the boundary between Cth and normal space. "He's practically sidelined us."

A violent jolt rocked the cruiser. Metal screamed and tore as the ship, struck by a mine at the fringe of Cth, was driven downwards into breakout. Blinding flashes and whirls of light burst before Davenport's eyes as the ship spiraled uncontrollably back into normal space. The talker's robotic tone jolted him back to awareness. "Enemy cruiser, range three-fifty steady."

Davenport swore softly at the monotone voice as a muffled explosion rocked the ship from midsection. The cruiser lurched sideways, unleashing a broadside. Davenport snapped to full consciousness. Beside him, Pedersen, his face a bloody mask, was still calmly managing the control board.

A chunk of his scalp had been torn away, dangling down his neck, mingling with the shattered ruins of his helmet.

"Take a break, Pete. I'm back. Patch up that scalp and grab a new helmet. You'll suffocate if they puncture the hull up here."

"I thought you had it, skipper," Pedersen said with a blood-streaked grin. "That last maneuver was a bit intense."

"What's going on?"

"I'm not sure. Our Eglan friend's been taking potshots from long range. He's not keen on getting closer. Came within three fifty and has been shadowing us ever since. Seems like he's waiting for backup."

"We can't let this drag on. What's our status?"

"Damage control says we're about eighty percent operational. They're working on the number three converter, but it'll take at least an hour. We've lost two secondary batteries, but the mains are fine, and our screens are fending off his attacks."

"Our drives?"

"Running okay, aside from the converter issue."

Davenport leaned over the plotting tank. "Full right turn," he commanded. "If he won't close in, we will."

"Skipper!" the intercom buzzed. "We've got that tape loaded. Ready to roll down here."

"Then get on with it," Davenport snapped. "Do I need to explain everything?"

"No, sir, but we thought—"

"Stop thinking and start that broadcast!"

"Yes, sir!"

"Eighty-five-degree right turn, down five," Davenport said. "Full drive, execute!" He bent over the tank, his eyes locked on the Eglan ship. The enemy's response was sluggish. "It's working," Davenport mumbled with satisfaction. Even a novice could see the alien's operations were off. His maneuvers were clumsy, his fire scattered, inaccurate. As the Dauntless's shells punctured his secondary screens, there were no evasive moves or reinforced defenses. Davenport's grin widened, predatory. A few more volleys and it would be over.

Suddenly, a violent impact threw the Dauntless sideways, and another sent her thrusting forward with an explosive surge of acceleration. Then, the drives cut out completely.

Propelled solely by its own momentum, the cruiser glided forward.

"We're done for, Captain." Sandoval's voice crackled with grim finality. "A torpedo hit us right on the drive lattice. The engines are kaput."

"Enemy cruiser approaching from behind," the lookout added. "Range: eighty and closing slowly."

The "Dauntless" floated lifelessly through the void. The faint hiss of leaking air and the clatter of booted feet were the only signs of life in the hull. Emergency lights flickered, but the drives and powerplant were gone—rendering the "Dauntless" unable to fight back. Captain Davenport stared blankly, perplexed by the ship's stubborn refusal to disintegrate in a fiery explosion, a fate typical for battle-scarred vessels. The guns were silent, every mine and torpedo spent. The intercom system was a tangled mess of dead circuits. A gaping hole, a foot across, marred the right side of the control room, exposing the blackness of space. One more shell, Davenport thought, and they'd be reduced to cosmic debris. But the final blow never came. The Eglan ship matched their speed, hovering just a hundred yards away, as a stunned communications officer reported, "Sir, they've opened a channel—they want to surrender!"

Davenport exchanged a bewildered glance with Pedersen. The shock on one man's face mirrored the other's disbelief. This was impossible! The Eglan cruiser was unscathed, while the "Dauntless" was a ruin. And yet, these aliens, who never surrendered, were offering to do just that.

"A trap?" Pedersen speculated.

"Why? They've got us. They know we're defenseless." Davenport turned to the intercom. "Tell them we accept. Instruct them to lower their shields and prepare to receive boarders." He looked back at Pedersen. "Any idea how we're set for a boarding party?"

Pedersen shook his head, his expression grim.

"I'm going to check it out." Davenport unfastened his safety harness and stood, wincing from the effort as he moved towards the manway leading aft to the main gun batteries and the drives. Carnage lay in his path. Bodies were strewn everywhere.

The sick bay had been obliterated by a direct hit. Guns and torpedo mounts lay in twisted ruin, interspersed with the bodies of the fallen. The communications center, by some stroke of luck, remained untouched, still operating on emergency power, still broadcasting incessantly over the all-wave transmitter as the endless tape looped through its guides. A hulking figure hunched over the transmitter, using a torch and welding rod to fix tie-downs that had snapped from the concussion. To his dull surprise, Davenport recognized Sandoval. The big man turned and gave a weak grin. Remarkably, he hadn't been seriously injured, though his battered armor showed several minor tears patched up with sealant. His helmet was dented, and the short-range communicator on its back had been blown away. Davenport shook his head as he approached and pressed his helmet against the engineer's.

Sandoval's voice came through, cracking slightly, "I've got what's left of my team working on the drive. Give us an hour, and we'll be moving again."

"Call them off, Sandy. There's no need. The Eglan has surrendered."

"They've what?"

"Surrendered. Quit. Given up. We've won!"

"You sure you're not in shock, skipper?"

"Just get your men together. We've got to form a boarding party from this mess somehow. We've got to gather the wounded and get them out of this wreck. Since the Eglan's still intact, we're going to take over their ship."

"But skipper, everybody knows the Eglani don't "

"Break it off, Sandy, and do as you're told. That's an order."

Shaking his head, the big man floated away as Davenport shrugged and turned upward toward the gun decks, navigating through torn and splintered metal, gathering survivors, and issuing orders similar to those he had given Sandoval. In the next twenty minutes, Davenport irrevocably shattered his carefully built reputation for compassion and humanity.

They assembled on the main deck, those who were left. The whole and the wounded, barely thirty men from a crew that had numbered over a hundred. They clustered together, staring at the vision screen that displayed a clear view of the alien vessel pulled up alongside.

The Eglan ship loomed in space, a dark, formidable presence with smooth, impenetrable sides, distinguished only by the bright circle of an open airlock. It didn't shimmer with the reflections of starlight; instead, it exuded a stillness profound enough to be almost terrifying as it drifted closer to the battered hull of the "Dauntless."

"Boarders away!" Davenport commanded, and the ragtag group of survivors, escorting the wounded, opened the airlock and launched themselves across the gap between the two ships. Davenport lingered until the last of his men vanished into the glow of the Eglan's airlock before making the jump himself. He blinked a few times, clearing mist from his eyes as he took a final look around the empty, silent remains of his ship. It wouldn't do for the men to think he was not only soft but also a crybaby. The Eglan vessel featured a double airlock, and as he stepped through the second seal, he was met by Olaf Pedersen, who had removed his helmet, a strange expression on his face.

"Well? What did you find?" Davenport asked, his voice edged with tension.

"She's all ours. There's no fight left in them," Pedersen replied, his voice strained. "We just moved in and took control. The men are rounding up the prisoners now, what's left of them." He gestured down the broad, low corridor leading into the ship's heart. "Control room's down that way."

"I know." Davenport glanced around with keen interest. The ship bore the typical features of other captured Eglan vessels he had seen. Even the two decapitated Eglani on the deck didn't surprise him, nor did the other dead enemies he passed en route to the control room. Their presence was to be expected on a captured Eglan ship. What unnerved him were the living: stern-faced, thick-bodied, rigidly standing aliens and their human captors who stood silently in the passageways, watching him pass. Davenport shuddered. He had never before encountered eyes so tormented and haunted as those of the Eglani gazing back at him.

The aliens seemed like they might crumble at the slightest touch, fragile shells held together by something stronger than sheer willpower.

"Gives you the creeps, doesn't it?" Pedersen murmured.

"It's worse than anything I've ever encountered," Davenport replied. "These people are on the brink of collapse. This is pure chaos!"

The sense of brittle tension grew as they stepped into the control room at the ship's core. A short, stout Eglan stood beside the master console. He raised his arm in a clear salute, which Davenport respectfully mirrored. A muscle in the Eglan's cheek twitched uncontrollably. His fingers were clenched, the knuckles pale against his greenish skin.

"I am Sar Lauton of the Eglan Directorate, the commander of this ship," the alien said in flawless Terran.

"And I am Commander Alton Davenport of the Confederation Navy," Davenport replied. "I've moved my men to this ship since you didn't leave much of mine intact."

"For that, I am sorry," the Eglan said solemnly. "You fought bravely and deserved a better end. However, you have still won. It's over." The Eglan smiled bitterly. "You see, Commander, we never realized war could be so horrific. For many of my crew, it was unbearable. You probably saw some of them on your way here."

Davenport nodded. "Now about the surrender terms," he began.

"There are no terms," the alien said flatly. "You have won." His face twitched again. "Can't you understand what your weapon has done? I am an Eglan. An Eglan never surrenders. Yet, I and half my crew have surrendered. Don't you grasp the implications of that?"

"Don't you see? The Directorate is finished. This victory is more complete than anything we've achieved in a thousand years of warfare."

"But..."

"From birth," the Eglan continued, ignoring the interruption, "we warriors have been taught there's no glory but in battle, that the Directorate's honor and its supremacy must be upheld, that it must expand to bring order to those less fortunate, that a superior's orders are to be obeyed without question. We are taught that it is only right to subordinate ourselves for the greater glory of the Eglan race, dedicating our minds and lives to this service. There is no higher honor, no greater glory than to die for the Eglani." He spoke as if reciting a creed that had lost its meaning.

"But this, I find, is a lie. Such a belief leads not to life, but to death—the death of the soul first, then the mind, and finally the body. Your weapon struck us at the core of our convictions, exploited our weakest link—a link we maintained because, paradoxically, it was our source of strength and unity. Through our neurocommunicators, your feelings, emotions, and beliefs clashed with ours. And yours prevailed because they were purer, more righteous than our own. You disarmed us. We were left bewildered, unable to maintain control. In the end, we couldn't even bring ourselves to kill—not even ourselves!" A muscle in his cheek twitched.

Davenport inhaled sharply. He suddenly understood, remembering his own reaction to hearing Shelia on that recording. But it had to be more than just Shelia. It was all of them, and somehow the Eglani had grasped the true significance behind that chaotic broadcast! And that meaning had shattered them! This act wasn't the end of the war, but it was certainly the beginning of the end.

The battle would continue, but now it wouldn't be humanity standing on the brink. The Eglani, too, would taste the sting of defeat. Davenport sighed. Oddly, he felt a bit of pity for them. They understood too well.

"Thank you," Sar Lauton said unexpectedly. "Your empathy does not go unnoticed."

Davenport glanced at him with unease. "Oley, take him away and put him with the others. I'm getting this ship out of here." Davenport settled into the control chair and reviewed the instrument panel. No issues here. He was nearly as familiar with Eglan centralized controls as his own. One person could navigate this vessel if necessary, though it required many to fight and maintain it. He activated the drives, and the ship advanced. The view-screens glimmered, framing the star-studded expanse and the battered silhouette of the "Dauntless" as it slowly fell behind. The old girl drifted silently through space, faintly shimmering in the cold light of distant stars. Gradually, she shrank to a mere toy as the Eglan ship pulled away. It was time, thought Davenport, as he adjusted a dial and pushed a small lever. The faint ion trail of the torpedo glowed like a pale sword in the darkness, vanishing toward the derelict in their wake. Seconds ticked by before a massive fireball obliterated the stars, and with its dissipation, the "Dauntless" was gone, leaving only a fiercely radiant cloud of molecules spreading through the vastness of space.

Pedersen quietly entered and sat opposite Davenport. "The prisoners are secure, sir, and our men are prepped for the Cth jump," he reported.

"Good. We'll commence familiarization once we reach cruising speed."

"Aye, sir."

"The 'Dauntless' is gone," Davenport said absently as he engaged the converters and the ship shivered on the edge of hyperspace.

"I know. I watched her go down."

"She was a remarkable ship."

"The best. She victoriously ended our war."

"I hated to destroy her, Oley."

"I understand. But it was necessary."

Davenport sighed as he guided the ship through the Cth components.

The controls felt responsive, though not as seamless as those on the "Dauntless." The two men sat quietly, the control panel between them. Davenport finally broke the silence. "You know, Oley," he said, "I thought it was a disaster when Bordoni's recordings got destroyed."

Pedersen looked at him seriously. "You might still be right," he replied. "We're going to win this war now. We're going to win it completely. They can't stop us now that we know their vulnerability."

"And that's a disaster?"

"It could be. After all, what happens when we win? What kind of conquerors will we become? How will we treat them and the other races they've subjugated? We have no guidelines. We've steered clear of other intelligent species in our domain. We left them alone because we didn't know how to engage with them, and we knew we didn't know. But we can't ignore the Eglani. They'll be our responsibility, and we've never learned to rule."

Davenport stared, shrugged, and grinned. "Maybe the Eglani will win after all, even if we beat them in battle. They have the administrative know-how."

Pedersen chuckled, though without joy. "You get my point? It still might be a disaster, after all."

THE END.

Printed in Great Britain
by Amazon